DEEP HOUSE

OTHER WORKS BY THOMAS KING

FICTION

Medicine River

Green Grass, Running Water

One Good Story, That One

Truth and Bright Water

A Short History of Indians in Canada

The Back of the Turtle

Indians on Vacation

Sufferance

DREADFULWATER MYSTERIES

DreadfulWater

The Red Power Murders

Cold Skies

A Matter of Malice

Obsidian

NON-FICTION

The Truth About Stories

The Inconvenient Indian

POETRY

77 Fragments of a Familiar Ruin

CHILDREN'S ILLUSTRATED BOOKS

A Coyote Columbus Story, illustrated by William Kent Monkman

Coyote Sings to the Moon, illustrated by Johnny Wales

Coyote's New Suit, illustrated by Johnny Wales

A Coyote Solstice Tale, illustrated by Gary Clement

Coyote Tales, illustrated by Byron Eggenschwiler

GRAPHIC NOVELS

Borders, illustrated by Natasha Donovan

DEEP HOUSE

A DreadfulWater Mystery

THOMAS KING

HarperCollins*Publishers*Ltd

Deep House
Copyright © 2022 by Dead Dog Café Productions Inc.
All rights reserved.

Published by HarperCollins Publishers Ltd

First edition

HarperCollins books may be purchased for educational, business or
sales promotional use through our Special Markets Department.

HarperCollins Publishers Ltd
Bay Adelaide Centre, East Tower
22 Adelaide Street West, 41st Floor
Toronto, Ontario, Canada
M5H 4E3

www.harpercollins.ca

Library and Archives Canada Cataloguing in Publication

Title: Deep house : a DreadfulWater mystery / Thomas King.
Names: King, Thomas, 1943- author.
Identifiers: Canadiana (print) 20210321997 | Canadiana (ebook) 20210322004
ISBN 9781443465601 (hardcover) | ISBN 9781443465618 (softcover)
ISBN 9781443465625 (ebook)
Classification: LCC PS8571.I5298 D44 2022 | DDC C813/.54—dc23

Printed and bound in the United States
LSC/H 9 8 7 6 5 4 3 2 1

For the in-laws and the outlaws.
You know who you are.

1

Frank Dodge watched the digital display on the gas pump count up the gallons. At least the van took diesel. He had a friend who owned an Audi. It was an expensive piece of junk, and it took premium. Give him a Ford any day.

Dodge in a Ford.

Dodge in a Dodge.

Not that he cared. It wasn't his van. He wouldn't own one. The only people who drove vans were plumbers and frazzled mothers with noisy brats.

American muscle cars. Those were the only things worth driving.

1966 Shelby Mustang. 1970 Baldwin-Motion Corvette. 1978 Pontiac Firebird. 1970 Oldsmobile 442.

He had been all set to close a deal on a 1971 Plymouth Hemi Cuda when the virus arrived and shut everything down.

Then he got sick. Almost died. Hospital, intensive care, pneumonia. Flat on his back for a month. Another month in his apartment watching *Columbo* reruns.

And then no job.

Shield was downsizing, he was told. No more long-distance driving needed. So long, and thanks for all the fish.

So when the chance for a decent payday had come along, he didn't hesitate. Okay, there were lines to bend, corners to cut, but it was the company's fault. They had thrown him out with the garbage.

He didn't owe them squat.

Getting the van out of the plant had been easy enough. Disconnecting the GPS, child's play. And in less than a week, he would be long gone. Someplace warm with enough money to kick-start the rest of his life.

Dodge felt the lever disengage. He replaced the hose and glanced at the window. Christ, he could remember when you could fill a tank for ten dollars.

AT THE TRUCK STOP outside Lovelock, he had overheard a couple of long-haul boys blame the pandemic on the Chinese and the U.S. military.

As if diseases had a nationality. As if they had a flag.

But that didn't stop the one guy from swearing off Asian restaurants, and it didn't keep the other guy from explaining how the virus had escaped a government installation in the Utah desert just southwest of Salt Lake City.

Dodge was pretty sure he knew how those two had voted.

A rising tide. That's what they were calling the recovering economy. And it was supposed to float all boats.

Eventually.

Of course, the yachts had done just fine. While everyone else was drowning, the pirates in Washington stood on the poop deck and gave away billions of dollars of public money to private enterprise. So CEOs could continue receiving their bonuses, and shareholders could continue to get their dividends.

Dodge wasn't against public investment in private enterprise. But if you were going to give public money to corporations, you should at least get something for it.

Boeing wants sixty billion of public money? American Airlines wants fifty billion? Fine. Use the money to buy shares in the company. Or buy the company outright. Other businesses did that all the time.

Think Bank of America would give away that kind of money out of the goodness of their heart? Think Citigroup would pony up grants and loans with no hope of a return on the investment?

DODGE GOT THE MAP and laid it out on the hood. The drive from Sacramento to Reno had been scenic enough, but once he got to the east side of the Sierra Nevada, the landscape had gone to shit.

Flat, dry, deserted.

Winnemucca, Battle Mountain, Elko.

So far as he could tell, these towns were simply gas stations, casinos, and whorehouses. He had stopped at one of the brothels in Battle Mountain for a beer and some company.

A little boughten friendship.

He had dated a woman who was into poetry. Before the relationship went tits up, she gave him a volume of Robert Frost. Dodge had been attentive enough to see that Frost was the price of admission. So he gave it a read. And discovered that he actually enjoyed some of the poems.

Boughten friendship, indeed.

The Calico Club was dark and dingy. Cheap beer, country music, tired women in baby-doll pyjamas coming at him in slow, stagnant waves. It was hot inside the brothel. And dark. An air freshener was plugged into a receptacle behind the bar. Dodge watched it puff out clouds of fragrance in a futile attempt to cover up the smell of sweat and the stink of lives going nowhere.

But he hadn't been in the mood. More than that, he still wasn't feeling well. Yes, he had survived the pandemic, but it had left him with dizzy spells and dull pains in his chest. The aftermath of the virus. A little damage to his heart. Nothing to worry about, the doctor had told him. A couple of pills each day would control the discomfort.

Along with flushing his libido down the shitter.

So the Calico Club had been one beer and gone.

He stayed in Battle Mountain that night. At the Big Chief Motel. Pool, WiFi, ESPN, and a continental breakfast. The bed was okay, but the sheets and the pillows left him feeling apprehensive.

He had seen a documentary on the hygiene of motel beds, watched as the investigative team played the black light across the dry pools of saliva, the urine stains, the crusty smears of semen, and other bodily fluids.

He should have brought his own sheets.

The next day, he got up at dawn and drove to Wells before he stopped for breakfast and made the call.

It's me.

Wells.

This evening.

Yeah. Everything's good.

From there, he took 93 to Twin Falls, cut over on 86 to Pocatello and Idaho Falls and across the edge of the Caribou-Targhee National Forest. The second night, he stopped in West Yellowstone at the Brandin' Iron, another generic motel in another generic town, and had dinner at the local Dairy Queen.

As he was finishing the double cheeseburger, he wondered once again what the hell had happened to America? How had the country become a nation of cheap franchises? Kentucky Fried Chicken politics. Burger King morality.

Dodge had gone to Quebec once, and not even the French had fallen this low.

Chinook.

Nice name. Probably friendly in the way Western towns in this part of the world were friendly. Not that he was planning on sticking around long enough to find out. He'd grab a meal, have a little fun, good night's sleep.

He caught his reflection in the rear-view mirror. There he was. Frank Dodge. Nothing much behind him. Nothing much ahead. The hired man.

Maybe Frost had been talking about him.

2

Thumps DreadfulWater had every intention of sleeping in. He didn't have anywhere to be. He didn't have anything he needed to do. And yet, here he was wide awake. And alone.

If he had been at Claire's house, he'd be changing Ivory's diaper about now. She was walking and talking at the same time. Thumps didn't know a great deal about babies, but Ivory seemed to be a punctual child. To bed by seven, up by five.

Some of the time.

Claire was taking the second run at motherhood in stride. Originally, the plan had been for Thumps to move in and take up residence with Claire and Ivory on the reservation. But after Claire officially adopted Ivory, and had no legal need for a father figure, she suggested that Thumps might want to spend some time at his place in town.

And to tell the truth, he wasn't sure whether he was disappointed or relieved.

Maybe a little of both.

What did he know about being a father? Claire had already raised one child on her own, so she had experience on her side. True, Stanley Merchant was self-centred. True, he could be a pain in the ass. True, he had, from time to time, made Thumps's life a misery.

But if Thumps was being honest, Stick, as he was known to everyone except his mother, hadn't turned out all that bad. And what Claire learned from raising Stanley could now be applied to raising Ivory.

If you actually learned anything from one child to another.

And Claire hadn't said that he *couldn't* be in Ivory's life. What she said was that she wanted space, that she had lived by herself for so long that having another person in the house— another adult person—was disconcerting.

That's the word she used. "Disconcerting."

Thumps could understand the desire. A quiet house, the day to do with as you chose, was mildly exhilarating. Not as in having escaped any obligation or responsibility, but just in the knowledge that you were in complete control of your life.

At least for that moment.

So why was he awake?

The sheriff had survived his prostate operation and was back at work. Duke had given up his short-lived fling with gourmet coffee beans and was back to making the foulest brew east of the Rockies. Still, it was good to see the man up and around.

Beth Mooney and Gabby Santucci had moved in together and, from all accounts, the relationship was a winner.

Archie Kousoulas was back to the business of running the bookstore, starting a restaurant, and saving the world with his usual vengeance.

Life was good again. At least for the people around him.

So why was he awake?

He didn't think the insomnia was tied to his cat. During one of Thumps's absences, Freeway had taken up residence with another family a couple of blocks over, and when the Passangs left Chinook to return to Tibet, they hadn't taken the cat with them.

Thumps had been sure that Freeway would come slinking home, full of apologies, riddled with remorse. Instead, the cat had disappeared. And the only reason he could come up with to explain her not returning was that she was dead.

Hit by a car. Eaten by a coyote. Starved to death in a culvert by the side of the road. Or some other equally distressing end.

He had always been ambivalent about the cat, and Freeway certainly hadn't exhibited any filial fondness for him, at least not the kind of affection Thumps associated with small children and dogs. But he and the cat had lived together for a number of years, and there was something to be said for the familiar.

And now that he did think about the cat, as he ran through

the possible scenarios, each one more gruesome than the next, he found himself slipping into a minor depression. Another discouragement. Another failure on his part.

It was a good thing that he did not believe in making lists.

Thumps rolled over, arranged the covers and the pillows in an effort to take another run at sleeping in, and felt his stomach rumble.

Hunger.

There it was. He was hungry. Okay. This was the kind of problem that Thumps enjoyed the most. A problem that could, with minimal effort, be solved.

3

Al's sat between Fjord Bakery and Sam's Laundromat. The café had originally been an alley that was turned into a dead-end alley when the chamber of commerce built the Chinook Convention Center and blocked off one end. Nobody could figure out what to do with the space until Alvera Couteau bought it from the city for a dollar and built a narrow café that had all the ambience of a Northern Pacific boxcar.

The place was little more than a cooking area with a coffee machine and a grill, a lime-green counter, a row of red Naugahyde stools, and a run of plywood booths reserved for any tourists brave enough to come in off the street.

It wasn't that the place was scary. But it was dark. There was a plate-glass window at the front, and whatever light got in was quickly swallowed up by the steam and fat that rose off the grill like a fog.

But while Al's wasn't going to be a Tripadvisor pick any time soon, it served the best breakfast in town and probably the state, and if you wanted to start your day off right, this is where you came.

When Thumps got to Al's, the café was packed. Wutty Youngbeaver, Jimmy Monroe, and Russell Plunkett were perched on their usual stools, across from the grill, where they could keep track of the food. Chintak Rawat, Big Fish Patek, and Stas Black Weasel were clustered on the middle stools and deep in a heated discussion.

Thumps tried to slip by, but the big Russian turned and blocked him with an elbow.

"Here," said Stas, "is the impractical voice."

"Impartial," said Big Fish.

"We are debating the existence of god," said Rawat. "Perhaps you have an opinion?"

Thumps kept his face flat. "Nope."

"Mr. Black Weasel is proposing that god, in any form, does not exist," said Rawat. "A most radical view."

"Yes," said Stas, "but accurate. People create gods to maintain order and power. Very effective. A powerful myth. The divine cop."

"And Mr. Rawat," said Big Fish, "is of the opinion that there is a power in the universe that transcends humankind, something that we call 'god.'"

"And for Mr. Big Fish," said Stas, "god is good movie, cold beer, sex. Watch, drink, wookie-wookie, go to sleep."

"You see," said Rawat, "we are at an impasse."

Al strolled along the counter with the coffee pot. "They've been going on like this since they arrived. About ready to kill the lot of them."

"Breakfast," said Thumps. "The usual. Please."

"How's the blood sugars?"

"Fine."

"'Cause I don't want Claire to think I'm catering to your carbohydrate addiction."

"I'm not addicted to carbohydrates." Thumps slid onto his favourite stool. "So don't cut back on my potatoes."

"God and the Machine," said Rawat. "Perhaps this is where you wish to take the discussion."

"Yes, yes," said Stas. "These are the same thing. Both created by humans."

"Garbage in," said Big Fish. "Garbage out."

"Exactly," said Stas. "Every Russian knows this."

"A most depressing vision of the world," said Rawat. "Where is universal beauty and love?"

"BMW," said Stas. "The 507 Roadster."

"I wouldn't encourage them if I were you," said Al. "It's like putting peanuts out for squirrels."

"Speaking of food . . ."

"And I'd stay away from Wutty."

Thumps looked down the counter. "What's he up to now?"

"He saw a video on the internet." Al rolled her eyes. "Electroshock for drunks."

"What?"

"Seems that in Mexico there are guys who wander around bars with portable electroshock units."

Thumps rubbed his face.

Al lowered her voice. "He figures he'd make a killing."

"Shocking drunks?"

Al wandered back to the grill. "Enough to make you give up on the human race."

The philosophers were hard at it. Thumps closed his eyes, pulled his neck down into his shoulders, tried to pretend he was a turtle.

"The unavoidable conclusion," said Rawat, "is if there is no god, then there is no moral centre in the universe."

"People do not need god to know what is right and what is wrong," said Stas.

"Beer," said Big Fish. "The moral centre of the universe is a cold beer."

Maybe, Thumps considered, he should get his breakfast to go. He could take the eggs and sausage and hash browns over to the park, sit under a tree by the pond, and enjoy the day, away from the discussions of electrical sobriety and the divine.

"There are many atheists in potholes," said Stas.

"Foxholes," said Rawat.

"Beer," said Big Fish. "There's nothing like a cold beer."

Or he could take his breakfast out to Claire's. The food would be cold by the time he got there, but he could put it in the microwave. Ivory would be glad to see him, would want him to chase her around the house and listen to her murder "Twinkle, Twinkle, Little Star."

Claire *had* said that he could come out whenever he wanted. What if this was a test to gauge the level of his commitment?

He hadn't thought of that.

Al wiped the countertop. "Good news is the electroshock thingy is out."

Thumps tried to look interested.

"Wutty was looking for investors and ran into Dolores Cardoza."

"Chinook Insurance?"

"Dolores gave him a brief lecture on the subject of legal liability."

Thumps felt a smile form on his face. "As in, what if he shocked someone and they had a heart attack?"

"And that was the end of Captain Electrode." Al shook her head. "Now he's got a new scheme."

Almost on cue, Wutty abandoned his seat and began making his way along the stools.

Al pushed away from the counter. "Forewarned," she said, "is forewarned."

"Thumps!" Wutty grabbed Thumps's neck with both hands and began rubbing his shoulders. "How's life as sheriff?"

"Not sheriff anymore."

"Then this is your lucky day."

Thumps moved the sugar jar from one side of the chrome napkin dispenser to the other.

"Imagine being independently wealthy."

Then he moved the sugar jar back.

"What do you do with your money? Leave it in a bank where it earns, what, one percent?"

Wutty stopped rubbing and slipped a brochure under Thumps's elbow. It was a single sheet of paper, folded into thirds.

"WindArrow." Wutty tapped the brochure with a finger. "Opportunities like this don't come along but once in a lifetime."

On the front was a badly Photoshopped image of Wutty standing next to a large passenger van.

"Think Uber, DoorDash, FedEx, and Greyhound," said Wutty, "all rolled into one."

Al was back with the coffee pot. "Ask him about the van he doesn't have."

"But I will," said Wutty. "Soon as I get all the investors lined up."

"It's not much of a line," said Al. "Not like the ones outside the Cash and Carry during the pandemic."

"Transport and tourism," said Wutty. "The new buffalo."

Al filled Thumps's cup. "Shares are five hundred dollars a pop."

"It sounds like a lot," said Wutty, "but only when you say it out loud."

Thumps sighed. "Not interested."

"That's because you haven't thought it through yet," said Wutty. "Look over the brochure. It will answer all your questions."

"I don't have any questions."

"Let's say you're out drinking with friends."

Al shook her head. "Thumps doesn't have any friends."

"And I don't drink."

"There's that," said Al.

"How you going to feel when all your friends have a piece of WindArrow and you don't?"

Thumps tried to think of a more neutral term than "relieved" or "fortunate."

"Moses Blood bought shares."

"Moses?"

"Don't wait too long," said Wutty. "Week or so, and all the shares will be gone."

Thumps closed his eyes and tried to pretend he was still in bed, asleep.

"Okay," said Al. "He's gone."

Thumps opened his eyes.

"I hate to say it," said Al, "but Wutty might be on to something."

"You going to buy shares?"

"Does my head look like it zips up the back?"

"Did Moses really buy shares?"

"Word is the old man bought ten."

"That's five thousand dollars."

"I hear Beth and Gabby are thinking about investing as well."

Thumps's stomach rumbled. "I'm thinking about investing in eating."

"You want your breakfast?"

"I do."

Al shrugged. "Why didn't you say so?"

THE EGGS WERE MOIST, the potatoes crisp, the honey-garlic sausages fried to perfection. Thumps wiped his plate with the last of the toast and settled in over his coffee.

"You plan on sitting there all day?"

"In Paris, meals can last for hours."

"This ain't Paris."

Rawat, Stas, and Big Fish left when Wutty came along the counter with his brochure a second time, and Jimmy and Russell dragged Wutty off shortly after that.

"I'm your only customer."

It was amazing how much better the day looked once you were fed. Maybe he should consider investing. Tourism was a growth industry. He had a little money in the bank. Wutty was right. The banks didn't give you much of a return.

Al filled his cup. "You keeping up on the news?"

"Such as?"

"Bookstore is open again," said Al. "Your little buddy is back in business."

Chinook had not been hit by the virus as hard as New York City or San Francisco. Toronto or Montreal. Certainly not as bad as northern Italy, Spain, India, and Russia. But businesses in town had closed, and people had gone into hiding.

"You were closed for a while."

Al shrugged. "Don't know that it did any good, but that's what happens when you do something right. You don't know."

The town had been in quarantine for most of the winter and early spring, and, all in all, it had been a remarkably generous time. People had helped each other. Businesses had banded together to provide the necessities of life. Hardly anyone had complained.

"You think it's going to happen again next year?"

That was the worry, that the planet was going to be faced with wave after wave of new viruses, year after year.

"Can't keep closing like that and stay in business."

Not that Chinook hadn't taken a hit. There were businesses along Main Street that wouldn't be open again.

"Things aren't back to normal just yet," said Al, "but maybe this is the new normal."

Through the plate-glass window at the front by the grill, Thumps could see the street. Sitting there on the stool, he felt as though he were on a spaceship looking out at another planet.

"You heading to Claire's?"

Thumps took in a deep breath and let it out slowly.

"That Ivory is one cute kid. Bet she's talking up a storm."

Thumps checked his plate to see if there was anything left that he could wipe up with a finger.

"But once they find their feet," said Al, "it's all over."

"You know, in Paris, no one bothers you while you eat."

Al took Thumps's plate and dumped it into the tub with the rest of the dirty dishes. "In Chinook," she said, "nobody gives a shit what they do in France."

Thumps yawned and put his head down on the counter.

"That the diabetes talking?"

Thumps sat up straight.

"I knew I shouldn't have given you a full serving of hash browns."

"Blood sugars are fine."

Al whacked him on the shoulders with the towel. "Go see your daughter."

"Not that easy."

Al tossed the dishtowel over a shoulder and headed back to the grill. "Nothing much is."

4

Anyone who lived on the high plains for any length of time knew better than to turn their back on May. Rain, blizzards, wind, hail. If there was a volcano in the area, May would have been the month it chose to erupt.

Just ask the folks on Hawaii's Big Island.

Today was pleasant enough. Warm with the edge of a chill. Fresh and crisp, smelling of promise, as though it had been washed and hung outside to dry in the sun.

Thumps stood on the sidewalk outside Al's under a thin, cloudless sky and tried to reconcile his mood with the weather. There was every reason to be cheery and hopeful, and yet here he was, come to the end of a long, hard road only to discover a cliff.

A *Thelma & Louise* moment.

Thumps supposed that such imaginings qualified as depression, though putting a name to them didn't soften the effect in the least. Having somewhere to go, having something to do—that might help.

There was the reservation, Claire and Ivory. There was his darkroom with negatives waiting to be printed.

And there was standing in one spot and doing nothing.

But that wasn't really an option. Was it?

A CAMERA STORE had finally come to town. Langfield's on Main Street. Thumps had been at the grand opening, had spent a good deal of time browsing the newest offerings from the major photographic companies.

Digital, digital, digital.

There were film cameras on display. Lovely manual mechanisms in black leather and chrome. But they weren't for sale. They sat on shelves, high above their computerized cousins, much like the trophy heads of animals from a bygone era, when such indulgence in art and craft had been the norm.

In the last couple of years, he had started to worry about the effect wet-room photography was having on his body. Developer, stop bath, fix. Chemicals of a decidedly dangerous nature. Most were contact poisons of one sort or another, poisons you could breathe in or absorb through your skin, if you were foolish enough to stick your hand into something as nasty as Pyro.

Digital photography certainly appeared to be safer in terms of personal health. The problem was, he didn't understand photography via a computer, had no sense of the algorithms that made up the mystery that was Photoshop, thought of a digital file and the ease with which it could be manipulated as a cheat.

He was, after all, a traditionalist, a practitioner of the art that Man Ray and Dorothea Lange, Edward Steichen and Gertrude Käsebier, Edward Weston and Berenice Abbott had made famous.

A standard bearer. A knight errant.

Well, not a knight errant. More a living dinosaur. Lumbering toward the brink of extinction. Out of step with the times. Unwilling to embrace the new advances in the field.

Stuck, literally, in the dark.

LANGFIELD'S WAS JUST opening. There was a poster in the window for the new Fujifilm. Thumps had read a couple of reviews that compared the camera to the Sonys and the Ricohs, the Canons and the Nikons that were trying to occupy the same market space.

Street photography. That seemed to be all the rage. Photographers leaving their studios, roaming the streets, looking to capture the pulse of humanity. Thumps had seen a number of examples of street photography, and some of the shots were interesting.

Though he wondered how people in the shots would feel if they knew they were being photographed without their permission.

There was a photograph of a woman hanging out a window in a most unflattering pose. Another was of a young Black man pointing a gun at the camera. An old woman sitting on a stoop amidst a herd of cats.

Thumps supposed that street photography was akin to going hunting. You walked around with a camera or sat in a blind somewhere, looking for inspiration, waiting for something to move, waiting for something to shoot.

LYNN LANGFIELD WAS behind the counter. His wife, Lilly, was stocking the wire hangers with photo accessories.

"Mr. DreadfulWater."

Thumps had told the Langfields to call him Thumps. Any number of times.

"You're open again."

"Last week," said Langfield. "And none too soon."

Lynn was an older man, tall and stooped, as though he had spent too much time in a low-ceilinged house.

"You see the new Fuji?"

The X100 series was designed with a 1950s retro look that suggested film instead of pixels. The X100V was the fifth iter-ation. Not quite as artistic as the one before it, but that was the idiocy of marketing. No matter how perfect the design, it had to be changed with each new cycle. God forbid that this year's camera look exactly like last year's camera.

Cars, televisions, cellphones, running shoes. In the world of business, keeping the same design year after year was an unconscionable and unforgivable sin. Even if it was perfect. Such a thing might suggest corporate complacency.

Or socialism.

Lilly came back to the counter. She was a solid woman, and if there was heavy lifting to be done, Thumps imagined that it was Mrs. Langfield who would do it.

"You still dragging that 4x5 around the countryside?"

Thumps wanted to tell Lilly that he enjoyed hauling a forty-five-pound pack and a twelve-pound wood tripod up mountains, along rivers, and across the high prairies, but the truth of the matter was he had begun to notice the weight.

"Archie says you've gone back to your Rolleiflex." Lilly took a camera off the shelf and set it on the counter. "The f3.5 Xenar, right?"

"F3.5 Planar."

"Did you know that Lilly used to work at the Hasselblad factory?" Lynn put an arm around his wife. "She knew Erna and Victor Hasselblad."

"Long time ago," said Lilly.

"The Rollei is a lovely camera," said Lynn. "You still do all your own developing and printing?"

"Rolleiflex is German," said Lilly. "Hasselblad is Swedish. You'd be surprised how many people don't know that."

"We had a darkroom." Lynn sighed. "The good old days. Chemical fog almost killed me."

"So now," said Lilly, "it's all digital."

Thumps picked up the Fuji and turned it over in his hands.

"It won't beat your big rig," said Lynn, "but it'll come close."

"Fuji rep is supposed to stop in this week," said Lilly. "Nice young man. Ameet something or other."

"Maybe we can get you a loaner," said Lynn. "Field test it. See what you think. I'll even process the files. Print off a couple of the shots, so you can see what digital is all about."

"Sure."

"Sheriff just bought a very nice Panasonic," said Lilly.

Thumps held the camera up to his eye.

"More for his wife, I think," said Lynn. "Hear she's itching for a vacation."

Thumps pressed the shutter release. The camera was almost dead quiet.

Lilly smiled. "Feels good in the hand, doesn't it? Rangefinder. More or less. Like the old Leicas."

Thumps swung the camera around and watched the auto-focus snap into action.

"When Ameet comes in," said Lynn, "I'll ask him about a loaner."

***

THE WINDOWS AT PAPPOUS'S were still covered. The pandemic had kept the restaurant from opening, had kept Archie Kousoulas from introducing Chinook to the delights of Greek food. Thumps wasn't sure what constituted Greek food, but he knew that Archie would fill in the blanks once the place was up and running.

Thumps cupped his hands, put his face against the window, tried to peek in through the gaps in the brown butcher paper.

Nothing.

If he knew the little Greek, there would be a flashy grand opening with food and music. But for now, the place was quiet, and as he stood at the window trying to see in, Thumps found himself getting melancholic. As though looking into the empty restaurant was the same as looking into his life, looking into his soul.

If there was such a thing.

Being at loose ends didn't help. He had just decided to bite the bullet and go out to the reservation to see if Claire and Ivory wanted company when he remembered that they had gone to Great Falls to visit friends.

And to shop.

That left Archie and the bookstore. Thumps hadn't seen the man in over a week, and he couldn't think of a good reason to go see him now. Archie would tell him about the new restaurant, give him advice on his social life, ask him probing questions about his health, and generally make a nuisance of himself.

Sometimes Thumps didn't mind.

Or he could drop in on Beth Mooney, medical doctor and county coroner. Beth would have painted the walls of her apartment again and would ask him if he liked the colour.

That never went well.

And she would want to give him advice on his social life, ask him probing questions about his health, and generally make a nuisance of herself.

That left the sheriff. Duke Hockney made the worst coffee Thumps had ever tasted, but Duke didn't care about his social life or his health. And he did have a new camera.

If nothing else, Thumps could give him tips on taking photographs.

THE SHERIFF'S OFFICE was dark and looked as though it was closed. Thumps tried the door. It was locked. But he could see the sheriff sitting in his chair, staring at something on his desk. Thumps tapped on the glass. Hockney stayed staring. Thumps tapped again.

This time, Duke looked. And scowled. He pushed himself out of the chair and lumbered to the door.

"Door was locked."

Hockney did his dead face. "That's because I locked it."

"But you're open."

"Just so you remember that this is an office for sheriff business and not a coffee shop."

"I don't want to drink your coffee."

"And it's not a lounge." Hockney ambled back to his desk. "Coffee's fresh, so it's a little on the weak side."

The sheriff's idea of weak coffee was fifty-weight motor oil. At the height of its perfection, the coffee would come out of the old percolator in sludgy lumps.

"How's the prostate?"

Duke's face turned into a storm cloud. "Still can't sit on my ass. Had to get one of those pillows with a hole in it."

"Could be dead."

"There's that."

There was a box on the sheriff's desk. Sitting next to it was a small camera.

"That the new camera?"

"No," said the sheriff, "it's a computer with a shitty disposition."

"Can't make it work?"

"I can barely turn it on."

"Want me to give it a try?"

"No, I want Macy to call off the vacation."

"Where does she want to go?"

Duke sighed. "Vietnam."

"What happened to New Zealand?"

"Last year. Virus saved me from that."

Thumps glanced at the coffee machine. It was making its burbling, molten lead sounds. Still, if the sheriff had just made the coffee this morning, it might be drinkable.

"My older brother went to Nam in '68." Duke swivelled in his chair. "He wasn't impressed."

"You say you made the coffee this morning?" Thumps started to rise from the chair.

"More or less."

Thumps settled back into the chair. "You try the camera yet?"

Duke slid the camera across his desk. "Knock yourself out."

The Panasonic was small, ridiculously small.

"The button on top turns it on," said Duke. "But don't press the red button. That's for video."

"Video?"

"Yeah," said Hockney. "That's what I said."

Thumps pressed the on button and the lens slicked out.

"Book says to press the shutter release halfway down and it will focus," said Duke. "Then you can take the picture."

Thumps brought the camera to his eye. "It says, 'Pictures will be stored in intelligent memory.'"

"Right," said Duke. "That's because it doesn't have an SD card in it right now."

The sheriff held up a tiny black piece of plastic. Thumps knew what it was, but he hadn't seen one up close and personal.

"The new negative," said Duke.

The card was no bigger than a postage stamp.

"What say we take a drive, give it a field test?"

"Has someone been murdered?"

"Don't be like that. It's a nice day. Thought I'd take a ride out to Deep House. Figured you might like to come along and try out the camera."

"You want to go hiking in Deep House?"

"You nuts?" Hockney pushed out of the chair, hitched his pants. "Got to check on something near there."

Thumps brought up a mental map of the area. "There's nothing near Deep House."

"*Au contraire.*"

Thumps closed his eyes.

"That's French for 'on the contrary.'"

Thumps opened his eyes. "And no one has been murdered?"

"You make it sound as though I drag you off to every crime scene that comes along."

"You do."

"You enjoy the excitement."

"No, I don't."

The sheriff grabbed his hat. "Come on. It'll be fun. We can do a little bonding, and you can show me the tricks of the trade."

Thumps stayed in the chair. The old percolator had picked up speed, gurgling away as though it might erupt at any moment.

"And there's no dead body?"

"Nothing but sunshine and blue skies." Duke slipped into his jacket. "Sunshine and blue skies."

5

Sheriff Duke Hockney was not particularly talkative, and he generally kept his personal life to himself. Thumps liked that about the man.

"So here's what you need to know about prostate operations."

"Don't need to know."

"Not sure which was worse." Duke glanced at Thumps to make sure he was paying attention. "The anticipation, the operation, or the aftermath."

Thumps put his head on the dash.

"According to Macy, if I had eaten a bunch of turmeric, I might have been able to avoid the surgery."

"Turmeric?"

"Supposed to protect you from prostate problems." Duke drummed his fingers on the wheel. "Turns out the stuff is better for you than burgers and fries. Who knew?"

"You might want to watch the road."

"There are a couple kinds of prostate operations. There's the one where they open you up, take out the prostate and your balls, along with a bunch of the surrounding tissue. Sort of like excavating for a septic system."

Thumps concentrated on the mountains in the distance, imagined that he was in one of the high valleys, walking through a meadow. Alone.

"If it's just an enlarged prostate, then they stick a wire in through your penis and carve off layers until they get whittled down to size. Like peeling an onion."

In his meadow, Thumps could see wildflowers. Butterflies. A doe and her fawn.

"So now Macy has me on the turmeric. Dumps it in my oatmeal every morning."

Thumps opened his eyes. "You eat oatmeal?"

Duke grimaced. "And ginger. Macy boils up this god-awful concoction of ginger and green onions. I mean, the horse is already out of the barn, right? But she makes me drink it anyway."

"What say we talk about photography?"

"You ever had to wear an adult diaper?"

"Duke . . ."

"Damn things are hot as hell."

"Duke . . ."

"Don't you want to know about erectile dysfunction?"

* * *

THUMPS LEANED AGAINST the door and watched the land fly by. There was a lonesome majesty to the high prairies, a sensation he had never been able to capture in a photograph. Even from inside the car, Thumps could feel his body open up to the space that stretched out forever.

"Almost there."

As far as he could figure, they were on the eastern edge of the reservation, an area that had little to recommend it. Mostly flat, empty, windswept land, baked and frozen by the seasons.

"And we're here."

Thumps had no idea what "here" was. First impression was a compound of some sort, a large enclosure with hundreds of uniformly spaced panels, set at angles to the ground. Each of the panels was painted a different colour. From a distance, the overall effect was that of driving into a cubist painting. Or a riot of wildflowers.

Much like his imaginary mountain meadow.

All surrounded by a high, chain-link fence with a rolling gate.

Duke pulled the cruiser up to the gate. "You got a favourite colour?"

Through the chain link, Thumps could see a pickup parked next to the remains of a burned-out vehicle. Farther on, at the back of the enclosure, was a dirty, white single-wide. The trailer was leaning from back to front, as though it were poised for a sprint.

The gate was closed. There was a keypad on a post. Duke

rolled down his window, punched in numbers, and the gate rolled open. The sheriff eased his cruiser forward. As he cleared the entrance, the gate rolled shut behind him.

"Could use one of these at my place."

Duke slowed to a stop, set his hat on his head, and stepped out.

The woman leaning against the truck reminded Thumps a bit of Judi Dench when she played M in the Bond series.

"You the sheriff?"

"Duke Hockney," said Duke.

"Bargain Hall," said the woman, extending her hand. "See you didn't forget the code."

"Bargain's different," said Hockney.

"That it is," said Hall. "I was the first baby born in Nevada that year. Hospital covered all the costs. Mom said I was the best bargain she ever got."

Hockney stuck his thumbs in his belt. "And this is Special Deputy Thumps DreadfulWater."

Bargain's face broke into a smile. "Thumps? DreadfulWater? Shit, I guess you got me beat."

"Special Deputy DreadfulWater helps me from time to time."

Thumps made a mental note to hurt Hockney when a good opportunity presented itself.

Bargain walked over to what was left of the van. "Mercedes," she said. "Late model from the look of it."

The star on the hood was black and sooty. The van was pitched to one side, windows blown out, tires melted.

"Real waste," said Bargain. "Why the hell would anyone do something like this?"

Duke rubbed the back of his neck. "This place got a name?"

"Used to be Main Street Paints," said Bargain. "Family-owned business. Plant is in Sacramento."

"California." Duke rolled each syllable around as though he were trying to get something nasty out of his mouth.

"Paint," said Bargain. "Home, high-end commercial. This is one of the company's test facilities. Weather in this part of the world can suck the black out of tar."

"And now?"

"Old man Eshelman died, and the company got kicked around the family for a while." Bargain took out a handkerchief and blew her nose. "Then it all got sold to an outfit called Shield Industries. One of those conglomerate boogers."

Hockney gestured to the rows of panels. "And they send you sample panels to leave out in the elements."

"Not anymore," said Bargain.

Duke waited.

"Got the paint store over in Glory. MSP used to pay us to come out here regular like to look after the facility, check the panels, keep the grass down, do the rotations, organize the deliveries and the pickups."

"But not now."

"Main Street did good business." Bargain shielded her eyes. "Then Shield took over and everything went to hell in a hurry. Don't make a lot of sense."

"So they closed this facility."

"About eight months back."

"Yet here you are."

Bargain shrugged. "Anyone opens the gate, alarm system sends a notification to my cellphone."

"But seeing as the place has been closed . . ."

"Guess the keypad didn't get the memo."

Hockney smiled. "So you got a notification."

"Nope," said Bargain. "I got five."

Duke set his feet and folded his arms on his chest. "Why don't you tell us how this all works."

"Pretty simple," said Bargain. "One way in, one way out. Gate's got a keypad and an electric eye. You punch in a code, the gate opens, you drive in, the electric eye shuts the gate behind you."

"Self-serve."

"There's a keypad on the inside as well. If you want to leave, you just reverse the process."

"And each time the gate is opened, you get a notification ringy-dingy?"

Bargain nodded. "When I got the first notification, I thought it might be a false alarm. But then I got four more."

"In a row?"

"Nope," said Bargain. "Got the first one late Friday. The other four early Sunday morning."

"So someone came in on the Friday and didn't leave until Sunday?"

Bargain shrugged. "Your guess is as good as mine."

"But you were curious," said Duke.

"My husband says I'm nosy," said Bargain.

"So even though you no longer worked for the company, you came out to see what was what."

"Not right away," said Bargain. "Couldn't get out on the Sunday or the Monday. Had some time today. Figured I'd check the facility and get in a little birdwatching while I was at it."

"Birdwatching?"

"Be surprised what you can see around Deep House."

Thumps glanced at the sky, just in case something interesting might be on the wing.

"Woodpeckers, grackles, red-tailed hawks." Bargain shaded her eyes. "Last year, I saw a bunch of pelicans."

"Pelicans?"

"The American white," said Bargain, "as well as the occasional Caspian tern. The thermals over the canyon are great for hawks and vultures."

"So you came out and found this." Duke paused and did a quick visual sweep of the compound. "Don't suppose there are any surveillance cameras."

"Not exactly a top-secret, black ops site, now is it?" said Bargain. "Not much point in keeping track of prairie grass and the wind."

Duke turned to Thumps. "Any thoughts, Special Deputy?"

Thumps decided to start with the obvious. "Anything missing?"

Bargain chuckled. "You mean like a paint panel?"

"Sure," said Thumps. "Like a paint panel."

"Not that I can tell," said Bargain. "Got most of the records in the trailer."

"They valuable?"

"The records?"

"The panels."

Bargain rolled her shoulders. "What's the price of plywood?"

Hockney stepped back into the conversation. "So there's nothing here worth stealing?"

"Trailer's a piece of shit." Bargain kicked at a pile of ash. "Van had value, I guess."

Duke nodded. "You call the folks at Shield Industries yet?"

"Not yet," said Bargain. "Reception out here is crap. I'll call them when I get back to the store."

Duke hitched his pants. "When you reach head office, have them call me."

"Maybe you can tell them how to run a successful business," said Bargain.

Thumps had never seen a test site for paint, but he could

see where such testing would be handy. You wouldn't want to paint your house a stylish red and, in a few years, have it fade to a tired pink. Buy a metallic blue pickup and watch it turn into a dead-lead lump.

Duke kicked at the ground. "Be nice if we knew what happened to the driver."

"Didn't go up with the van," said Bargain. "Had a house fire down the street from me couple years back. Family of four. You don't forget that smell."

"No," said Duke. "You don't."

Thumps looked at the panel field and then back at the remains of the van. "Why was it here? If the facility is closed, what's the van doing here?"

Bargain took a moment. "Only two reasons I can think of. First would be to deliver new panels."

"Which wouldn't make much sense," said Duke. "Why bring new panels to a facility that's closed?"

"Second reason," said Bargain, "would be to pick up the old panels."

"That makes more sense."

"Not much," said Bargain. "This van wasn't large enough. If you wanted to pick up all the old panels, it would make more sense to bring in a moving truck big enough to do the job in one shot."

"Seems as though you're suggesting that the van shouldn't be here," said the sheriff.

"Yeah," said Bargain. "That's what I'm suggesting."

Thumps turned around and faced the gate. "So if the driver wasn't burned up with the van, where is he?"

Duke squeezed his lips together. "Chinook's one hell of a hike."

Thumps turned back to Duke and Bargain. "Someone picked the driver up."

"See," said Hockney. "Mind like a steel trap."

"Sure," said Bargain. "But why the delay? Driver comes in on the Friday and doesn't get picked up until the Sunday? That don't make any sense."

Duke tried to contain a yawn and failed. "It's all interesting as hell, but I'm not sure any of this qualifies as a crime scene."

"Arson," said Bargain. "Destruction of private property. Leaving the scene of a crime."

"True," said the sheriff. "I guess we'll lock it down until we hear from the folks in Sacramento. That work for you?"

"Not my circus," said Bargain. "Not my monkeys."

Thumps walked around the remains of the van and sorted through the most likely scenarios.

The driver arrives, opens the gate, parks the van. Maybe he calls a friend who drives out and picks him up. That was the most likely answer. But if that is what happened, there should have been at least two gate notifications.

But, according to Bargain, Friday only had one, which would seem to suggest that the driver drove in and stayed until Sunday morning. Which made little sense. The test facility was not exactly an all-inclusive resort in the Caribbean.

Thumps squatted down on the ground so he could get the angle right and let the shadows do their job. There were tire tracks in the dirt, but no way to tell how many vehicles had come and gone.

And no footprints.

Thumps ran through the other possibilities, and when he got to alien abduction, he gave up.

"You figure it out yet?"

"Alien abduction," said Thumps.

Duke nodded. "Leaning in that direction myself."

"You want me to take pictures with your new camera?"

Duke reached into his pocket. "I thought you'd never ask."

"If you don't need me," said Bargain, "I'm going to head home."

"Head away," said Duke.

"Let me know what happens," said Bargain. "I love a good mystery."

THUMPS AND THE SHERIFF spent the next hour playing *Forensic Files*. The sheriff collected samples of the burn debris in plastic sacks, while Thumps took photographs of the van from different angles. Then he took shots of the prairie landscape through the fence, the clouds in the sky, along with a couple of his shadow stretched out across the ground.

The camera worked well enough. It was quick and silent. And the reach of the lens was amazing.

Of course, the quality wasn't going to be anywhere near the resolution of a 4x5 or even a 2 1/4 negative. But you could slip this camera in your pocket and take it anywhere.

Just for fun, Thumps stood off at a distance and used the telephoto to take several shots of the sheriff as he roamed the facility, searching for clues.

And he took photographs of the paint panel field, just to check the camera's colour rendition.

Hockney caught up to him by the fenceline. "How you like it?"

"It's small."

"You can take about a thousand pictures with that puppy."

"Not if you shoot in RAW," said Thumps, in an attempt to demonstrate some knowledge of the digital world.

"JPEGs. Low-res JPEGs." Duke slid in behind the wheel of the cruiser. "That way, Macy can shoot till hell freezes over."

"Won't get as good quality with JPEGs."

"You ever seen her photographs?"

Thumps climbed in the other side. "We done here?"

"What say we put a nifty crime-scene sticker on the gate?"

"Then we're going home? Right?"

"You worried that I'm going to make you work up a sweat walking the rim of the canyon, looking for vultures and pelicans?"

"Yes."

"Or that I'll drag you into Deep House itself? Make you hike the canyon, in case our missing driver fell in?"

"That too."

Hockney rolled the cruiser out through the gate. "You know what they say about the solution to any problem?"

"The simplest solution is normally the correct solution."

Duke tapped the side of his head. "Which means?"

"The guy called someone in town, and they came and picked him up."

"As in someone special?"

"Maybe," said Thumps.

"That someone special being a woman?"

"Probably."

"See?" said Duke. "Mystery solved."

"And the fact that the gate was only opened once?"

"Driver could have vaulted the fence."

"It's eight feet tall."

"The things we do for love," said Duke. "The things we do for love."

6

eep House was not one of the hiking attractions here-
abouts. In fact, there was a large sign at the entrance that
warned against going into the canyon.

"Restricted Access," the sign said. "Unstable area."

Thumps knew the answer to the question, but he asked it anyway.

"Why are we here?"

"There was some talk about putting in a parking lot." The sheriff stepped out of the cruiser. "Then that kid got himself killed, and they put up the sign instead."

The entrance to the canyon looked benign enough. A narrow dirt trail that ran in between two sheer rock walls and disappeared into the darkness beyond. As though you were about to enter a lost world.

Lasciate ogni speranza, voi ch'entrate.

Duke took his time, walking a grid at the entrance to the canyon.

"Why would the driver come here?"

The sheriff held up his phone. "Here we get cell reception."

"You think he walked here," said Thumps, "in order to make a phone call?"

"Got footprints." Duke stopped in the shade of a large boulder. "Not all that new."

"Could have been anyone."

"Candy bar." The sheriff fished a plastic bag out of his pocket. "Guess they didn't see the sign about littering."

"There is no sign about littering."

"Still, you'd think folks would know better." Duke picked up a foil wrapper and dropped it in the bag. "Course, this is nothing compared to the dumping."

"That still going on?"

"Cooled off a bit after that pumper got shot up," said Duke. "But we still get the occasional asshole who tries to use the canyon as a garbage can."

"Deep House is tribal land," said Thumps. "Part of the big land claim."

"That ever get settled?"

"Not yet."

Duke stuffed the bag in his pocket. "Hall said she got a gate notification on Friday evening."

"She should have gotten two."

"Driver comes in Friday evening." Duke kicked at the ground with his boot. "The next gate notification comes on Sunday morning."

"Maybe the first notification was a false alarm."

"See, now you're thinking like a cop." Duke checked the sky. "Can you imagine a pelican in this part of the world? I saw a bunch when I was in Seattle. But here?"

"How about we go home, and you can watch pelicans on the nature channel."

"You sound grumpy."

"I'm not grumpy."

"Be nice if we knew who the driver was and where he went." Duke opened the door to the cruiser. "What do you figure?"

"Someone came out and picked him up," said Thumps. "Only thing that makes any sense."

"Man or woman?"

"Doesn't matter. The gate would have had to be opened a second time. Whether the driver came out or someone came in, the gate would have had to be opened."

"Maybe he disabled the alarm," said Duke.

"Why would he do that?"

"How about we put the how and the why to one side for the moment and concentrate on the where?"

"Where?"

"Let's assume someone picked him up Friday evening. And let's assume that someone was a woman."

"That's a lot of assuming."

Duke slid in behind the wheel. "Where might our missing driver take her for a good time?"

THE ONLY SPECIAL someone Thumps had in his life at the moment was Claire, and if he was going to take her somewhere, the Mustang wouldn't have been at the top of the list.

Not that there was anything particularly wrong with the place. The Mustang had been a Texaco gas station until Delroy "Hack" Chubby bought the property at auction and turned it into a Western saloon and biker bar. He dragged in a double-wide, cut out one wall, and spliced the trailer up against the station's service bays so the place had enough room for a couple of pool tables and a dance floor.

And in a moment of decorator madness, Hack hung the original Texaco sign from the ceiling and nailed the grille of a 1965 Mustang to the wall behind the bar.

The saloon was famous for fist fights and arm-wrestling contests, with the occasional range war between the men in pickups and the men on bikes.

Hack was killed while trying to pass a semi on the long grade north of Chinook. There was a huge and noisy wake that lasted the weekend, and when Monday rolled around, Hack's daughter moved the Texaco sign and the Mustang grille and the pool tables into the parking lot and burned the place to the ground.

***

"YOU THINK THE DRIVER and his 'special someone' came to the Mustang?"

"No idea," said the sheriff. "I just want to say hello to Lorraine and see the baby."

Lorraine Chubby and Big Fish Patek. Thumps still couldn't see the attraction. Lorraine was a sturdy, no-nonsense woman, and Big Fish was an amiable flake. Still, they had stayed together long enough to produce a son.

Hack. After his grandfather.

"I hear the kid is cute as a button."

Hack was cute. But then most baby animals were cute. Except pigeons. Try as he might, Thumps couldn't work up any parental feelings for the squabs.

"Hear Big Fish has settled down." Duke pulled into the parking lot and stopped. "Hear he's a regular entrepreneur."

LORRAINE HAD HER MOTHER'S BRAINS, and before the ashes of the old Mustang had gone cold, she brought in a bulldozer, levelled the site, and started work on the new Mustang, a high-tech, red prefab building with a herd of wild horses painted across the front, and a satellite-receiver array on the roof.

It was an all-purpose bar where you could drink with your buddies, watch sports, and stay connected with free internet.

Lorraine's philosophy was that cowboys and bikers deserved

the same consideration as bankers and hedge-fund managers. And she had only four rules.

If you wanted to fight, you did it outside, where Lorraine had thrown up a rope ring around a sandpit, complete with lights and benches for the spectators. Along with a remarkably well-stocked first-aid station.

Lorraine's second rule was no puking in the bar. Anybody who couldn't hold their liquor was expected to make it to one of the bathrooms or take their stomach contents to the parking lot.

You threw up in the Mustang and you were thrown out.

Lorraine's third rule was sacred. There was to be no noise while she was singing. She didn't have a particularly good voice, but she liked to sing, and when she sang, she expected everyone else to shut up and listen.

THE MUSTANG WAS almost empty. Since it was a weekday, Thumps took the low turnout as an encouraging sign that sobriety and good sense did keep business hours.

Big Fish Patek was behind the bar. With a baby carrier strapped to his chest.

"Hey, guys." Big Fish bounced in place, patting his son on the bottom. "What's up?"

Hockney touched his hat. "You know that it's against the law to allow minors in a bar."

"You met Hack?" Big Fish was all smiles. "Kid's not even one, and he can already speak two languages."

Thumps tried to keep "dubious" off his face. Hockney was not as considerate.

"Really."

"English and French," said Big Fish. "It sounds like gurgling, but he's really bilingual."

The sheriff stepped in, leaned to one side. "Thank god, he looks like Lorraine."

"Sure," said Big Fish, "but he's got my eyes. They're just closed right now, so you can't tell."

Hockney looked around the bar. "Lorraine here?"

"Sleeping," said Big Fish. "Something wrong?"

"Looking for someone," said Duke. "Probably a couple. Thought they might have dropped in here this last weekend."

"We've only been open for about a month," said Big Fish. "People are slow getting back to normal. Haven't been many customers other than the regulars."

"The guy wouldn't be a regular."

"You got a picture?"

"Nope."

"That makes it harder," said Big Fish. "But I can ask Lorraine when she wakes up."

Hack was starting to squirm in the carrier.

"Feeding time," said Big Fish. "Kid has one hell of an appetite."

Suddenly, Hack's arms were out of the snuggly and the bilingual gurgling turned into a surprisingly loud wail.

"Got great lungs too. Lorraine says he sounds like Willie Nelson."

Big Fish wrinkled his nose. Duke and Thumps took one step back.

"Probably should change him while I'm at it."

"Let me know if Lorraine remembers anyone new showing up," said the sheriff.

"Next time you come by," said Big Fish, "he'll be singing."

7

The sheriff's office was as they had left it. The percolator was still bubbling away, smelting coffee beans into asphalt ingots. Hockney went straight to the pot and poured himself a cup.

"I should get going."

"Where?" Duke let the coffee vapours rise up and wash over his face. "You don't work."

"Are adult diapers really that uncomfortable?"

"Amazing what you can get used to. You ever find your cat?"

Thumps took the camera out of his pocket.

"Keep it," said Duke. "Maybe take it by Langfield's in the morning. Lynn offered to print off a couple of shots, so I could see how good the little bugger is."

"You want me to talk Lynn into giving you free crime-scene photos?"

"Not sure it's a real crime scene," said Duke. "And my budget is tight as hell."

The bungalow was where Thumps had left it. But in his absence, someone had thrown a large bag of laundry onto his front porch. He was halfway up the walk when the bag came alive.

Pops.

Virgil "Dixie" Kane lived next door. Dixie was a tall, thin man with a quiet, soft-spoken nature. His dog, Pops, was a very large, farty Komondor who weighed as much as his master.

The dog was normally on his own porch. When Freeway was alive, she and the dog had been best friends, and seeing Pops without the cat made him a little sad.

"Hello, Pops."

The dog came alive, wiggling the way an elephant might wiggle, if an elephant could wiggle.

"Where's Dixie?"

Pops licked Thumps's hands until they were gooey with dog saliva, and then he wiggled over to the door and waited.

"You want to come in?"

More wiggling. Pops's tail began banging against the siding and shaking the house and rattling the windows.

"I don't think so," said Thumps. "You're a little big for my place. You need to go home."

Pops didn't seem inclined to do that. He lay down in front of the door and waited.

"I have to go inside."

Behind him, Thumps heard a door open.

"Pops!" Dixie was standing on his porch, a towel over his shoulders. "Get over here."

"Afternoon, Dixie."

"Afternoon, Mr. DreadfulWater," said Dixie. "I was in the shower. Hope Pops wasn't a bother."

"No bother."

"Don't know what's gotten into him," said Dixie. "Last day or so, every time I turn around, he's at your place. You got raccoons?"

"What?"

"Raccoons," said Dixie. "Pops loves to chase raccoons. He never catches them, but he has aspirations."

Thumps reached for the doorknob, and the dog got to his feet, stuck his nose in the jam.

"Pops," Dixie shouted. "Bad dog. Leave Mr. DreadfulWater alone."

"Thumps," said Thumps.

"That's right," said Dixie. "After all, we're neighbours."

Pops didn't move. Dixie held up a box and shook it. The dog looked at the box and then back at the door. Box, door, box, door. And then he loped off the porch and back to where Dixie was standing.

"Doggie Bon-Bons," said Dixie. "Gets him every time."

"Thanks."

Dixie stood at the railing. "You ever find out what happened to your kitty?"

Thumps shook his head.

"You got to stay positive," said Dixie. "Maybe she'll come back. Like in the song."

THUMPS GOT AS FAR AS the kitchen table before he realized that he was tired. Dead tired. He got out his testing kit and stuck his finger. Blood sugars were a little low, but nothing to worry about. He didn't think that the lack of energy was age. In fact, he didn't want to think about age at all.

He could stop by Beth Mooney's office and report on the malaise, but then Beth would order up tests, and suddenly there would be strangers snooping about his body, taking pictures of his organs, sticking needles in his arm.

Along with other forms of medical torture.

Thumps was of the general opinion that health science and medical interventions were useful. He just wasn't sure that, in the end, they did any good.

People got sick. People got healthy. People lived. People died.

So he was tired, and the best cure for exhaustion, at least the best cure that he had found, was a nap. Curl up in bed in a dark, quiet room with a pillow under your head and another stuffed against your side.

Heaven.

Thumps was halfway down the hall, closing in on his pillows, when he heard the door open and shut.

"Hey, Thumps. You home?"

Cooley Small Elk was standing in the kitchen, next to the refrigerator. Thumps wasn't sure which was larger. He decided to call it a tie.

"You know you got a really big dog on your porch?"

"Next-door neighbour's dog," said Thumps. "He and Freeway were friends."

"Always nice to have a big dog for a friend."

Thumps tried to come up with a reason that would explain Cooley Small Elk's stopping by out of the blue, and there was only one answer that came to mind.

"Moses okay?"

"That's why I stopped by," said Cooley. "He's been feeling pookily. He was sick for a while, you know."

Moses not feeling good was bad news. The old man had always seemed to be indestructible. But when the virus had come through Chinook, Moses got it, almost died.

"He still sick?"

"You busy tomorrow morning?"

"Tomorrow?"

"Around five?" Cooley opened the refrigerator and looked in. "Moses says that some people are still asleep at that hour, and that I should ask."

Freeway used to get Thumps up early. The cat would climb

onto the bed and sit on his chest. Close to his face. And purr. In the silence of the bedroom, Freeway had sounded like a jet plane preparing to take off.

"If Moses needs me, I can be up at five," said Thumps, putting all the stress on the dependent clause.

"Great." Cooley closed the refrigerator and ambled to the door. "You want me to let the dog in?"

THUMPS PADDED INTO the living room and sat down on the overstuffed chair and swung his feet onto the ottoman. Five in the morning? The only reason for him to be up at five was if he had to pee.

During the pandemic, when people were supposed to stay in their homes, Thumps had rediscovered the pleasure of sitting and reading. Archie had helped. The Aegean had been closed for much of the contagion, but the little Greek had dropped off care packages of books on Thumps's porch.

The man could be a pain with his incessant interest in the lives of the people around him, but there was nothing wrong with his generosity.

Thumps settled into the chair and opened *Love in the Time of Cholera*. He was about a third of the way through the book. It was a bit slow, but interesting, and the love story of Florentino and Fermina reminded him a bit of his long-running relationship with Claire Merchant.

As he sat in his chair, he tried to imagine what it would be like if they were all living in the same house. Claire and Ivory. What it would be like to go to sleep and wake up each morning with the two of them in his life.

But his eyes began to droop and the image faded away. He yawned once, set the book on his chest, and went to sleep.

8

Thumps was still in the chair with the book on his chest when the phone rang. The phone did this from time to time, and most of the time, he ignored it. He'd had an answering machine for a while but quickly discovered that its main purpose was to create obligations. If someone called and left a message, there was the unspoken expectation that he would call back.

Then the phone company came along with a special package. Call display, call forwarding, three-way calling, answering service, all rolled into one low price that would have necessitated a second mortgage.

Thumps told the young woman that he didn't want any of these services, that he just wanted a home phone that was a home phone, and the young woman transferred him to Retentions and Rewards, where another young woman offered him the same package along with a new cellphone on a two-year contract.

"How does that sound?" the young woman asked.

Of course, the call could have been from Claire, just back from her shopping trip to Great Falls. Maybe she was hoping he'd come out to her place for dinner. A chance to see her and Ivory, kick-start their on-again, off-again romance, an opportunity to practise his fatherhood skills, in case there was a need for them in the near future.

That was wishful thinking, of course. That Claire would call. For much of their time together, Thumps had done the lion's share of the calling. More likely it was a scam of some sort. Duct cleaning. Driveway paving. A warning about an overdraft on his bank account. The IRS poised to repossess the house.

During the pandemic, a herd of hyenas had descended on frightened and vulnerable people with offers of surgical masks, overpriced hand sanitizer, toilet paper. One enterprising couple from Texas blew through town selling photocopied prints of healing hands that you could put under your pillow, and plastic packets of miracle water to protect you from the virus.

The worst of the bunch was the gang in white lab coats pretending to be from the World Health Organization. They arrived on doorsteps, talked their way into homes on the pretext of checking the premises for the virus, and then robbed the place.

The sheriff caught them on their way out of town.

"Husband and wife. Guy claimed he had lost his job and was desperate." Hockney shared the details. "Thought they were going to get off with a fine."

So it was just as well he hadn't answered the phone. He'd call Claire a little later, make sure she had gotten back safely, ask about Ivory, suggest that they might get together for lunch.

He had just settled back into his comfortable complacency when the phone rang again.

"How come you're not answering your phone?"

Archie Kousoulas.

"I am answering my phone."

"Sure," said Archie, "but I called a minute ago, and you didn't answer it."

"I was asleep."

"In the afternoon? You're supposed to sleep at night."

"Archie . . ."

"So it's just as well you're awake."

Thumps could hear banging noises in the background and someone shouting in a language other than English.

"'Cause you need to be here."

"Here?"

"Pappous's."

"The restaurant?"

"Yes, of course the restaurant. You sure you're awake?"

Thumps put the bookmark in the book. "I don't think I should be going out."

"The pandemic is over," said Archie. "At least for the time being. Now we have to re-establish our relationship with humanity."

"And I'm tired."

"I'll feed you," said Archie. "An hour. Don't be late."

Thumps wasn't sure he wanted to re-establish his relationship with humanity. He had seen more than his fair share of the human race, and truth be told, most of it wasn't all that pretty.

"And don't show up looking like a *vlákas*."

Thumps stayed under the shower until the hot water disappeared. He had read somewhere that draining the tank every so often helped to get rid of the sediment. Thumps wasn't sure where sediment would go. Except to the bottom of the tank. But he was willing to do his part for the vague promise of hot-water-tank integrity.

The mirror was fogged up when he stepped out of the shower. Just as well. This way he could continue to pretend that he was in great shape, that age and diabetes hadn't begun to chip away at his stony veneer.

He wiped a round hole in the glass, just large enough to allow him to shave. Not large enough to be confronted by unpleasant vistas.

He was selecting a shirt from the closet when he heard something in the spare bedroom. He waited for the sound to repeat itself, and when it didn't, he went to the room and stood in the doorway.

The sound had been singular and distinct, as though someone had shut the door or moved a piece of furniture. He waited. Of course, it could have been a joist expanding, a pipe rattling, the house tired of standing in one place too long.

Thumps laid two shirts out on the bed. Blue or white. Casual or business. He put on a pair of dark pants. Dark colours were supposed to be slimming. Ora Mae Foreman had told him this and, say what you would about the woman and the world of real estate, she knew clothes.

Now that he was fully dressed, he risked stepping in front of the hall mirror. Not all that bad. A little loose at the edges, but no real collapse. Thumps turned sideways.

Okay.

Except for the adorable swell at the brink of his belt. As though he were hiding a small puppy under the shirt. Three-quarters angle. Stand at a three-quarters angle. Stand up straight. Hope for the best.

THE RESTAURANT WINDOWS were still covered, but now Thumps could see light leaking out around the edges of the paper. He tried the door. It was open.

He hadn't given much thought to how Archie might decorate the place, but as he pushed through the door, he braced himself for walls covered in scenes of the Acropolis, the Parthenon, Delphi. Along with ocean panoramas of Corfu or Mykonos or Zakynthos.

With a grape arbour, wine bottles in wicker baskets, and waiters in dresses and pointy shoes. The soundtrack from *Never On Sunday* playing softly in the background.

Along with any number of other equally inane clichés.

"Thumps!"

What he hadn't considered was that there would be anyone else in the restaurant.

"You're late."

Let alone a small party.

"Come, come." Archie took Thumps's elbow and dragged him into the festivities. "The grand opening will be later. Tonight is just for friends."

About thirty of them, if Thumps's quick count was accurate. Beth Mooney and Gabby Santucci, Ora Mae Foreman, the sheriff and his wife, Al, Chintak Rawat, and Stas Black Weasel. Big Fish Patek and Lorraine Chubby. Vernon Rockland. The mayor.

Archie held out his arms. "What do you think?"

"What happened to social distancing?"

If there was a Greek platitude in the place, Thumps couldn't find it. Archie had gone with a mix of modern chic and early twentieth-century elegance. Muted walls, exposed brick columns, hardwood floors, white marble tables with metal frames, and a high ceiling set off with copper tiles. There was a small bar in the corner with an array of liquors and an espresso machine with dark red end-panels.

Unless Thumps was mistaken, Archie had Chet Baker on the sound system.

"Maxim's," said Archie, "meets Studio Munge."

Against one wall was a buffet table. Whatever was in the steam trays smelled delicious.

"I figured we could put some of your landscapes on the walls."

"We?"

"And if I sell any, the restaurant would get forty percent."

"What?"

Archie frowned. "When you show at Shadow Ranch, how much does Vernon take off the top?"

"That's a gallery."

"What do you think this is?"

"A restaurant."

"Okay," said Archie. "Thirty percent. But that's only because we're friends."

Rawat and Stas were huddled around the buffet, along with Beth and Ora Mae. Thumps floated in that direction, Archie steaming along in his wake.

"You must try these." Rawat held up something that looked like a short cigar. "Dolmades."

"And these," said Stas. "Little meatballs."

"You're out of the moussaka," Ora Mae sang out. "Someone ate it all."

Beth Mooney joined him at the table. "Have the lamb," she said. "Stay away from the baklava."

"Thumps isn't hungry," said Archie. "He wants to see the place."

"Thumps is hungry," said Thumps. "Is that shish kebab?"

"Souvlaki," said Archie.

"Same thing," said Ora Mae.

"No, it's not," snapped Archie. "Souvlaki is Greek. Shish-whatever is from that other place."

"Turkey," said Rawat.

"Language," said Archie. "Please."

Thumps stopped, took a moment to look around the restaurant a second time.

"I invited her," said Archie, "but I guess she couldn't make it."

"She's got Ivory now," said Thumps. "That keeps her busy."

"Sure," said Archie. "Kids are a big responsibility."

"Place looks good." Thumps grabbed a plate and moved along the line of trays, taking a little of everything.

"You were expecting Greek ruins, marble statues, and grape arbours?"

"Great-looking espresso machine."

"Anthony Quinn doing the sirtaki?"

A man Thumps didn't recognize stepped out of the kitchen and waved at Archie.

"Somebody wants you."

Archie returned the wave. "Beth is right," he said as he headed back. "Stay away from the baklava."

Thumps found a place against the wall, out of harm's way, and sorted through the offerings on his plate. The meat and rice wrapped in grape leaves was delicious, as were the meatballs. He had taken something that looked like a chunk of tandoori chicken and had it in his mouth before he realized that it was probably octopus.

"Pretty good food." Duke had snuck up on him when he wasn't looking. "I could get used to this."

"And you a turmeric and oatmeal kind of guy."

Thumps was sorry that Claire hadn't come. It would have given them a chance to reconnect. During the time that the virus had everyone in lockdown, they hadn't seen much of each other. And now that the pandemic had subsided, Claire hadn't seemed to be in any hurry to get the relationship back on track.

If there was a track for it to get on.

"You like mysteries?"

Thumps shook his head. "No."

"Come on," said the sheriff. "Everyone likes mysteries."

"No, they don't."

"Take the case of the disappearing driver."

"It's a case now?"

Duke helped himself to one of Thumps's meatballs.

"You heard from Sacramento?"

"I did," said Duke. "They were very pleasant."

"And?"

"And according to one Carl Mobley, there was no delivery scheduled for the test facility."

"You told them about the van?"

"Of course." Duke took a sip of his coffee. "And they said that they haven't lost a driver or misplaced a van."

Thumps waited. "Okay."

"Okay, indeed." Duke settled against the wall. "Let's say you're a company that has not lost a driver or misplaced a van. What do you do?"

"Nothing," said Thumps.

"Exactly," said the sheriff. "You do nothing, because nothing is wrong."

"But that's not what head office did?"

"Guy I talked to, this Mr. Carl Mobley, thanked me for my concern, asked me to lock the place down and post a guard."

"Post a guard?"

Duke nodded. "Said that they were going to send a *liaison* to look into the matter."

"To investigate the 'not my driver, not my van' matter."

"A *liaison*. Don't know I've ever had one of those stop by." Duke began humming along with the music. "Bound to be more exciting than a representative or a spokesperson."

"And when you asked him why he was sending someone for nothing, he said?"

"A *liaison*." Duke let the word drip out of his mouth.

"Right," said Thumps. "A *liaison*."

"He said he couldn't tell me," said the sheriff. "Can you imagine? And me an officer of the law."

"You tell him about the fire?"

Hockney licked his fingers and grinned. "Darn, I knew there was something I forgot."

The sheriff finished what was on his plate and headed back to the hot trays for seconds. With Thumps right behind him.

"Let's say that a guy did take a van from this Shield Industries in Sacramento, and let's say that he drove it cross-country to our beautiful part of the world."

Duke put a large piece of lamb on his plate.

"And let's say that the company knows all this," said Duke, "but are pretending that they don't."

"This is why you're sheriff."

"Which would mean that there is more here than meets the eye."

"And you don't like it," said Thumps.

"I don't like it." Duke took several of the little meatballs. "I especially don't like someone trying to tell me that bullshit is fudge."

"And yet all you really have is a possible case of arson and a missing driver who might not be missing."

"You mean a driver who is not missing and who is probably off somewhere having a good time."

"Probably." Thumps helped himself to several more meatballs and another dolmade.

"So what do you think?" said Duke. "Any of this smell like fudge to you?"

9

When Cooley arrived the next morning, Thumps was in the kitchen. Coffee on, breakfast made and waiting.

He had gotten home from Pappous's in good order, had gone straight to bed. Where he spent the next hour counting paint panels.

Cooley was visibly surprised. "You're up."

After he had counted paint panels, he got out of bed, settled in the chair, and followed the continuing adventures of Florentino and Fermina until he had to pee. Then he went back to bed, where he listened to every sound the house made when no one was looking. Most distressing, he could hear Freeway's voice in the floorboards and the wallpaper, as though the bungalow had retained a memory of the cat.

"And you made breakfast."

By three thirty, Thumps could see that sleep was not going to be one of the evening's activities. So he got up, showered, cleaned the darkroom, sorted his camera equipment, read some more about García Márquez's star-crossed lovers, and watched part of *A Night in Casablanca*.

"I figured you'd still be in bed."

"Up with the crows," said Thumps.

"They're still asleep," said Cooley.

Thumps didn't ask if Cooley was hungry. He simply set the plate of sausages in front of the big man, along with a stack of toast, and quickly scrambled half a dozen eggs.

"You eat already?" Cooley helped himself to the toast and the sausages. "You want me to save you some?"

"Maybe a little."

"There any pancakes?"

The inside of Cooley's truck was warm and comfy. Thumps leaned up against the door. He wasn't going to sleep, but maybe he could meditate on the drive to Moses's place. Or just relax. He had read somewhere that sitting very still with your eyes closed, with no distractions for twenty minutes, was as good as a nap.

When Thumps woke, he realized that the truck had stopped moving. It took a moment for his brain to organize itself.

"Wakey-wakey," said Cooley.

Thumps wasn't exactly sure where they were, but wherever this was, it wasn't Moses's house on the river bottom.

"Truck break down?"

"Nope." Cooley opened the door and got out.

In the early sunlight, the warning sign looked larger than it had the day before.

"Deep House?"

Cooley stood beside the truck and stretched, turned from side to side. "You know, you snore pretty loud."

"I thought we were going to see Moses."

"We are," said Cooley. "But first we have to get his tea."

"His tea is in the canyon?"

"It's not as bad as people say." Cooley pushed the oilskin hat off his eyes. "Just watch your step. It's early for snakes, but you never know."

THE FIRST HUNDRED YARDS was wide and flat. And then the trail turned, dropped into a tight chute and the first of the boulder fields.

"Came here a lot when I was a kid," said Cooley. "Great place for playing hide and seek."

The walls of the canyon narrowed and squeezed all the warmth out of the morning.

"Couple of times, we camped out in the caves."

"There are caves?"

"You bet." Cooley worked his way around a boulder the size of an apartment house. "Didn't Archie ever tell you about this place?"

There was only one reason that the little Greek would be interested in Deep House.

"This about that Aztec gold?"

"He used to come out here and poke around."

"But he never found anything?"

"Guess not." Cooley slid down a rock face to another rock. "But there's lots to find. People throw stuff off the rim all the time."

A path opened up and ran out for about fifty yards and then disappeared into another boulder field.

"Mattresses, sofas, refrigerators, stoves. You could outfit a couple of houses with the appliances that get dumped. If they weren't so beat up from the fall."

Thumps tried not to reflect on the stupidity of human beings and concentrated on his footing.

"Had a real problem with this one clown who thought Deep House was a good place to dump sewage. Another guy pushed his car into the canyon. Reported it stolen. Tried to collect on the insurance."

For the next twenty minutes, Thumps followed Cooley as the big man made his way up and over boulders, down into crevices, and out the other side. And then suddenly, the canyon opened up.

"We call this shelter the Porch."

"Shelter?"

"The next one in is the Kitchen."

"Parts of a house?"

"There are six shelters in the canyon. Places where it opens up," said Cooley. "This is the smallest."

The Porch was a bowl between two boulder fields. Here, the air was heavy and moist.

"There's an underground spring that comes up into a crevice over there." Cooley pointed his lips at the canyon wall. "But you have to know what you're doing to find it."

The second rock field was more difficult than the first, the boulders the size of houses with no easy path through them.

"Come on," said Cooley. "The easy part is almost behind us."

"How much farther?"

"You know why we call this the Kitchen?"

Next to one of the more impressive boulders was a rectangular depression in the ground that was covered in tight, grey lichen.

"Is that supposed to be a sink?"

"That's right," said Cooley. "Course, you have to use your imagination."

At first, it was a bit of an adventure, following Cooley up and down the boulders. But after the third or fourth slip, after tearing his jeans on a stumble and trapping an ankle in a crevice, Thumps had had more than his fair share of derring-do.

By the time they got to the Living Room, he was ready to call it quits.

"How much farther?"

Cooley began walking along the cliff wall. "We can start here."

The Living Room was larger than the other shelters, a place where the canyon widened out to a point so that the midday sun actually reached the bottom.

"Look for a small bush with dark red berries," said Cooley. "So far as Moses and me can figure, Deep House is the only place they grow."

"In the canyon."

"Sometimes, we'll find a few here in the Living Room," said Cooley. "But generally, we have to go in further. The Bedroom and the Bathroom."

"And if we don't find the tea in either of those shelters?"

"Then we'll go to the Basement."

"That sounds ominous."

"You know people." Cooley smiled. "They tend to exaggerate."

Thumps and Cooley went over the ground twice, but there was no sign of the bush. The Bedroom and the Bathroom yielded no better results.

Cooley brushed off his pants and surveyed the boulder field in front of him. "You probably should stay here. The next part changes from year to year."

"Changes?"

"The Basement gets more water than the rest of Deep House." Cooley nodded to himself. "Some years, the runoff will move things around."

Thumps looked at the rocks in front of him. He couldn't imagine anything moving them. Other than the end of the world.

"Or you can come along." Cooley began climbing the face of an enormous boulder. "Not many people ever make it as far as the Basement."

For the better half of the next hour, Thumps followed Cooley through the boulder field, wedging himself up crevices, sliding down rock faces, trying to find ways around sheer stone walls.

Cooley was encouraging.

"Use your legs. Press your back into the crack. Don't forget to bend your knees when you land."

It had been a mistake. Thumps should have stayed in the Living Room and waited. He was no longer twenty. He wasn't even thirty. What the hell was he thinking? Climb around on rocks? Sprain an ankle? Break a leg?

It had been Cooley's fault. The challenge of the thing. The right to wear the "I Made It to the Basement" T-shirt.

At one point, he realized that he had misplaced Cooley and was lost amongst the building-high boulders. He didn't want to call out, to let Cooley know that he had failed, and so he kept climbing and sliding and wedging until his pants and his hands were in shreds and he could no longer feel his toes.

At the bottom of one of the descents, he finally gave up. He was stuck in a hole with no way out. Stupid, stupid, stupid.

"There you are."

Cooley popped out from between two enormous boulders that looked as though they had been slammed together tight.

"Come on. We're almost there."

What Thumps hadn't been able to see was the narrow passageway that ran in behind the first boulder. It was a crack in the rocks that tunnelled through the field. Cooley was waiting for him when he stepped out into a broad flat.

"The Basement." Cooley held up a small plant with red berries. "Good crop this year."

Thumps wondered if he looked as bad as he felt.

"We use the whole plant, so we don't need many."

The Basement was dark and damp. A thin waterfall tumbled off the canyon wall and splashed over the smaller rocks.

"I'm thinking we should get about four," said Cooley. "That'll do the trick."

Thumps bent over, put his hands on his hips. A hot meal, a cup of coffee, a soak in the tub, a good night's sleep, and maybe he'd recover.

"Going back is easier," said Cooley.

Thumps followed the big man as he selected and gathered the plants.

"You don't want to take the big, established plants," he said, "and you don't want to take the little ones."

Cooley took a piece of cloth out of his jacket pocket and wet it.

"You want to keep the roots moist," he said. "That way, the plants won't lose any potency."

Thumps tried to pay attention, but if he was being honest, he didn't really care. He just wanted to be back at the truck, standing upright in the bright sunlight.

"Hey, look at that."

Thumps followed Cooley's eyes. There was something yellow lying on the canyon floor.

"And over there."

"Are those paint panels?"

"Be my guess," said Cooley. "Most times, what you find are washing machines and car parts."

Cooley gathered up some of the panels and set them against the rocks.

"The yellow's okay, but I wouldn't want a room painted in this shade of brown."

"The silver's not much better." Thumps picked at the edge of the panel. The paint was thicker than he would have expected. "These have to be from the testing facility."

"Be my guess," said Cooley.

Cooley stacked several more panels up to form an abstract mural, something Mondrian might have considered.

"I left my cellphone back at the truck," said Cooley. "Too bad you didn't bring your camera."

Thumps patted his pocket. It was still there. The sheriff's point-and-shoot.

"All right." Cooley stood next to the panels and struck a pose, one foot on a rock, hand on his hip. "Home is the hunter, home from the hills."

THUMPS WAS RELIEVED that Cooley didn't suggest they try to carry the panels out of Deep House. Even better, the big man was right about the return trip. It was easier. And by the time they finally slid down the last boulder and emerged at the entrance to the canyon, Thumps had put his failures behind him, was busy removing the more embarrassing moments from the story he would tell.

The story that would focus on his fortitude and endurance.

"Your elbows are pretty beat up."

Cooley slapped him on the shoulder. The kind of slap that was reserved for teammates in sports. A gesture of masculine brotherhood.

Thumps ignored the ache in his legs. He flexed his stomach muscles. Stood up a little straighter.

"And," said Cooley, "you got one hell of a hole in your pants."

10

Moses Blood lived by himself on bottomland that fronted the river. His house was backed against a run of cottonwoods that provided shade in the summer. In good weather, he spent almost all his time outdoors.

Today, the air was warm enough, but there was no sign of Moses.

"He's staying indoors," said Cooley, by way of explanation. "Still having some trouble getting around."

"Maybe I shouldn't come in."

"Should be okay," said Cooley. "Moses got the virus, but he recovered, so he's probably not going to get it again. And he's been wearing a mask."

"Good thinking."

"I wanted to tell you that ahead of time. So you're not startled."

"Why would I be startled?"

* * *

THUMPS HAD BEEN inside Moses Blood's house, but as he followed Cooley, he realized that he couldn't remember much about the place.

A kitchen. Thumps remembered a kitchen.

"*Na-ahks*."

"In here, *nissohkowa*."

The living room was small and dark, the air still, as though time had decided to pause and rest. Moses was sitting in a recliner, a blanket over his legs.

"Wonderful," said the old man. "You brought your uncle."

Cooley held up the bundle. "We went to Deep House."

"Ah," said Moses. "Good. I'm almost out of tea."

"Thumps helped me," said Cooley. "They're getting harder to find."

"World's changing," said Moses. "Human beings have stopped paying attention."

Thumps looked at the old man and tried not to smile.

"How do you like my mask?" Moses started to chuckle, and then he started to cough. "Roxanne Heavy Runner's sister works at the hospital. She said I should wear one."

"I don't think she meant a Lone Ranger mask."

"She wasn't specific," said Moses. "So I improvised."

"Tell Moses what else we found," said Cooley.

"Let me guess," said Moses. "A refrigerator."

"Nope," said Cooley.

"Once," said Moses, "I found an ambulance."

Thumps looked at the old man to see if he was joking.

"In the Basement," said Moses. "That's where most of the stuff winds up. There's a spot on the rim where you can back a truck up and dump in anything you like."

"An ambulance?"

"One of those older models. The ones that look like a long station wagon." Moses took off the Lone Ranger mask, set it to one side. "The good news is there was no one in it."

"That would be a surprise," said Cooley. "You're on your way to the hospital and, bam, you're at the bottom of Deep House."

Moses's face had lost some of its strength, the skin around his jaw loose and grey. His eyes had a pale yellow cast to them.

"Was I right?" Moses pushed the blanket to one side. "Was it a refrigerator?"

"Paint panels, grandfather," said Cooley.

"Like the ones at that test facility?" Moses leaned back in the chair. "Were they nice colours?"

"I didn't much like the brown," said Cooley, "but the yellow was okay."

"Yellow is always a good colour," said Moses. "For some of the people in the southwest, yellow is a sacred colour."

"That's right," said Cooley. "There was a Hopi guy I met in Salt Lake City who told me about pollen."

"I'm partial to red myself," said Moses. "What about you?"

Thumps didn't know if he had a special colour. As a photographer, he mostly saw the world in black and white. Course, you could use colours to change the grey spectrum. Put a yellow filter on your lens and you would get a greater visual separation between the sky and clouds. Put on a red filter, and any reds would turn white and any foliage would go dark. Yellow, orange, green, blue, red—they could all change a black and white image by degrees.

And then there were neutral density and polarizing filters.

"The berries are red," said Cooley. "That's why you like red."

Moses pushed himself out of the chair. "Your woman stopped by with your little girl."

Thumps sat up. "Claire and Ivory?"

"They were coming back from Great Falls." Moses opened the refrigerator. "They brought me some beef stew."

"Claire cooked a beef stew?"

"I don't think so," said Moses. "But only because it came in a can."

The beef stew was quite salty, and it had an aftertaste that made Thumps think of the compost pile in his backyard. The vegetables were soft and soggy, but it was a hot meal, and he was hungry.

"The bread is from that bakery in town," said Moses. "It's sourdough."

"I saw a cooking show on television," said Cooley. "The guy said that sourdough is good for your health."

"So long as you don't eat too much," said Moses.

"He also said you should eat the bread with oil instead of butter."

Thumps tried to imagine bread without butter. He knew that restaurants in places such as Italy served bread with olive oil, but he couldn't see the attraction.

Cooley tore off a huge hunk of bread and buttered it. "We should have brought the yellow panel out. We could have stuck it next to the picnic table for a little colour."

Thumps was working on the last of his stew when it occurred to him that finding the paint panels at the bottom of the canyon was odd. He waved his spoon at Moses.

"You know anything about the test facility?"

Moses nodded. "Marvin Old Person and me used to hunt antelope in the area, around the rim of the canyon. Was pretty strange to see that place go up all of a sudden."

"Especially as it's unceded reservation land," said Cooley. "And part of our land claim."

"That too," said Moses.

"You ever meet any of the people at the facility?"

"Nope," said Moses. "Most of the time we went by, there was no one there. Then Marvin got sick, and we stopped hunting. Now I do most of my hunting at the meat counter in the Cash and Carry."

The test facility was a simple enough arrangement. Thumps had no trouble with the logic. The company would send out new panels and bring the old ones back. They would want to see how the various colours held up, how the surfaces had survived the weather.

But then why would you throw them away?

"The ambulance was a surprise," said Moses. "But I wouldn't have expected to find paint panels in the canyon."

"I don't think they were supposed to be there. I think they were supposed to be sent back to head office for testing."

"Someone didn't get the memo." Cooley went to the stove. "You want more stew?"

"I'm fine."

Moses put down his spoon and wiped his mouth. "Okay," he said, "I guess we got to talk business."

"Business?"

"You know all about the White world."

Thumps waited.

"Cooley's pretty good, but he's not sure he can do the job."

Thumps waited some more.

"Roxanne tells me that I'm old, and I guess she's right." Moses covered a burp with his hand. "And she figures that I'll probably die pretty soon."

"She's been wrong before," said Cooley.

"No one's wrong all the time," said Moses. "And with dying, you're going to be right at least once."

Thumps wasn't sure he was liking where this was going.

"Auntie said that Moses needed to make a will."

"So I did that," said Moses. "Last year."

"Now all he needs," said Cooley, "is an executor."

Moses nodded. "Roxanne says that everyone has to have one of those."

Roxanne was the band secretary, and she handled all of the reservation's business affairs. She might be difficult, but the woman knew her way around the ins and outs of the modern world's legal niceties.

"Normally," said Thumps, trying to sound as though he knew what he was talking about, "you only need an executor if you have an estate."

Moses looked at Cooley. Cooley looked at Thumps.

"Like land and a house?" said Cooley. "A car? Investments?"

"That's right," said Thumps.

"Oh," said Moses, "that stuff."

"But all this is reservation land, right?"

"That's right," said Cooley.

"So, technically, the land and house really belong to the tribe."

"That's true," said Moses.

"And you don't have a car."

"Nope," said Moses, "not anymore."

"He used to have a Corvette," said Cooley. "But I wrecked it."

"It was when he was young and foolish," said Moses. "He was trying to impress a woman."

"Turned out," said Cooley, "she wasn't all that impressed."

"So you don't have a house or any land to pass on to someone. And you don't have a car." Thumps paused to make sure he wasn't missing anything. "I don't see where you need an executor."

"What about the investments?" said Cooley.

Thumps looked at Moses. "You have investments."

Moses got out of his chair and opened a drawer next to the stove. "I get treaty payments from time to time. Roxanne does something with the money, and every month I get a letter."

Moses set the envelope on the table.

"This one came a couple of days ago."

Thumps opened the letter. It was a summary of the money in the account and the interest it had earned.

"Roxanne said she'd be my executor, but since she invested the money, she said she would have a conflict of interest."

The total was astonishing.

Thumps sat back and let the amount wash over him.

"Course, I'm starting to feel good again," said Moses, "so I may not need you for a while."

Thumps put the letter back in the envelope. "And that's fine with me."

Moses reached out and patted Thumps's hand. "But when I do die, you can be my executor."

Thumps nodded. "I will."

"Roxanne says that executors are supposed to get paid for

being an executor," said Cooley. "Maybe you'll want to buy a new car."

"I don't need to be paid."

"If I were you," said Moses, "I wouldn't get a Corvette."

11

Cooley was quiet on the drive back to Chinook. Thumps let his mind drift and began imagining ways in which he could rearrange his kitchen. It would help to have a proper pantry, somewhere to put all the boxes and cans, get them out of the cupboards so there would be more room for plates and bowls.

Not that he needed more than one place setting at a time. There was nothing to keep him from using the same plate, the same bowl, the same knife and fork. Nothing to keep him from washing everything, setting it all to one side, and using it again as required.

Unless he had company.

"In Moses's will," said Cooley, "there's a list of disbursements."

"Disbursements?"

"Yeah," said Cooley. "I had to look it up to make sure I

wasn't confusing it with something else. It means 'to pay out.'"

"Right."

"For instance, I get the Corvette."

"I thought you wrecked the Corvette."

"I did," said Cooley. "Moses got it fixed. But I don't get it until he dies."

"Okay."

"He doesn't want to be around to see me hurt myself again."

Thumps tried not to smile.

"I love my grandfather." Cooley took his foot off the gas and let the truck coast down the hill into town. "So I'm not real anxious to get the car."

MAIN STREET WAS SURPRISINGLY QUIET, and there were parking spaces every so often. Some of the smaller businesses hadn't made it through the bad times. Café Brasilero, the fancy coffee place, had had to close its doors, as had the Asian grocery and Blue Bell consignment.

Still, there was hope. Pappous's would be opening soon. Langfield's was managing, and Al's wasn't going anywhere. The downtown would survive. It would just be different.

Thumps wasn't sure if Wild Rose Realty was open. Until he tried the door and discovered that it was. Ora Mae Foreman was sitting behind her desk, staring at a monitor. The desk was remarkably clean. No papers or folders. Just a keyboard, two monitors, and half a dozen pencils in an "I Love Real Estate" coffee cup.

Ora Mae was not a cheery person in general. She wasn't mean or rude. But she did lean toward efficiency and bluntness, and this tended to put some people off.

Thumps included.

"Afternoon, Ora Mae," said Thumps, putting as much good-will into his voice as he could muster.

Ora Mae didn't look up. Thumps glanced over his shoulder to see how far away he was from the safety of the front door.

"DreadfulWater." Ora Mae's voice was a cleaver in a slaughterhouse. "You got any secretarial skills?"

Thumps stopped and waited in place.

"You know, answer phones, type up offers, look after the website? Bring me coffee?"

"You lose your secretary?"

"We don't have secretaries anymore," said Ora Mae. "We have administrative assistants."

Thumps slipped into the chrome and leather chair.

"Don't be getting too comfy," said Ora Mae. "You better be here to buy something, 'cause I'm ready to shoot the next cowboy who comes in, wants to kick my tires."

"I already have a house."

Ora Mae looked up and smiled. It was not a happy smile. In fact, it could have been a grimace. Thumps wasn't about to ask.

"You know how many properties I've listed in the last month?"

Thumps was pretty sure this was a rhetorical question.

"You know how many properties I've sold?"

As a rule, Thumps tried not to answer rhetorical questions.

"Here's a hint. The answer to both questions is the same."

"Business not good?"

"There would have to be a business for it to be good. Or bad, for that matter." Ora Mae turned in her chair. "The houses aren't sick. You're not going to get COVID-whatever from a bungalow with a two-car garage and a fenced yard."

"People are still worried."

"You know how many cases were reported in the last six months? Nationwide?"

"Nope."

Ora Mae took a pencil out of the coffee cup and tapped the pointy end on the desk. "You know what scares me?"

Here was a question that Thumps could answer. "Nothing?"

Ora Mae smiled in spite of herself. "Well, aren't you just the apple in my crisp."

Thumps pressed his advantage. "Sheriff was hoping you could help him with an investigation."

"What? That nice Sheriff Hockney sent you all the way over here to ask me for some help?"

"He values your knowledge."

"The same nice Sheriff Hockney who called this morning, asked me what I might know about the test facility out by Deep House?"

"He called?"

"If you two plan on dancing together," said Ora Mae, "you better be listening to the same music."

Thumps waited.

"You want me to tell you what I told him?"

People liked to say that honesty was the best policy. It was a good theory, but Thumps hadn't seen many practical or successful applications.

"Actually, Duke wanted to know about wills and executors."

"Wills? Thought they got all the cancer."

"He was just wondering."

Ora Mae cocked her head. She reminded Thumps of a large bird looking at a worm.

"You're not thinking about dying on me, are you?"

"Me?"

"'Cause this is beginning to sound like one of those 'I got a friend who is . . .' and then you fill in the blanks."

"No. It's for the sheriff."

Ora Mae put the pencil back in the coffee cup.

"Okay," she said. "Here's the short course. Everyone should have a will. No exceptions. You die without a will, and it's like putting a cow carcass out in an open field."

"Cow carcass?"

"Your estate," said Ora Mae. "Intestacy attracts all sorts of vultures."

"We talking lawyers?"

"You know the difference between a lawyer and a vulture?"

"What about executors?"

"Only better job is printing money."

"Okay."

"And you got no interest in the property out by Deep House?"

Thumps tried to look nonchalant. "Part of the tribe's land claim, isn't it?"

Ora Mae cocked her head. "Well, listen to you. Wills? Executors? Treaties? Land claims? Damn. You sure you're a photographer?"

Thumps fished the sheriff's camera out of his pocket. "Guilty," he said.

Ora Mae shook her head. "I got a cellphone that's bigger."

Thumps held the camera up so he could see the screen and focused on Ora Mae.

"You threatening me with that dinky camera?"

"I could take your portrait."

"Not if you want to go on living."

Thumps got to his feet. "Hope business picks up."

"How's Claire?"

"Fine."

"That cute baby girl?"

"Ivory's fine too."

"You and Claire?" Ora Mae interlaced her fingers. "You can tell me to mind my own business."

"Mind your own business."

Thumps could see that he was about to be dragged into a discussion of personal relationships. If he wasn't careful, Ora Mae would be pumping him for information about Beth Mooney and Gabby Santucci.

Ora Mae looked off into space. "You think Beth's happy?"

Beth and Ora Mae had been lovers. And now they weren't. Thumps had never understood what it was that brought people together or what pushed them apart. He didn't think anyone did. It just seemed to happen.

"I hear she painted the apartment again."

"I better get going."

"Why do men say that?" Ora Mae frowned. "It makes it sound as though you're on your way out of town, heading west, riding off into the sunset."

"Headed home."

"But then we look up, and you're still here."

Ora Mae walked Thumps to the door. She stopped in a pool of light that was streaming in through the window. "Is here good?"

"Good?"

"For my photograph," said Ora Mae. "You mess it up, and you can kiss body parts goodbye."

"Maybe I should come back with my other camera."

"So which do you think is more flattering?" Ora Mae pulled her shoulders back, lowered her chin, and struck a pose. "Full face or profile?"

12

Thumps took his time walking home. The light in the western sky had hunkered down along the horizon, a thin gold glow at the edge of the world, and the air had stopped moving altogether. Thumps paused on the bridge and watched the water beneath his feet.

Even now, with everything that had happened, there were still perfect moments.

THE EVENING LIGHT bathed his bungalow in a brilliant warmth. The house had never looked better, and Thumps had to check twice to make sure that this was where he lived.

The pile of laundry on the porch removed any doubts.

Pops.

The large Komondor was stretched out, blocking the screen door, as though he were guarding a castle.

"Hello, Pops."

Nothing.

"You think you could move?"

More nothing.

Thumps didn't want to go next door and enlist Dixie and his box of doggy whatnots, but there was no way he was going to be able to move the dog to one side. Even if Thumps could clean and jerk the mutt—which he couldn't—he was sure he didn't want to wind up with his face buried in doggy fur.

"You know, I have to get into the house."

Pops's tail moved.

"And you need to go home."

Thumps waited to see if the logic had any effect. Which is when the air on the porch went black.

"Jesus!"

Thumps stumbled backwards, momentarily blinded by the smell that had exploded out of the dog.

"You okay, Mr. DreadfulWater?"

Thumps held on to the railing and tried to get his eyes to focus.

"Pops is upset." Dixie kneeled down next to the dog. "When he's upset, he has problems with his digestion."

Thumps had been sprayed by a skunk once. He had taken out the garbage late one night and had found the animal lurking next to the can. That had been bad. This was worse.

"He's really sorry," said Dixie. "He just hasn't been himself lately."

Thumps steadied himself.

"Every time I let him out, he comes to your place and lies on the porch." Dixie stroked the dog. "You know what I think? I think he misses your kitty. I think his heart is broken. He might still be able to smell her on the porch. You know, doggy memories."

Thumps stayed at the railing.

"You got to watch his tail," said Dixie. "That's your clue."

THUMPS LOOPED AROUND the side of the house and went in the back door. He stripped off all his clothes and padded naked into the shower, where he stayed until the tank ran cold. He dried himself and took the towel straight to the laundry room, where it joined his clothes in the washing machine, with the cycle set on "sanitize."

If that didn't work, he would just burn the lot.

There was leftover meatloaf in the refrigerator and a couple potatoes in the basket. A simple dinner tonight. Were there any green beans? Thumps dug around in the crisper and came up with a red pepper.

Perfect.

He had just sliced the potatoes and was taking the pepper to the sink to wash it when he heard the noise. A shuffling sound, as though someone were rearranging the furniture. He waited, and the sound came again. From the back of the house. From his bedroom.

"Hello."

The best outcome would be to find Claire in his bed, waiting for him. Thumps was sure this wasn't the answer, but it would be a nice surprise.

And something Claire would never do.

A raccoon.

Thumps kept the knife in his hand. That's why Pops had been on his porch. The dog knew that there was a raccoon in his house. Thumps had read about raccoon infestations and how they never ended well.

There had been a guy in Livingston who had discovered a family of raccoons in his attic. Mother, father, four babies. They tore up his insulation, fouled the lath-and-plaster ceiling with their urine and feces, and attacked him when he tried to drive them out with a broom.

Maybe he should go next door, borrow Pops, and give him the run of the house. One good doggy fart and goodbye raccoons. Of course, it would be goodbye house as well.

Thumps took the thick dowel he used for drying fresh pasta off its hook. Club in one hand, knife in the other, he advanced toward the sound.

The bathroom was clear. So was the guest bedroom. That left the master. How could he have slept in a room with a family of raccoons and not known it? And now that he was in the room, he wasn't sure how to proceed. For a moment, he entertained the idea of backing out into the hall, going to the living room, and looking up various solutions on the internet.

Type *how to get rid of raccoons* into a search engine.

The noise came from the closet. The door was open. The raccoon had pushed his runners and his slippers out into the room. Thumps gripped the dowel a little tighter and held it out in front of him to fend off the animal if things went south.

"I'm not here to hurt you," he called out. "I just need you to leave."

What he should do is call Moses. Surely the old man would have had some experience with this kind of situation.

"I'm going to step back, and you can come out."

The cat door. That's how they had gotten in. That was dumb. He should have locked it when it was clear that Freeway wasn't coming back.

"It was my fault. So no harm, no foul."

The inside of the closet was pitch black. He had always meant to install a light but had never gotten around to it. As he opened the door even wider, he made himself the promise that installing a light would be the first thing he did, once the raccoon problem was behind him.

"Come out, come out."

The sound was sudden. A hissing snarl that crackled in the quiet confines of the room like ball lightning.

"Shit!"

Thumps leaped backwards and tumbled onto the bed. But he was up in a flash, knife at the ready, waving the dowel in front of him in little figure eights.

And then silence.

"It doesn't have to end this way."

He tried to put some real commitment into his voice, but it was just for show. Standing there on the bed, he had already decided to get out of the room and call an animal-removal service.

"Okay," he called out. "You win. I'm leaving."

Another hiss, this one less threatening. And then movement. And then a face.

"Meow."

It took a moment to register.

"Freeway?"

"Meow."

The Freeway in the closet was thinner than the Freeway who had disappeared, but it was Freeway nonetheless.

"What the hell." Thumps put the knife and the dowel to one side and sat on the edge of the bed. "What the hell."

Freeway wandered over and began rubbing herself up against

his leg. Thumps reached down and ran his hand over the cat. She was skin and bones.

"You scared the shit out of me."

More rubbing, joined by loud purring. And a second sound. Higher pitched than Freeway's voice. Bright and tinny and quick.

Freeway left his leg and returned to the closet. Thumps slid off the bed and sat on the floor. Freeway hadn't died. She'd come home. That's what Pops had been trying to tell him.

"Meow."

And she hadn't come home alone. Freeway sat at the entrance to the closet with four tiny kittens pressed up against her.

"You're kidding."

"Meow."

The kittens couldn't have been more than a couple of weeks old. One of the kittens began mewing and was quickly joined by the other three. Freeway reached down and grabbed a kitten in her mouth.

"You're going to put them back in the closet, where it's safe," Thumps said, by way of encouragement. "That's a good idea."

But that's not what Freeway had in mind. She carefully carried the kitten over to where Thumps was sitting, climbed up over his legs, and deposited the kitten on his lap.

And then she went back and got the other three.

Thumps started to say something clever, but nothing came

out. And then tears. He tried to control the emotion, to tamp it down, but once it was out, there was no stopping it.

Freeway stepped onto his lap, rolled on her side so the kittens could nurse. And they sat there in the bedroom until evening ran to night and all the babies were full and sound asleep.

13

Thumps didn't get any sleep.

When he crawled into bed that night, Freeway and the kittens followed, decided that they were most comfortable tucked in around his neck. Whenever he moved, they moved with him. When he got up to go to the bathroom, they tumbled off the bed and staggered along behind him.

Freeway was the anxious mother, meowing, prowling the cardinal points of the bed, rearranging the infants in a variety of patterns that only a cat would understand.

Still, having Freeway back, safe and sound, even with kittens in tow, was an unexpected delight. He had had one cat and had been ambivalent about that. Now he had five and was enchanted. He knew it wouldn't last. The kittens were cute as all baby animals were cute, but by the time he got out of bed the next morning, reality had returned to the world.

There was the matter of a litter box. Should he have one or several? How much waste could one adult cat and four very small kittens produce? What about vet bills? Who would want a kitten? Should he name them?

Thumps stood in front of the refrigerator, tried to imagine what he might feed kittens. He knew that regular milk could cause diarrhea. He had ruled out eggs and bacon and cottage cheese when Freeway came out of the bedroom by herself. She rushed to her dish and began to vacuum up the food.

"Slow down," Thumps cautioned. "You know what happens when you eat too fast."

And then, on cue, the kittens spilled out of the bedroom, mewing for their mother. Freeway redoubled her efforts to eat, as her family plowed into her side and tried to push her over.

Thumps sat at the table and watched Freeway nurse her babies, watched as she licked each one clean, until they snuggled into a knot on the kitchen floor and went to sleep.

He was already in the bedroom, looking for his jeans, when Freeway appeared in the doorway. The cat gave a sharp meow and walked into the closet. Then she meowed again and walked out. Another meow and back into the closet.

"You've been watching too much *Lassie*."

And out she came again.

"Am I supposed to follow you?"

"Meow."

The floor of the closet was strewn with shoes. Freeway stepped over a pair of wing tips and disappeared into the deep shadows. Thumps got down on his knees so he could see better.

"Okay," he said, "I'm here."

It took a moment for his eyes to adjust. Freeway was lying on the floor next to the body of a kitten who hadn't made it. A tiny black and white female who looked as though she might be asleep.

Freeway stared at Thumps for a moment and then gently licked at the body. Thumps felt the air leave his body. He sat back on his heels, leaned against the door frame, and closed his eyes.

BY THE TIME he got to Al's, the place was mostly empty. There was a young woman standing at the counter, waiting for a cup of coffee to go.

"Hi, Mr. DreadfulWater."

Thumps didn't recognize the woman. "Oh, hi, how you doing?"

The woman smiled. "You don't recognize me, do you?"

"Thumps doesn't remember much of anything," said Al as she handed the woman her coffee. "It's the artistic temperament, you know."

"Tess Duval? I work at Café Brasilero." Tess struck a pose. "Forty-eight kinds of coffee?"

"Right."

"What I mean is, I used to work there."

"Tess is at the Tucker now."

"It's not the same. Big corporation." Tess sighed. "They really took advantage of the pandemic. I'm getting about half of what I got before. Lots of people looking for work, so they got you over a barrel."

"Banks did really well," said Al. "Remember that guy from Wells Fargo who said that we're all in it together? Guess the 'we' didn't include them."

"Most of my friends haven't found jobs." Tess put two dollars on the counter. "It's really bad out there."

Al pushed the money back. "You keep it. I just won't give Mr. DreadfulWater here a refill."

THUMPS FOUND A STOOL and settled in. There was a great appeal to a quiet place. It was akin to being in church, Thumps decided, if church had a grill and a coffee machine and wasn't under the illusion that god existed.

Al set a cup in front of him. "You look like you slept with the dogs."

"Cats," said Thumps.

"Cats?"

"Freeway came home." Thumps could feel his whole body smiling.

Al grinned. "So the cat came back."

"She did." Thumps watched Al pour the coffee into the cup.

"I thought she was a goner."

"She had kittens,"

Al set the coffee pot down with a bang. "The hell you say."

"I thought she was spayed," said Thumps, "but it appears I was wrong."

"So you're a father."

"More like Freeway's a mother."

"How many did she have?"

"Five," said Thumps. "But one died."

"That's always heartbreaking." Al started back to the grill. Halfway there, she stopped and came back in a rush. "I hope to hell you didn't throw it in the garbage."

"No."

"I hope you buried it in the backyard."

"I did."

"You and Freeway, right?" Al looked at Thumps hard. "Freeway was there when you buried her child?"

"She was."

"Okay," said Al, "then I'll make you breakfast. With kittens, you're going to need your strength."

Thumps leaned over the coffee cup and let the warmth drift across his face. He'd have to buy kitty litter, some more food for Freeway, maybe a couple of toys for the family.

And he'd have to name the babies. That would be fun. But he didn't have to do that right away. It might be better to wait to see if the kittens' personalities suggested names.

"Roxanne Heavy Runner stopped in this morning, looking for you."

"Roxanne?"

"Don't panic," said Al. "She wasn't here to hurt you."

Roxanne was a large woman with the personality of a cruise missile. She had been the band secretary long before Thumps arrived in Chinook, would probably be the secretary long after he was dead.

"She wanted me to tell you that Claire is expecting you for dinner tonight," said Al. "Early evening. Around six."

"Dinner?"

"Maybe Ivory would like a kitten."

"Claire's going to cook?"

"Yeah," said Al, "that could be a problem."

Claire Merchant was many things. A fine administrator, who had been tribal chief on several occasions. A mother to a worrisome son. A sometimes lover. And now a mother a second time around.

"I'm guessing a frozen dinner of some sort," said Al. "So you're probably safe."

What Claire wasn't was a cook. The woman just had no aptitude for cooking. And little interest in learning.

"Roxanne said you should bring flowers and something sweet." Al put a plate in front of him. Eggs, sausage, hash browns, toast, salsa. All the major food groups in one place. "Almost forgot, Wutty is now the proud owner of a bus."

"Wutty?"

"Don't be like that," said Al. "The man tries."

"He bought a bus?"

"Not exactly," said Al. "You remember that big yellow school bus been sitting behind Stas Black Weasel's garage?"

Thumps put his head in his hands. "The one with no engine and no tires?"

"Now it has an engine," said Al, "and tires as well."

"Stas repaired the bus?"

"He's Wutty's new partner," said Al. "Wutty runs the tours, and Stas looks after the maintenance."

"You fill Stas in on Wutty's other enthusiasms?"

"Sure," said Al, "but Stas said that the bus wasn't doing anything, and fixing it up wasn't a big deal. And he gets a fifty-percent stake in the business."

"What happened to the Uber/DoorDash/FedEx look-alike plan?"

"Going to concentrate on tourism instead."

Thumps pushed his coffee cup to the edge of the counter.

"No can do," said Al. "I gave your refill to Tess."

THUMPS TOOK HIS TIME with breakfast. Langfield's would be open soon. He'd stop in early, show Lynn the shots he had taken at the test facility and in Deep House, see how the camera had managed the colour rendition of the paint panels and the surrounding rocks and canyon foliage. If nothing else, it would be a pleasant conversation, a chance to find out just how far photography had moved on into the future without him.

Al was back with the coffee pot. "I decided to relent," she said as she filled his cup. "And just so you know, I wouldn't object if you named one of the kittens after me."

14

There was a young, dark-haired man behind the counter at the camera store.

"I'm guessing you're Mr. DreadfulWater," said the man. "Lynn said you'd be in first thing."

"Thumps," said Thumps.

"Ameet," said the young man. "Ameet Zalera. Fujifilm rep extraordinaire."

There was a laptop on the counter. Thin and sleek, with a soft black finish that made you want to rub it in the hope that a genie would pop out, the kind of laptop Thumps might like to have if he wanted a laptop.

Which he didn't.

"People hear my name and want to know where I'm from." Ameet opened the laptop. "Bet you get that too."

"DreadfulWater's Cherokee," said Thumps.

"Oklahoma, right?"

Thumps nodded. "Never lived there. Born and raised in California."

"East Indian," said Ameet. "Zalera is more a Portuguese last name. Grandparents are from Gujarat state, north of Mumbai, but I was born and raised in Saskatoon. You ever go back to Oklahoma?"

Tahlequah. And Park Hill. His mother had told him that he had relations in the area. But that was a lifetime ago.

"Nope. Family's all gone. Nothing left for me there."

"I got an uncle in Rajkot," said Ameet. "But that's about it."

Thumps tried to remember the other family names in Oklahoma. The grandparents. The uncles and aunts. The Phillips? The Hunts?

"Lynn says you're a film guy. Medium format? Large format?"

"Guilty."

"It's not dead." Ameet took several cameras off the shelf. "Got a lot of customers who still shoot film. Some shoot both."

"Both?"

"Sure," said Ameet. "I have an old Nikon film camera with a fifty-millimetre lens, and a Fuji mirrorless with a twenty-three millimetre. You do mostly landscape, right?"

"Mostly."

"Lynn says you're interested in giving digital a look."

"I'm curious."

"I have a loaner that's out with a photographer in Helena.

Soon as it comes back, I'll drop it off with Lynn. He'll set you up. Next time you're in the field, take a couple of shots with it and take a couple of the same scene with your rig."

"Can't get a better deal than that." Lynn had come out of the back. "I'll be curious to see how the two compare."

"In the meantime," said Ameet, "Lynn tells me you're looking to score some free crime-scene photos."

Thumps took the Panasonic out of his pocket and set it on the counter.

Ameet slid the SD card out of the camera and slipped it into the side of the laptop.

"All right, so we have a . . ." Ameet turned the computer so Thumps could see the screen.

"Burned Mercedes van."

"Don't see that every day." Ameet scrolled through the photos. "And these are?"

"The paint panel field out at the test facility."

Lynn made a popping sound with his mouth. "Is that Deep House?"

The photo on the screen was of one of the shelters. A dark, damp landscape. Confined and slightly disturbing. Thumps couldn't remember which one. Not that it mattered.

Lynn pushed his glasses up his nose. "You actually went hiking in the canyon?"

Thumps was surprised at the sharpness and clarity of the shots.

"Couple of these are underexposed," said Ameet, "but that's the beauty of digital photography. With digital, you can change the exposure." The young man moved a slider on the screen and the image brightened. "It's that easy."

"Great."

"And that's before you get into the various filters and algorithms."

Thumps watched as Ameet changed the saturation and the intensity of the image.

"Bada bing, bada boom."

Or, Thumps thought to himself, you could expose it correctly the first time and not depend on a computer to do it for you.

"And if you don't like colour, you can switch to black and white."

Thumps had to admit that he was impressed. All this without having to put one foot in a darkroom. All this without having to mix chemicals and hope that the fumes didn't destroy your liver.

"What I like best," said Ameet, "is that you can enlarge sections. Course, you can do the same thing with an enlarger, but this is so much quicker."

The image on the screen was of Cooley standing next to the paint panels. The big man was smiling, one hand resting on the silver panel, as though it were something he had bagged on a safari.

"Depending on the size of the sensor and the file, you can go as large as you want."

Cooley suddenly disappeared, and Thumps realized he was looking at the rocks in the background.

"Like this," said Ameet.

Lynn leaned in. "What's that?"

"What?"

"There."

Ameet squinted at the screen. Then he worked a slider and made the image larger and smaller, larger and smaller, trying to get the correct magnification.

"Shit," said Lynn. "Is that what I think it is?"

Sheriff Duke Hockney was enjoying a cup of coffee, and he was not amused.

"A body?"

Thumps handed him the photograph that Lynn had printed off.

"In Deep House?" There was a small bag on the desk. Duke pushed it to one side and studied the photograph. "You sure Lynn isn't pulling your leg?"

"What?"

"I've seen some of the things you can do with digital. They got tidal waves breaking over Manhattan, whales in a bathtub."

"Don't think he's fooling around."

"Dinosaurs walking across the Golden Gate Bridge."

"I think that's an arm."

"You know that this is my first cup of coffee?" Duke turned the photograph upside down. "And in this bag is a raisin Danish. From the new bakery."

Thumps glanced at the bag.

"I have a routine to my day," said the sheriff. "And I don't like it interrupted."

"Could be a dead body."

Duke snorted. "Damn it, DreadfulWater, you sure know how to ruin a man's pleasure."

"I could stay here and guard the Danish."

Duke reached for the phone. "You know what misery loves best of all?"

Two hours later, there were four vehicles and six people at the entrance to Deep House. Cooley Small Elk and his pickup truck, Sheriff Duke Hockney and his cruiser, Deputies Lance Packard and Deanna Heavy Runner, Beth Mooney in her station wagon.

And Thumps DreadfulWater.

"Why am I here?"

"You're a material witness," said the sheriff. "You and Cooley found the body."

"The only thing we found," said Thumps, "was a bunch of busted paint panels."

"Everybody knows everybody," said the sheriff. "So let's not waste any time. Canyon's no place to be after dark."

"Thumps doesn't have to come," said Cooley. "I can show you where the photograph was taken."

"He interrupted my morning routine."

Thumps held his hands out. "Sitting in a chair is a routine?"

"And he ate part of my Danish."

"Unfortunately," said Beth, "I seem to have worn the wrong shoes. So I'm going to wait here until you bring the body out."

"Don't you want to see the crime scene?" said the sheriff.

"Take lots of photos," said Beth.

"I'll stay and protect her," said Thumps.

"Don't need protection," said Beth.

"I'll stay anyway."

Duke pulled his hat down on his head. "Going to be boring just standing around."

Beth's face brightened. "I can give Mr. DreadfulWater his annual physical."

Thumps didn't waste any time. "She's kidding."

"No, I'm not," said Beth.

"Now there's a difficult choice," said the sheriff. "Don't suppose you could wait until I get back?"

"Canyon gets dark quick," said Thumps. "You guys are burning daylight."

"You know," said the sheriff, "one of these days, I'm going to arrest you for aggravated annoyance."

"I'll be happy to testify for the prosecution," said Beth.

Hockney pulled the backpack out of the cruiser. "About that physical," he said to Beth, "if there are sharp instruments involved, I'd appreciate it if you'd use your cellphone to capture the moment for later viewing."

Thumps walked with the sheriff as far as the first boulder field. "You thinking what I'm thinking?"

"You mean our missing driver?" Duke stopped and considered the mountain of rocks in front of him. "In law enforcement, we call that 'jumping to conclusions.'"

"Could be a tourist," said Lance. "Got too close to the edge."

"Or it could be a hiker," said the sheriff. "Though why anyone would go into Deep House for shits and giggles is beyond me."

Thumps looked up at a boulder the size of a three-storey building. "You're actually going in?"

"My job," said the sheriff. "I don't have to like it. I just have to do it."

"It's not that bad," said Cooley. "So long as you don't get hurt."

"It might not even be a body," said Deanna. "The photo isn't all that clear. It could be the arm from a mannequin. Maybe someone dumped a bunch of fixtures from a store that went out of business."

Duke's face darkened. "What was the most important thing they taught you at the academy?"

"Don't piss off the boss," said Deanna.

"And if it is a mannequin," said Duke, "who gets to carry it out?"

"I do," said Deanna.

"Only because Special Deputy DreadfulWater here has an appointment for a physical."

Deanna didn't even make an effort to keep the smile off her face. "Special Deputy?"

"It's honorary," said Duke. "It doesn't mean shit."

BETH HAD HER DOCTOR'S KIT OUT and was arranging the pieces on the tailgate of Cooley's pickup.

She motioned him over. "How long do you think they'll be?"

Thumps kept his distance. "Couple of hours."

"Then we have plenty of time."

"Not happening," said Thumps. "I'm thinking I should go back to town."

"You don't have a car." Beth set a small rubber hammer next to a tongue depressor.

"You have a car," said Thumps. "We could go back together."

"I'm an officer of the court," said Beth. "I can't leave my post."

"And I have to look after Freeway," said Thumps.

"Freeway." Beth stopped what she was doing. "Your dead cat?"

"She's not dead," said Thumps. "And she had kittens."

"Kittens?"

"Four," said Thumps. "It's my job to make sure that they're okay."

"So you're a father." Beth picked up the tongue depressor. "All the more reason to have a physical."

Thumps glanced at the entrance to Deep House. Maybe he could catch up with the sheriff.

"Don't do it for yourself," said Beth. "Do it for your family."

THE SUN WAS FADING and the shadows were gathering up the land when Cooley strolled out of Deep House.

"Took us longer than we thought." Cooley stopped and shook himself. "Carrying a body bag over the boulders is tricky."

Beth cocked her head. "Duke carried a body bag over those boulders?"

"Nope," said Cooley. "Me and Lance and Deanna took turns. Duke supervised."

"So it was a body?"

"It was." Sheriff Duke Hockney came out from the shadows on the canyon walls. "No wallet, so we're going to have to wait on a name."

Beth opened the back of her station wagon. "In the meantime, let's get John Doe somewhere more comfortable."

Thumps flashed on Beth's morgue. "Comfortable" was not the word he would have used for the basement room with its body lockers and stainless-steel table.

"Found more of those paint panels," said Duke. "Yellow was kinda nice. The silver was ugly as hell."

"Just painted my apartment," said Beth. "You wouldn't believe how hard it is to get the colour right."

Duke hooked his thumbs in his Sam Browne belt. "You got any other bodies on the go?"

"You don't know how long I've waited for a man to ask me that."

"Just need to know if we're looking at an accident or something more nefarious."

Thumps looked at Duke.

"Not my place to guess," said the sheriff. "That's the job of the county coroner."

BETH SHUT THE BACK DOOR of the wagon. "Let the guessing begin." Cooley headed home. Lance and Deanna drove back to the office. Beth set out for the old Land Titles building and the morgue. Thumps rode into Chinook in the cruiser with the sheriff.

"You missed all the fun." Duke brought the visor down to block out the last flash of the day. "Saw a porcupine."

"And a dead body."

"Heard an owl," said Duke, "but didn't see it."

"And a dead body."

"Paint panels were still there."

"Next to the dead body."

"Actually," said the sheriff, "the dead body was in the rocks behind the panels. You would have known that if you had come with us."

"Drop me at the house," said Thumps. "Please."

"Don't you want to attend the autopsy?"

"Beth's not going to do the autopsy tonight."

"She might if I ask her."

"I have a cat to take care of."

"I thought you killed your cat." Duke kept his eyes on the road ahead.

"Freeway came back," said Thumps. "And she had kittens."

Duke started chuckling. Then he started laughing. When the laughing turned to choking, he pulled the cruiser off to the side of the road.

"Damn it, DreadfulWater," said Duke, tears running down his face. "When you step in the shit, you step in the shit."

"They're cute."

"All kittens are cute," said the sheriff. "And then they grow up."

"If you're good," said Thumps, "I might give you one."

Duke shook his head. "You got names for them yet?"

"Not yet."

"Keep it that way," said Hockney. "You start naming them, and you'll never get rid of the little rascals."

Thumps rolled his hand backwards. "The dead guy?"

"If you had come with us," said the sheriff, "you'd have seen what we saw."

"Which was?"

"Well, between you and me," said Duke, "let's just say I don't think it was the fall that killed him."

15

There wasn't much left of the evening by the time the sheriff pulled up in front of Thumps's house.

"I'll call you when I know about the autopsy," he said.

Thumps opened the door and stepped out.

"Come on," said Duke. "You love autopsies."

"Tied up."

"How can you be tied up?" said the sheriff. "You don't do anything."

The lights were on at Dixie's. Thumps checked his porch. No Pops.

"You want to see the kittens?"

"Pass."

"They're really cute."

"So was I when I was a baby," said Duke.

Thumps shut the door of the cruiser. "Point taken."

There were no lights on in the house, and as he stepped onto the porch, Thumps reminded himself, once again, that it might be a good idea to leave at least one light on so when he arrived home after dark, the place would feel as though he were walking into a dinner party rather than an open grave.

Dinner party.

Shit.

Dinner at Claire's.

He had forgotten all about it. After seven.

Shit. Shit. Shit.

If he called and tried to explain, it would sound as though he was making an excuse. And besides, what was he going to say?

Duke dragged me out to Deep House to find a body.

I was at Deep House with the sheriff looking for a body we saw in a photograph.

No, I didn't go into the canyon. I had to stay with Beth.

God, Thumps thought to himself. At least try to be coherent.

Or he could just show up. He could claim that Roxanne had given him the wrong time. Which was a bad idea. Word would get back to Roxanne, and she would kill him.

And he didn't have flowers. Roxanne had said something about flowers.

Shit. Shit. Shit.

He jogged to his car and got in. Twenty-two minutes to Claire's place. Eighteen if he had lights and a siren. He hadn't been particularly comfortable playing sheriff while Duke had his surgery, but right now he would have welcomed a police cruiser and the right to break every and all traffic laws.

Not that a cruiser was going to be of any help once he arrived.

There were lights on at Claire's place. Thumps wasn't sure if this was good news or bad news. On the way out to the reserve, he had fantasized that the house would be dark, that Claire wouldn't be home, that she would be off somewhere, that Roxanne had been jerking his chain just because she could.

As he pulled into the driveway, he saw Claire pass in front of the kitchen window. Okay, this was the moment that separated the men from the other men, whatever the hell that meant. Stay or turn tail and run. Though it wasn't much of a moment. Claire would have seen him coming the moment his lights broke the ridge.

His opportunity to flee was long gone.

Thumps shut the car door with some authority and strode to the house, shoulders back, swinging his arms in what he hoped looked to be a confident manner.

If this were a scene in a romantic comedy, Claire would open the door just as he mounted the porch and reached for the bell. She'd be dressed in dark slacks and a silky blouse that hugged her body. She'd look surprised. Her face would soften with love and diffuse lighting as she stepped forward and melted into his arms.

In his dreams.

Claire was dressed in a pair of bib overalls and a blue work shirt. The overalls had seen better days. The top half was stained in various colours, while the bottom half was streaked with what looked to be dried glue.

"Hi."

Ivory was huddled behind her mother's leg, her face covered in something brown, which Thumps hoped was chocolate.

"You're late."

Thumps smiled. Sometimes it worked.

"Roxanne said you were bringing flowers."

Sometimes it didn't.

Thumps squatted down so he was on Ivory's level. "Are you the best little girl in the world?"

Ivory seemed to consider this for a moment.

"Dog," she said.

"You're a dog?"

"Dog."

"It's her new word," said Claire. "Last week, it was 'poop.'"

"I got tied up with the sheriff." Thumps tried to look contrite. Sometimes that worked better than smiling.

"I heard," said Claire. "Dead body in Deep House."

The kitchen was warm and bright. Thumps didn't see anything that resembled dinner, and there was nothing in the air to suggest a meal might be in the offing.

"That's not going to help the land claim any." Claire went

to the refrigerator. "They'll use it as another excuse to delay the implementation of the court order."

Ivory followed her mother, glancing over her shoulder in case Thumps tried to get too close.

"Right now, she's shy," said Claire. "In another five minutes, you won't be able to get her off your lap."

"Dog," said Ivory.

"Does the sheriff know what happened?"

"Don't think so," said Thumps.

"So he could have fallen?"

"Sure," said Thumps. "We don't even know who he is yet."

Claire took out an egg carton. "Thought he was the driver of the burned-out van at the test facility."

Thumps was always amazed at how fast information got around. He had expected that the van and the dead body would be the entertainment for the evening. Now, he would have to find other topics of conversation.

Relationships, for instance.

"We're not sure if the body has anything to do with the van," said Thumps. "They could be unrelated."

"We?" Claire put the bacon next to the eggs. "You still acting sheriff?"

Ivory took a couple of steps away from her mother. "Dog."

"Not anymore. Duke just likes to drag me along."

"And you went."

Thumps shrugged. "You know. Friends."

Claire took an onion out of the basket. "I figured we'd have omelettes."

Thumps cooked. It was faster this way, with the probability of edible results. He knew if he waited for Claire to prepare the meal, he'd starve. Thumps wasn't sure if she was really this incompetent or if she had learned the art of avoidance from the other men who had moved in and out of her life.

Ivory sat in her highchair with a bowl of Cheerios and watched him intently. Claire sat in her chair next to her daughter and watched as well.

"I love to see a man cook," she said. "Just don't burn the onions."

"Dog," said Ivory.

"So you won the court case."

Claire turned in the chair. "Won the court case a year ago. Big ceremony to officially return the land is supposed to be this month."

"Congratulations."

"But now the state is asking for a five-year moratorium, so they can consider their options."

"Options?"

"As in landfill."

"You're kidding."

"Just a rumour right now," said Claire. "But if you look

around, it appears that reservations make the best landfills. Nuclear waste, toxic waste, general garbage. New Mexico. Arizona. Utah. Supposed to be the new buffalo."

Claire picked up Cheerios and put them back in Ivory's bowl.

"Course, people been using the canyon as a dump site for years. You ever know Sonny Martell?"

"Don't think so."

"Probably before your time," said Claire. "Sonny owned a bunch of small companies. Construction mostly. Along with a septic service."

"This the guy who ran the real estate scam?"

"One and the same," said Claire. "He was dumping sewage into the canyon."

"Lovely."

"We complained, but no one did anything," said Claire. "And then one time, Sonny backed his pumper up to the rim, was ready to dump his load, when Earl Old Person shot the tires out with his deer rifle."

Thumps smiled.

"Put a couple of rounds through the radiator as well."

"Don't suppose Martell was all that happy."

"Tried to have Earl arrested."

"What happened?"

"Turned out Sonny had bigger fish to fry," said Claire. "Something to do with embezzlement. He took off before the case ever got to court."

"Using Deep House as a landfill is crazy."

"You don't have to convince me."

"Besides, you won the case. The matter is settled."

Claire smiled at Ivory and brushed the hair out of her face. Then she smiled at Thumps with the same expression.

"Mr. DreadfulWater is a funny man, isn't he, honey?"

"Dog," said Ivory.

THE OMELETTES WERE PERFECT, if Thumps did say so himself. The bacon crispy. The toast lightly browned. Claire ate her meal in silence, giving Ivory forkfuls of egg every so often. At first, she ate them, but then she spat them out onto the tray and mashed them with her fingers.

"She has to touch everything, and she has to put everything in her mouth." Claire used her finger to wipe away a rope of snot that had slid out of Ivory's nose. "Stanley was the same way."

Thumps used his fork to cut into the omelette and tried to ignore the visual similarities between baby snot and egg whites.

Ivory leaned forward in the high chair and held out her hands.

"She wants some of your toast," said Claire. "Just a small piece with no crust."

"How was Great Falls?"

"Great. Saw friends. Had a nice meal. Ivory got sick and threw up all over her car seat."

Thumps placed the square of toast on the tray. Ivory looked at the toast, and then she looked at Thumps.

"She's not quite sure what to make of you."

"I should come out more often."

Claire got up and came back with the coffee pot. "How would you feel if I was seeing someone?"

Ivory hit the piece of toast with a fist. And then she hit it again.

"Stanley used to do that too."

"Okay."

Claire sat back. "Okay that Stanley used to mash his food too, or okay that I'm seeing someone?"

"Both," said Thumps. "I guess."

"You upset?"

Thumps watched Ivory continue her assault on the toast. Babies, he decided, had one advantage over adults. They didn't have to answer rhetorical questions. Or in this case, land mines disguised as questions.

You upset?

Of course he was upset. But if he said he was upset, he would look like a jealous lover, petty and unreasonable. If he said it was no big deal, he would appear cold and distant.

"I guess it's a surprise."

"Good or bad?"

* * *

Ivory, as it turned out, liked having a man around. While Claire did the dishes, Thumps chased Ivory around the house. He was sure that he would wear her down eventually.

"Don't get her too worked up," Claire called out from the sink. "It'll be harder to get her to sleep."

Thumps did one more lap through the living room, down the hall, back into the kitchen, before he collapsed on the sofa. Ivory ran past him and did three more circuits before she realized that no one was chasing her.

Claire dried her hands and joined him on the sofa. Ivory climbed up and wedged herself between them.

"Do you want to know who?"

"Freeway's back."

"Your cat?"

"She didn't die," said Thumps. "She had kittens."

"Kittens?" Claire's face was all smiles. "You and kittens?"

"I thought maybe Ivory would like a kitten."

Claire ruffled Ivory's hair. "Did you hear that, honey? Mr. DreadfulWater wants to give us a cat."

"Dog," said Ivory.

"Well," said Claire, "I guess that settles that."

Ivory grinned and put her head on Thumps's thigh. She lay there quietly while he rubbed her back and marvelled how something so small could one day become an adult, tried to imagine what it would be like to raise a child.

The pain was immediate and unexpected, and Thumps screamed in spite of himself.

Claire rolled Ivory over and looked at her sternly. "We don't do that, do we?"

Thumps felt as though someone had grabbed his thigh with a pair of pliers.

"She's started biting," said Claire. "Stanley did that as well."

There was no tear in Thumps's pants, and he was pretty sure Ivory hadn't broken the skin.

"I'm sorry," said Claire. "I should have warned you."

Ivory huddled up against her mother, her lower lip starting to quiver.

"It's okay," said Thumps. "It was just . . . a surprise."

"More where that came from," said Claire. "You want to read her a book?"

THE BOOK WAS about a bunch of animals who didn't want to go to sleep. Ivory lay next to him and kicked the sofa with her feet.

"She's pretty good about sleeping once you get her down." Claire held Ivory's feet in place. "But most nights, I have to start her in bed with me."

Thumps finished the book and set it to one side. "I should probably get going."

Claire gathered Ivory in her arms. "You ever think about him?"

Thumps waited.

"Harold Shipman." Claire held Thumps with her eyes. "Our serial killer."

"Not even sure that was his real name."

"Don't know that the name matters."

"No," said Thumps. "Probably doesn't."

Thumps could see that Claire wanted to say more. And then the moment passed.

"You going to be at the autopsy tomorrow?"

"Don't think so."

Claire walked him to the door. "If you go, could you call me? I'd like to know what we're looking at."

"So you don't get blindsided?"

"State may try to use a death in Deep House as an excuse to stop the implementation of the court decision."

Thumps stepped out into the night. "I'll see what I can find out."

"No one likes to be blindsided." Claire turned so Thumps could see Ivory's face. "You know," she said, "if we both didn't know better, I'd say that she has your eyes."

16

Thumps drove back to Chinook slowly, letting the car drift along the road. He stopped at the overlook and got out to watch the Ironstone River cut through the prairies on its way to somewhere else, not here.

So Claire was seeing someone. Someone he didn't know. As though that made a difference. Or maybe it did. Thumps supposed that the moment in Claire's house would have been harder if her new man had been someone he knew.

If he was a man at all.

The night was cold, and as he stood by the car, he found himself mourning the loss of a relationship that had been tenuous at best. He and Claire had always stood at a distance from one another. Sometimes, the degree of separation was a creek they could step across.

Sometimes, it was an ocean.

And Ivory. She wasn't his child. So why would he feel this loss as well? After all, she *had* bit him.

Try as he might, he couldn't help but drag out the old cliché. What did this new person have that he didn't? Of course, the answer was simple enough. He had Claire and Ivory. And Thumps did not.

Harold Shipman.

Thumps had hoped that Shipman would fade into the past. It didn't look as though that was going to happen anytime soon. Thumps could see Claire's concern, could see the parallels between the Obsidian Murders on the California coast that had left Anna Tripp and her daughter, Callie, dead and Shipman arriving in Chinook to threaten Claire and Ivory.

Mother and daughter.

Mother and daughter.

One pair he had failed. The other he had saved. Not by himself, but saved nonetheless. And now Shipman was dead. The threat gone. Only the memory in the blood remained.

Thumps stood at the edge of the overlook and considered the river. It didn't have to worry about such things. It was content being a river. Happy to be flowing along. At peace with itself. It didn't have to drive a cold car back to a cold house and climb into a cold bed.

He could feel himself sliding toward depression when he

remembered Freeway and the kittens. His family. As it turned out, his only family. They'd be happy to see him. He'd be happy to see them.

WHEN THE SHERIFF had dropped him off at his house earlier, the place had been dark. Now there was a light on. In the living room. Thumps doubted that Freeway could have reached the switch, couldn't think of a reason why the cat would have bothered.

Maybe he just forgot and was now paying to light the night.

Still, he took his time opening the door. He had had enough surprises for the evening. He stepped into the kitchen and listened. No sounds. Nothing in the air. Still, someone was here.

"Lucy," he called out, "I'm home."

The man sitting on the sofa in the living room was dressed in jeans, a black T-shirt, a windbreaker two sizes too large, a silver pendant on a leather thong around his neck. Shoulder sling. Combat boots. His long, black hair slicked back for effect. All in all, he looked like a villain from a James Bond movie.

"Hey, Pancho."

Cisco Cruz.

Freeway was on Cisco's lap, the kittens tucked in around him.

"Miss me?"

Thumps looked at Cruz on his sofa and at his cat family on another man's lap.

"You know, I could have shot you."

"Would have to have a gun to do that." Cruz held up the García Márquez novel. "Any good?"

"You read?"

"Mostly mysteries."

"Then you won't like it."

Freeway stood up, stretched, jumped off Cruz's lap, and came over to turn figure eights around Thumps's legs.

"She's hungry," said Cruz. "I don't feed cats."

Cruz hadn't changed all that much, and so far as Thumps remembered, the man was wearing exactly what he had been wearing that last time Thumps had seen him.

"So you broke into my house in order *not* to feed my cat?"

"Door was open, *pendejo*," said Cruz. "Cat was lonely."

"No, it wasn't. No, she's not."

"The kittens can't get into the litter box," said Cruz. "There have been a few accidents, so I'd be careful where I stepped."

"You could have cleaned it up."

"Not happening."

Cruz stood up. The kittens tumbled into the depression he left in the sofa. "They're cute," he said. "The one with the pink nose has your eyes."

Thumps didn't want to ask the question. He was sure he wasn't going to like the answer.

"What are you doing here?"

"Aren't you supposed to ask me how I've been, if I'd like

some coffee, maybe whip up some food?" Cruz walked past Thumps and into the kitchen. "Didn't the concept of Western hospitality get its start with Native people?"

"We learned our lesson."

Cruz pulled out a chair and sat down at the kitchen table.

"Remember how much fun we had last time?"

"Fun" wasn't how Thumps would have described it. Cruz had come to Chinook in the employ of a billionaire, one Boomper Austin. Austin had been after a red beryl deposit on reservation land, and Cruz had been his shotgun.

"Oliver Parrish? Hot lead and generous women? Gunfights at high noon?"

"It was at night, and you almost got me killed."

Cruz sat back. His jacket fell open. Thumps could see the butt of a very large gun in the sling.

"*Cabrón*, I saved your life."

Thumps snorted. "Parrish had a gun to my head. Said he was going to kill me. And what did you say?"

Cruz shrugged.

"You said, 'Go ahead, he's not my friend.'"

"That was before we got to know each other, Pancho. Before we became good amigos."

"And when did that happen?"

"Besides," said Cruz, "I was the one who got shot."

"What's the difference?"

Cruz frowned.

"Between *cabrón* and *pendejo*?" said Thumps. "Don't they both mean 'asshole'?"

"Sure," said Cruz, "but one is affectionate and one is not."

"And which is which?"

"Depends," said Cruz.

"Okay," said Thumps. "Easy question. Why are you in my house?"

Cruz spread his arms. "I was passing through. Thought I'd stop in and say hello."

Thumps closed his eyes. When he opened them, Cruz was still there.

"I'm in town for a few days." Cruz got to his feet. "Maybe we can get together. Talk about old times."

"Sure."

"Let me have your cell," said Cruz. "I'll put my number in your phone book."

"Don't have one."

"You don't have a cellphone?"

Thumps put on his happy face. "Nope."

"I don't believe it." Cruz fumbled around in the pocket of his jacket. "Here," he said. "Carry this with you at all times."

"Don't want a cellphone."

"It's just a loaner," said Cruz. "So you can reach me, and I can reach you." Cruz started toward the door. "Oh, I had to take your cat door apart."

Thumps waited.

"Some kind of monster dog got his head stuck in the opening."

"Pops," said Thumps. "My next-door neighbour's dog."

"You need to tell your neighbour to get his hound checked out. Dog has a bad digestion problem."

Thumps followed Cruz onto the porch. The night was black and alive with stars.

"No moon," said Cruz. "I always like it when there's no moon."

FREEWAY WAS ON THE SOFA, the kittens curled up beside her. The frame for the cat door was on the floor next to the end table. Thumps would fix it tomorrow.

So that's why Pops had been so keen to get into the house. He knew that Freeway had returned and was anxious to see his friend. He probably knew about the kittens as well.

Thumps, Claire, and Ivory.

Pops, Freeway, and the kittens.

There was a parallel here somewhere. Not that Thumps was interested in pursuing it. What did interest him was the arrival of Cisco Cruz. The man didn't just pass through. Thumps couldn't see how the dead guy in the canyon and Cisco Cruz would overlap, but he didn't believe that the two things happening at the same time was a coincidence.

And if Cruz was in town, the chances of trouble showing up

were excellent. In fact, trouble had probably already arrived.

Thumps went back inside. Cruz was right. The kittens couldn't get into the cat box. The sides were too high. But they had tried. There were little bits of kitten shit by the side of the box to mark their efforts. And there were bits of shit by the sofa where they hadn't tried at all.

How could something so little produce so much waste? Tomorrow, he'd give the floor a good scrubbing and break out the spray bottle of odour enzyme. And he'd get a different box, something the kittens could manage.

He had just gotten comfortable in bed when he felt Freeway jump up. He kept his eyes shut, pretended that he was asleep as the cat deposited the first of the kittens on his neck.

And then she jumped off the bed to get the next kitten, repeating the process until everyone was cuddled up on the bed together. For the first little while, Thumps tried to imagine that it was Claire and Ivory in the bed with him rather than cats.

But there was the purring and the wiggling and the sharp little claws.

Thumps was sure that the kittens were happy. They sounded happy. And he liked that Freeway trusted him with their safety. He just wished the cats could manage their contentment quietly.

And somewhere else.

Later, when he got up to pee, Freeway wandered into the bathroom and rubbed herself against his leg.

"You pleased with yourself?"

Freeway rolled over on the floor, her belly exposed.

"Really?"

Freeway looked at him as if to ask if this was really a question.

"Okay." Thumps leaned over and gave the cat a quick tummy rub. "Let's talk about where you've been all this time."

THE REST OF THE NIGHT, as Thumps moved about the bed, the cats followed. He tried to get them to settle at his feet.

No dice.

He tried arranging them against his back.

No dice.

He even tucked them under the covers next to his belly, and for a while, they were content in this position. But then Freeway began licking at his belly button, her tongue as smooth as eighty-grit sandpaper.

In the time Freeway had been gone, Thumps had forgotten about this particular bad habit. Evidently, she had not. Worse, as soon as their mother began licking, the kittens joined in, forcing Thumps onto his stomach, a position he hated.

"Give it up."

The belly button no longer available, Freeway pushed her way out from under the covers and began dragging her brood, one at a time, to the top of the bed and packing them in against his neck.

Thumps lay in bed and wondered if this was the way it was with mothers and babies across the animal kingdom.

But when he got up the next morning, he was simply tired and no smarter.

17

A l's was busy when Thumps got there, and he had to wait to get a stool. Russell Plunkett and Jimmy Monroe were sitting in their usual spots across from the grill.

"You just missed him," said Russell.

"Your lucky day," said Jimmy.

"They're talking about Mr. Youngbeaver," said Al. "In case you weren't able to figure that out for yourself."

Russell Plunkett and Jimmy Monroe shook their heads collectively.

"He wants a favour," said Russell. "Just so you know."

"He said it isn't so much a favour," said Jimmy, "as it's an opportunity to improve your brand."

Laura Dickson, who worked in Parks and Recreation for the city, was sitting on his favourite stool. She looked to be ready to leave. Thumps sent mental encouragements into the universe to help her along.

"Wutty figures that you're desperate for exposure," said Russell.

Dickson came along the narrow aisle between the stools and the row of plywood booths. Thumps squeezed up against Jimmy, in order to let her pass.

"Wutty wants you to photograph him and his bus," said Russell. "And he wants you to do a bunch of on-site photographs for the brochure."

"For free," said Jimmy.

Thumps slipped away from Jimmy and headed for the safety of the stool. Al followed along on the other side of the counter, the coffee pot in hand.

"Screaming Eagle Tours."

"What?"

Al started chuckling. "That's the name of Wutty's company."

Thumps wrapped his hands around the cup. "What happened to WindArrow?"

"Said it didn't have enough *gravitas*."

"*Gravitas*?"

Al wiped at a spot on the counter. "It's Latin."

"Does he know what it means?"

"Evidently, some famous actor used it in an interview." Al sighed. "Wutty's taking pre-reservations for the first tour even as we speak."

"How about breakfast?"

"You want to guess where it's going?"

There weren't really that many scenic places around Chinook to interest a busload of tourists. There was the Buffalo Mountain Resort with its river trail and casino. Red Tail Lake was pleasant enough if you liked flat landscapes. And there were places along the Ironstone with decent panoramas.

"You might suppose he would run them up to that new dude ranch over by Glory, the Rocking something or other," said Al. "Hear you can drive around in golf carts and shoot at buffalo."

"What?"

"The Rocking A. That's the place." Al was having a good time just thinking about it. "They use paintball guns, and the buffalo are just bales of hay with targets stuck to the side."

"Wutty's taking tourists to a theme park?"

"Nope," said Al. "He's taking everyone to Deep House."

"Deep House?" Thumps sat back on the stool. "Is he nuts?"

"A fair question," said Al. "But in Wutty's case, rhetorical."

It took Thumps a moment to catch up. "Is this about the body?"

Al lowered her voice. "He's calling it the 'Canyon of Death' tour."

Thumps put his head in his hands and considered the counter.

"He's hoping that the guy was murdered," said Al. "'Cause murder would add an element of danger to the trip."

"Whereas wandering about in Deep House isn't danger enough?"

"He's not going to actually take them into the canyon," said Al. "Just going to stand around at the entrance and think about how he's going to spend all his money."

Thumps remembered reading an article about a guy who spent years trying to come up with a successful idea. In the end, he did, and when he was asked what had led to the breakthrough, he said he attributed his success to all his failures.

Thumps didn't think there was any formula for failures versus successes, but maybe the concept had merit. Maybe the more you tried and failed, the more you learned until you'd learned enough to succeed.

Given Wutty's track record of failures, this might mean that Screaming Eagle Tours had more promise than was immediately apparent.

And then again, maybe not.

"How are the kittens?"

"Cute."

"That goes without saying," said Al. "And if they stayed small and cute, there might not be a need to go looking for a burlap sack and an irrigation ditch."

"Jesus, Al."

"No sense honey-coating the world."

"Aren't you supposed to be making my breakfast?"

"Then again, I might be in the market for a kitten."

"You?"

"Seems as though I've got mice."

Thumps looked around. "Mice? In the café?"

"Keep your voice down." Al leaned over the counter. "Found a few droppings the other day. Might be nice to have a café cat that would patrol the place. Might could train it to pour coffee and collect money."

"Right," said Thumps.

"One of the females," said Al. "Don't want one of the lazy males, lying around on his back, looking for a tummy rub."

Thumps gave a quick salute. "Female hunter-killer. Check."

"Just make sure she's a mean little carnivore." Al headed back to the grill to get his breakfast. "And not one of those 'live and let live' vegetarians."

THUMPS'S PLAN FOR THE DAY was simple. Eat a good breakfast. Go home and disappear into the darkroom, where no one could find him. Not the sheriff, not Archie, not Freeway and the kittens. He'd turn on some soft jazz and sort through his negatives to see if there was something he had missed, an image that might have exhibition potential.

He had done this more than once already and knew that there was nothing of any import hiding in the negatives. Still, it would take his mind off the world, at least for an afternoon.

"Ah, Mr. Thumps."

Chintak Rawat, resplendent in his starched white pharmacist uniform, slid onto the stool next to him.

"I am hoping that we might have a conversation."

Thumps smiled. "Sure."

"Excellent," said Rawat. "As you will know, I am quite skilled in the management of medications, both over-the-counter and prescription."

"You're the best."

"Too kind," said Rawat. "But true. I spend each day sorting and counting and informing myself about all the new remedies for the various problems that afflict humankind. If something can be cured with a pill or a potion, then I will know of it."

Thumps pushed a forkful of egg up against the toast. "This about a woman?"

Rawat's face lit up. "Oh, my, no."

"Okay."

"In addition to the dispensing of pills, I am well versed in the particulars of heterosexual romance and procreative coupling."

"Good for you."

"Though, I must admit, considerably less experienced in the intricacies of alternative arrangements."

Thumps looked at his plate. He liked to keep everything even. Just enough toast to go with the remaining egg. Enough sausage so the egg wouldn't be lonely. There was nothing worse than winding up with one thing or the other alone on the plate.

"However," said Rawat, "I find myself at a loss to understand the complexities of male camaraderie."

Al appeared with the pot of coffee. "This about the hunting trip?"

"Yes, indeed," said Rawat. "It is very much about the hunting trip."

Thumps looked at Al.

"Don't look at me," said Al. "All I know is that Cooley and Stas are going on a big hunting trip, end of the month."

"Mr. Stas and Mr. Cooley and I are very good friends," said Rawat. "We do many things together. We are the three . . . three . . ."

"Musketeers?" offered Thumps.

"Stooges," said Al.

"Amigos," said Rawat. "Yes. We are the three amigos."

Thumps put egg and a piece of sausage on his fork together. "And they didn't invite you on the hunt?"

"Sadly," said Rawat, "no."

Thumps tried to imagine Rawat with a rifle in his hands. "Do you like to hunt?"

Rawat looked stricken. "Absolutely no. Shooting another creature cannot be a consideration."

"Maybe," said Thumps, "that's why they didn't ask you."

"But we're friends."

"Thumps is their friend too," said Al, "and I'll bet they didn't ask him."

Thumps tried to look forlorn. "Didn't even know they were going."

Rawat sat back. "You are suggesting that they are trying to accommodate my sensibilities."

"Absolutely," said Al.

"Ah," said Rawat. "Yes. I can imagine this. In theory."

Thumps ate the last bit of toast and got off the stool. "It's what friends do," he said.

"Then," said Rawat, "I will say no more about it."

18

As Thumps walked along Main Street, counting the empty storefronts, he ran through his options on how to spend the day. If he had gotten out of bed in good order, he could be on high ground above the Ironstone with his field camera, waiting for that moment when all the elements of landscape came together.

Now, that option was gone. By the time he drove out to the river, the sun would be directly overhead, the light baking all the contrast out of the river valley.

Or he could be in the darkroom printing up the photographs for a possible fall show at Shadow Ranch. That option wasn't much better. The resort had been hard hit by the pandemic. And while it was slowly coming back to life, there was no guarantee that Vernon Rockland was going to be in the mood to host a photography exhibition.

So he kept walking. It wasn't an option, but neither did it require any decision-making. And when he got to the corner, he stopped.

It was the car.

A limousine. Metallic black with privacy glass and a communications fin on the roof that made the vehicle look as though it were a close cousin to a shark.

And not just any limousine. This one was a stretch Porsche Cayenne, more a luxury family station wagon than sports car. When had the Germans stopped making high-performance sports cars and started making these clumsy lumps?

And what was it doing parked in front of the sheriff's office?

THE SHERIFF'S OFFICE was crowded. All the chairs were taken.

"DreadfulWater," said Duke. "About time."

Whenever Sheriff Benjamin "Duke" Hockney was annoyed, you could hear it in his voice. He'd slow down and flick each word off his tongue like a snake working a whip.

"This is Martha Burke, Graham Chandler, and Carl Mobley." Hockney snapped out each name. "These good folks are all from the paint company."

"Shield Industries." Burke stood up and stuck out her hand.

Hockney's company was a mixed bunch. Martha Burke was tall with good shoulders and auburn hair that had been cut for speed. Graham Chandler was wafer-thin with an oiled elegance that probably came from squeezing money. Carl Mobley was the odd man out. Walmart chunky, with a head like an anvil. Polyester wrapped around a pear.

"Ms. Burke is the plant manager at Shield Industries," said Duke. "Mr. Chandler here does consulting work."

"He's our liaison with General Dynamics," said Burke.

"Evidently, General Dynamics owns Shield Industries," said Duke. "Did I get that right?"

"Affiliated," said Chandler.

"While Mr. Mobley is head of security at the Sacramento facility."

Thumps made himself comfortable on the windowsill. So he could enjoy the show.

"And this is Special Deputy Thumps DreadfulWater," said Duke.

"And exactly why is he part of this conversation?" asked Chandler.

Duke left his gun in the holster. "You might say he's my consulting liaison."

"Thumps," said Burke, trying the name out on her tongue. "Italian?"

"Gosh, no," said Duke. "Thumps here is a genuine Indigenous warrior."

"Indian?" said Mobley.

"We call them 'Native Americans' these days." Hockney got out of his chair and wandered over to the coffee percolator.

"Anyone want coffee?"

Thumps waited for someone to take Hockney up on his offer of coffee. He knew he should say something, and after meeting the folks from Sacramento, he knew he wouldn't.

Burke wrinkled her nose. "Is that the coffee?"

Thumps wasn't sure what he thought of Martha Burke, but he was impressed with her sense of smell.

"I'll have a cup." Mobley got up and joined Duke at the old percolator.

"Don't have any cream or sugar," said the sheriff.

"Black's fine," said Mobley, taking the cup.

"You want a cup, Mr. Chandler?" Duke held up a mug.

"Do you have any tea?"

Duke didn't even try to keep the scowl out of his voice. "Tea?"

"Da Hong Pao or panda dung?"

Duke smiled. "What about it, Special Deputy DreadfulWater? We got any of that Da Hong or panda kicking around the office?"

Thumps smiled back.

"Graham's just being an ass," said Burke. "His way of letting you know that he's part of the aristocracy."

"I *am* part of the aristocracy," said Chandler.

Duke wandered back to his desk and took out his notebook. "The other day, you didn't have a missing van or a missing driver."

"Until you called," said Chandler, "we weren't aware that anything was amiss."

"But then you checked."

"Yes," said Chandler.

"And discovered that you're missing one van and one driver."

"Frank Dodge," said Mobley. "Worked for the company for eighteen years."

Thumps could hear the "but" at the end of the sentence. He was pretty sure that Duke heard it too.

"But?" said Duke.

"Mr. Dodge was not working for Shield Industries when he took the van."

"We have security footage of Frank taking the van," said Mobley.

"So you've got a former employee," said Duke, "who stole a company van?"

"That would appear to be correct," said Chandler.

Duke played with his pencil. "That happen often?"

Burke frowned. "What?"

"One of your former drivers takes off in one of your vans," said the sheriff, "and you don't know about it?"

"Of course not," said Burke. "There was a lapse in security."

Mobley reddened. "I've explained what happened. Not a damn thing anyone could have done."

"Relax, old man," said Chandler. "No one is blaming you."

Duke set the pencil on edge and tapped the desk. "So what did he take?"

Chandler was first off the mark. "Nothing."

Thumps watched the sheriff slowly lean back in his chair.

"Let me make sure I have this straight," said Duke. "Mr. Dodge comes to the plant one bright, sunny day, helps himself to an empty van, drives off into the sunset with nothing but a smile on his face and a song in his heart."

The sunrise, Thumps said to himself. Dodge would have been driving east into the sunrise.

Chandler turned to Burke and Mobley. "By Jove," he said, "I think he's got it."

Duke turned to Thumps. "What do we call that in police work, Special Deputy DreadfulWater?"

Normally, Thumps stayed away from the sheriff's games. Today, he was willing to make an exception.

"Fudge?"

"That's right," said Duke. "And how do we feel about fudge?"

"We think it smells like shit."

Burke took a long, deep breath. "Do people pay you two extra for this dog-and-pony show?"

"Nope," said Duke. "It's all part of the service."

"I think we're done here," said Burke. "We're going to go out to the test facility to survey the damage. If you have no objection."

"Survey away," said Duke. "Your property. Unless it turns out to be a crime scene."

"Crime scene?" Mobley sat up straight. "What the hell is that supposed to mean?"

The sheriff set his pencil down. "You folks staying at the Tucker?"

"We have suites there," said Chandler. "Such as they are."

"Well, that's absolutely peachy," said Duke. "Why don't you enjoy the amenities of our little town while Special Deputy DreadfulWater and I look into the matter."

Mobley was on his feet. "You do what you gotta do."

Hockney slid one of his business cards across the desk. "You wouldn't happen to have a photo of your missing ex-employee?"

Burke smiled, took a phone out of her jacket pocket. Thumps watched as her thumbs flew across the screen with practised efficiency.

"On its way." Burke's jacket caught the light and made the material shimmer. "We'd appreciate it if you could let us know when you find anything."

"It'll be my pleasure." If Duke had had his hat on, he would have touched the brim. "I'm sure we'll be talking soon."

Burke, Chandler, and Mobley were on their feet at the same time.

"I'm sure we will," said Burke.

Mobley set the coffee cup on the edge of the sheriff's desk.

"Damn fine coffee, by the way," he said. "Beats the hell out of that crap they serve at Starbucks."

THUMPS HELPED HIMSELF to an empty chair. He could see that Duke wasn't going to rush anything, that the man was going to take his time digesting the new information. Thumps could wait. It was one of a handful of things that he did well.

"I do enjoy it when the big city comes calling." Duke didn't change his position. "And it's not every day that you meet a plant manager, a security chief, and an honest-to-god consulting liaison. Sounds like the beginning of one of those bad bar jokes. What about you?"

"First time for me too," said Thumps. "But then I'm just a special deputy."

"No point being touchy." Duke took his feet off the desk and stood up. "We got work to do."

Thumps stayed where he was. "*You* have work to do. I get to go home."

"I told Macy about your cat problem."

"It's not a problem."

"She said she might be willing to take one."

Thumps took his feet off the chair. "But only if I help you find the driver."

"May have already found the driver."

"You think the body in Beth's morgue is Dodge?"

Duke put on his hat. "What is it they say about a photograph? Worth a thousand words?"

"Something like that."

"And while we're waiting for that photograph to arrive, let's go see if Dr. Mooney might have a word or two to share with us."

19

Beth Mooney's offices were in the old Land Titles building. She had her medical practice on the main floor. Her living quarters were on the second floor. The basement was reserved for bodies.

The front door was substantial and fitted with a security keypad and an intercom. There were three buttons on the pad labelled 1, 2, and B.

"Batter up," said the sheriff.

Thumps pressed the button for the second floor.

Nothing.

"Strike one."

Thumps pressed the button for the first floor.

Also nothing.

"Strike two." The sheriff reached out and pressed the button for the basement. "Trouble with the curve."

"Yes?" said the speaker.

The sheriff put his face close to the intercom. "Sheriff Duke Hockney," he said, "and Pedro Cerrano."

"Basement," said Beth.

Thumps had nothing against basements in general. His darkroom at home was in a basement. And he didn't mind the dark. In fact, he looked forward to those times when he could go downstairs, close the door, and spend hours alone and undisturbed.

But Beth's basement was not that kind of basement. Her basement was stark. White light, disinfectant, a ground fog of bodily fluids. Her basement had metal body drawers and a stainless-steel table, along with an assortment of tools designed to cut and probe.

At university, Thumps had read "Ulalume" by Edgar Allan Poe. *The dank tarn of Auber.*

Poe had never been in Beth's morgue, but each time Thumps had to visit her in her ghoul-haunted landscape, the place brought the line from the poem to mind.

Hockney made his way down the metal stairs.

"I don't want you passing out again."

"I don't pass out."

"You sometimes get woozy."

"That's low blood sugars," said Thumps. "I'm diabetic."

"And I just had my prostate ripped out."

Thumps's stomach did a flip.

Beth was at her stainless-steel table, working on the body

that Cooley and the deputies had dragged out of Deep House. She didn't look up.

"Wasn't Pedro Cerrano the character in *Major League* who couldn't hit a curveball?"

"The very same," said the sheriff.

Beth looked at Thumps. "He's funny, isn't he?"

"For a sheriff," said Thumps, "he's hysterical."

Beth put her scalpel to one side. "Gentlemen," she said, with no particular affection. "Meet John Doe."

Duke's phone dinged. He held it out so he could see it without having to put on his glasses.

"Well, would you look at that." Hockney turned the phone around. "It appears we have a name for our corpse."

"Saints be praised," said Beth.

"Frank Dodge," said the sheriff. "Not much doubt about it."

The picture on Duke's phone didn't do Dodge any favours, but all things considered, he looked better as a digital image than he did on Beth's autopsy table.

"One mystery cleared," said Duke. "Now all we have to do is find out why Mr. Dodge wound up here."

Beth picked up a tool that looked vaguely like long needle-nose pliers and inserted it into Dodge's chest cavity. A sweet, nasty tang filled the room. Thumps quickly switched to breathing through his mouth.

"Can't help you with the why," said Beth, "but I can tell you that Mr. Frank Dodge was not in the best of health."

"Because he's dead?"

"There's that," said Beth. "But I'm talking about his heart. You want to see?"

Thumps stepped back. "Absolutely not."

Duke stepped in. "He died of a heart attack?"

"See this." Beth shoved both hands into the dead man. "If I were guessing, I'd say that the scarring here and here is a result of COVID."

Duke stepped back from the table. "COVID?"

Thumps sat down on the bottom step of the stairs.

"There have been a number of studies on the virus and the damage it can do to various organs. Especially the heart."

"What about all the lacerations?"

"Probably from the fall." Beth covered Dodge's body with a sheet. "Was there much blood in the area?"

Duke scratched at his face. "Not much."

"And there's hardly any bruising," said Beth. "I'm guessing he was already dead when he went over the edge."

"So it's not murder?"

"That's your job," said Beth. "I'm just telling you what I found."

"You might tell me how long Mr. Dodge has been dead," said Duke.

"You mean based on body temperature, rigor, livor mortis, degree of putrefaction, corneal cloudiness, vitreous potassium levels, and insect activity?"

"How does last Friday evening sound?" said Duke.

"Sounds about right," said Beth.

The sheriff turned back to Thumps. "Why are you sitting on the stairs?"

Thumps considered his shoes. "I'm resting."

"You look unprofessional."

"Almost forgot." Beth wiped her hands on her gown. "State medical examiner's office called. About the autopsy on our Mr. Shipman."

Duke shifted on his feet. "Serial killer Harold Shipman? Or whatever the hell his real name was."

"Seems there's an anomaly in the autopsy results," said Beth.

"What the hell does that mean?" said the sheriff.

"No idea," said Beth, "but they're sending over a package for me to review."

Thumps started up the staircase.

Duke snapped his head around. "Where you think you're going?"

"Out."

Beth picked up a nasty-looking curved needle that had been threaded. "Should I be expecting more bodies? You guys tend to find them in bunches."

Duke touched the brim of his hat. "We appreciate your service."

"Get out of here," said Beth. "And take Pedro with you."

***

Every time Thumps escaped Beth's morgue and was safely back in the sunshine, he felt as though he had cheated death.

"Okay," said Duke, "so our Frank Dodge arrives at the test facility late Friday and drops dead of a heart attack."

"Which is why there was only one gate notification," said Thumps.

"And then Sunday morning, someone comes to the facility and finds our dead van driver, takes him to the canyon and throws him in."

"Then they go back to the compound and set fire to the van."

"You keeping track of the gate ringy-dingies?"

"In to find the body. Out to take the body to Deep House. In to burn the van. Out to drive away."

"Four," said Duke. "Nothing like simple math."

"Aside from the possibility of arson," said Thumps, "all we got is a bunch of misdemeanours."

"Indignity to a dead body and littering." Duke rearranged his hat. "And what did you think of our visitors from another tax bracket far away?"

Thumps filled his lungs with fresh air. "A little overkill."

"Can't imagine a missing van driver is going to get any one of them out of bed in the morning."

"You going to tell them we've identified Dodge?"

Duke looked down the street. "Probably should mosey over to the Tucker, drop in on our new friends. Let them know we're on the job."

"Be the neighbourly thing to do."

"Maybe they'll buy me dinner at the Mother Lode."

"Not outside the realm of possibility."

"Where I'll work the conversation around to just what the hell is going on."

Thumps let the breath out and took in another. He could almost smell the sunshine. "Wish I could stick around and watch you in action."

Hockney set his hat at an angle and started down the street. "Don't see where you've done enough to warrant a free meal."

There was a bench in front of the fountain that the city had put in during the last beautification push. Thumps sat down on one end, closed his eyes, and relaxed in the warmth of the day. He wondered how the kittens were doing. Probably sleeping. Or trying to get into the litter box. He'd need to fix that problem right away, before things got out of hand.

"Pancho."

Thumps kept his eyes closed.

"You're not asleep," said Cruz. "I can see your eyelids moving."

Cisco Cruz was at the curb. In a dark green Mustang.

"Get in."

"I'm fine here."

"We have to talk."

"No, we don't."

"Come on, *vato*," said Cruz. "Don't make me hurt you."

Thumps opened his eyes. "How about you tell me why you're in town?"

"*Vacaciones.*"

Thumps settled back in on the bench and closed his eyes.

"Really," said Cruz. "I'm on holiday."

"Frank Dodge." Thumps waited to see if the name got a reaction.

"Who the hell is Frank Dodge?"

"Shield Industries."

Cruz's face turned to stone. "Just get in the damn car."

20

Thumps had never found the bucket seats in vintage Mustangs very comfortable, and Cruz's ride was no exception.

"So where we going?"

Cruz kept his eyes on the road. "You remember that park you took me to when we first met?"

"The one with the ducks?"

Cruz smiled at the memory. "Let's go there."

THE LAST TIME Thumps and Cruz had been to the park, there hadn't been anyone else there but the ducks. Today, a mother and her two children were spread out on a blanket, and a large dog was standing in the water up to his belly.

Cruz headed for a picnic table at the far end of the pond.

"No ducks."

"They're around," said Thumps. "They return just before the ice melts."

"You ever wonder where they go?" Cruz looked out over the water. "I mean, they go south. But where south?"

"Pie Town?" offered Thumps.

"You remembered."

"If it's even true."

Cruz looked hurt. "You think I'd lie about where I was born and raised?"

"You might."

Cruz considered this for a moment. "I might. But I didn't. Pie Town, New Mexico. It's not much, but it's mine."

Thumps sat on the bench. "So why are you really in town?"

"You know why I like ducks?"

"Something to do with Frank Dodge and Shield Industries?"

"They're beautiful animals," said Cruz. "Especially the mallards and the mergansers."

Thumps leaned forward on his elbows and waited.

"And because they mind their own business."

"Sheriff finds out you're in town," said Thumps, "he's going to ask the same questions."

Cruz pushed off the picnic table and strolled down to where the river opened up into the pond. Thumps followed.

"So, *ese*, who's this Frank Dodge?"

"You're telling me you don't know?"

"Contrary to popular belief," said Cruz, "I don't know everything."

Thumps was of the opinion that it was the sheriff's job to pass out information. Still, Cruz was law enforcement. Sort of.

"Come on, Pancho," said Cruz. "You know you want to tell me."

"Dodge worked for Shield Industries. As a driver," said Thumps. "Evidently, he commandeered a van from the main plant in Sacramento and drove it to the company's test facility just north of here."

"What was in the van?"

"According to the people who would know, nothing."

"Nothing." Cruz made a noise that was between a chuckle and a snort.

"Then today, the company showed up at Duke's office for a chit-chat." Thumps tried to keep the pieces together on the fly. "Plant manager, a corporate liaison, and the head of security."

Cruz rubbed his eyes. "Seems a little excessive. All that fire-power for a transport driver and an empty van."

"Especially when Dodge was no longer working at Shield."

"Disgruntled employee?"

Thumps waved him off. "This is where you jump in and tell me what the hell is going on."

Cruz stared out at the water. "Okay, let's say that I have a friend."

"Besides me?"

"We were at Stanford together."

It took Thumps a moment to get his head around Cruz as a college student. It took several more for a school such as Stanford to register.

"Stanford? As in Stanford in Palo Alto, California. That Stanford?"

"There's only one Stanford, *cabrón*."

"This friend got a name?"

"Rajan Garza. Physics and bioengineering," said Cruz. "I was in law."

"Law?"

Cruz shrugged. "It didn't take."

"So you became a ninja assassin instead?"

"Hockney know I'm in town?"

"Not yet."

"I'd like to keep it that way. At least until I can talk to Raj."

"As in Rajan Garza."

"Raj is a bit of a genius," said Cruz. "Also paranoid. Doesn't play well with the other children."

Cruz picked up a stone and whipped it across the water. Thumps stopped counting the skips at seven.

"Called me a while back. A problem at Shield."

"Shield?" Suddenly the pieces were on the move. "Shield Industries?"

"Raj is their head of research and development," said Cruz. "Last week, I got another call. Full-blown panic. We were supposed to meet here."

"In Chinook?" Thumps didn't wait for an answer. "So where is this Garza?"

"That's my problem." Cruz stooped down and sorted through a handful of stones. "I don't know."

The mother began packing up the picnic. The dog bolted out of the water, ran back to the blanket dripping wet, and began shaking itself dry. Thumps tried to imagine himself on that blanket. With Claire and Ivory. With Freeway and her kittens.

"Pancho. Focus."

"What?"

"Wander off to dreamland on your own dollar," said Cruz. "I need to talk to this Frank Dodge. Where do I find him?"

"You remember Beth Mooney?"

"The lady doctor?"

"And coroner."

It took a moment for it to register. "Shit," said Cruz. "How?"

"Beth says heart attack." Thumps watched the mother herd everyone to the car, the dog racing back and forth, barking. "Dodge worked for Shield. Garza works for Shield. You like coincidences?"

"Not much."

"Neither does Duke."

"He still pissed about Oliver Parrish?"

"You did kill a man on his watch."

"Parrish was a killer." There was no give in Cruz's voice. "He murdered Jayme Redding. Remember?"

Thumps did remember. Oliver Parrish. The Kanji Killer. A psychopath who had marked his victims with a Chinese number. Four women dead before Cruz killed him.

Cruz skipped another stone. "You going to tell Hockney I'm here?"

"He's my friend."

"I'm your friend too."

Parrish would have killed both Thumps and Claire if Cruz hadn't shot him first. He was more than a friend.

Cruz flipped a stone into the pond and it sank immediately. "Why would an outfit such as Shield Industries send a trio of big guns to a one-horse town for a transport driver and a stolen van?"

"We have more horses than that."

"Shield know about their driver yet?"

Thumps guessed that Duke would have told Burke, Chandler, and Mobley about the body in Beth's morgue by now. There was no reason for the sheriff to keep it a secret.

"Probably."

Cruz skipped the last stone, wiped his hands on his pants.

"Too bad about the ducks," he said. "I was hoping we'd have ducks."

21

There was no small talk on the way back to town. Cruz watched the road. Thumps dozed against the door of the car. He didn't remember closing his eyes, but when he opened them, the car was just pulling up in front of the Aegean.

"Thought you were taking me home."

Cruz opened the door and slid out.

"You want to buy a book?"

"Do I look like the kind of guy who buys books?"

IN ADDITION TO the only Greek restaurant in town, soon to be opened for business, Archie Kousoulas had the only real bookstore in a hundred miles. The building had originally been a Carnegie library that Archie had bought and renovated.

Before the pandemic, the Aegean had been the de facto cultural centre of Chinook. Thumps wondered if that kind of community would ever recover, if that kind of community would be able to survive in whatever the new normal might be.

The sign in the window said "Closed." Thumps tried the door. It opened.

"Business doesn't look all that good." Cruz went to the front desk and tapped the bell. The *ding-ding* echoed in the open space and disappeared into the stacks.

"He might be at the restaurant."

"He has a restaurant?" said Cruz.

"Yes, he has a restaurant." As if by magic, Archie appeared in the doorway to his office. "Good food. Good music. Opening soon."

Thumps waved a hand at the little Greek. "Hi, Archie."

"Thumps?" Archie squinted over the top of his glasses, took a step forward. "And Cisco Cruz?"

Cruz gave a nod. "In the flesh."

Archie stared at Thumps. "What the hell is he doing here?"

Cruz looked around the bookstore. "I was just wondering what one might read during a pandemic."

"Try *A Journal of the Plague Year* by Daniel Defoe," said Archie, "*Pale Horse, Pale Rider* by Katherine Anne Porter, and *The Plague* by Albert Camus."

"*Love in the Time of Cholera*," said Thumps. "I'm reading that right now."

"Yeah," said Cruz, "but you said it wasn't a mystery."

"We're closed," said Archie. "There's a big sign in the window that says 'Closed.'"

"Thumps was hoping you might be able to help us," said Cruz.

"No, I wasn't," said Thumps.

Archie pushed his glasses up his nose. "Are you here to kill the pope?"

Thumps had never heard Cruz laugh out loud before.

"One of my favourite movies." Cruz did a full circle. "I love what you've done with the place."

"If it weren't for mail order," said Archie, "I'd turn the place into a mausoleum, and they could bury me here."

"The Pharaoh of Information."

Archie shook his head. "So you're not here to buy a book."

"Need some assistance," said Cruz.

"And you brought Thumps with you in case I said no."

"It'll be fun," said Cruz. "Just like the good old times."

Archie peered at Thumps over his glasses. "You remember the 'good old times' he's talking about?"

"Can't recall any offhand."

"Last time you were in town," said Archie, "didn't you kill someone?"

"And I could use a cup of coffee."

* * *

THERE HAD BEEN a long library table in the middle of Archie's office. Now the space was taken with opposing sofas and a coffee table.

The room had always been on the sombre side with its dark panels and beamed ceiling, but now it felt more oppressive, as though the breath had been sucked out of it.

"Coffee machine doesn't work." Archie sat down behind his desk and turned the two monitors on. "You'll have to pretend."

"Pretend coffee." Cruz smacked his lips. "The new post-pandemic drink."

Archie ran his fingers over the keyboard. "Am I participating in a misdemeanour or a felony?"

"Public domain only," said Cruz.

"What are we looking for?"

"Shield Industries." Cruz came around the desk and stood at Archie's shoulder. "Facts and rumours. Whatever you can find."

Archie worked the keys. "How about problems and lawsuits?"

"Sure."

Thumps leaned toward the door. "You guys don't need me."

"Thumps has kittens," said Cruz. "You need a cat?"

Archie turned on Thumps. "Kittens?"

"Freeway came home," said Thumps. "She had kittens."

"And this you don't tell me?"

"I just found out." Thumps slid his hands into his back pockets. "I should probably go home and feed the family."

"Stick around," said Archie, "and tell me about the dead guy in the canyon."

"This the driver?" said Cruz.

Archie stopped typing. "You tell the ninja assassin about the dead man and your cat, and you don't tell me? I have to hear these things from strangers?"

Thumps held up his hands. "Frank Dodge. Former driver for Shield Industries. Found dead in Deep House."

Archie pushed back in his chair. "Murder?"

"Bad heart." Thumps could feel the conversation getting out of hand fast. "It appears someone dumped Dodge's body into the canyon."

Cruz and Archie turned on Thumps at the same time.

"Guy dies of a heart attack," said Cruz, "and then someone dumps the body into a canyon?"

"Maybe he was walking along the rim, enjoying the view." Archie was out of his seat now. "And, wham, he has a heart attack and falls in."

Thumps floated toward the door. "Call me if you find anything."

Archie went back to his chair. "Stay," he said. "I may need you."

"For what?"

Archie tapped more keys. "Someone has to take notes."

Cruz moved in behind Archie. "Okay, so what do we have?"

*　*　*

THUMPS AND CRUZ sat quietly as the little Greek worked his way through websites and news stories, stopping every so often for a moment of social and political commentary.

"That's interesting," said Archie. "Shield Industries is a wholly-owned subsidiary of General Dynamics, the company that made the Abrams tank."

"Wouldn't call General Dynamics a company," said Cruz. "They're more like a medium-sized country."

"One of the founding fathers of the military-industrial complex." Archie thumped a finger on the monitor. "You believe this? Shield got a grant from the state to clean up one of their holding ponds."

Thumps squinted at the screen. "Paint factories have holding ponds?"

Archie sat back. "Okay, so what else aren't you two telling me?"

"Ask Thumps," said Cruz.

"Me?"

"He had a meeting this morning with the sheriff and three of the company big shots."

Archie arched his eyebrows.

"Nothing to tell," said Thumps. "Shield executives are in town. Martha Burke, the plant manager, Graham Chandler, General Dynamics liaison, and the chief of security, Carl Mobley."

Archie sat back. "All that weight for a driver?"

"Ex-driver," said Thumps.

"I don't think they give a damn about the driver," said Cruz. "I'm guessing they're looking for Raj."

"As in Rajan Garza," Thumps explained. "Garza and Cruz went to university together."

"There's a school for assassins?" said Archie.

"Stanford," said Thumps.

"Why not," said Archie. "There was an article in *The Washington Post* about how U.S. universities have become ground zero for recruiting spies. Hell, some of the academic courses at institutions such as Harvard and Yale are funded by the CIA."

"Allegedly," said Cruz.

"Is that a no?" said Archie. "Is that how they recruited you?"

"I'm not CIA."

"Which is exactly what a CIA agent would say," said Archie.

Thumps wondered what Freeway was doing at this moment, if she was napping with the kittens or if she had taken them outdoors to see the world. And what was he going to do with four kittens? Even if Al did take one and the sheriff took another, that left two. Freeway was problematic. Freeway plus a bunch of little Freeways would be impossible.

"Raj is a friend," said Cruz. "I could use your help."

Maybe when he got home, he'd line the kittens up and try to decide on names for the little bundles of fur. Nothing too cute such as Baby Cakes or Chubby Bunny. And nothing silly such as Killer or Picatso or Cameow. Maybe he'd name them after the seven dwarfs. Happy, Sneezy, Doc, Dopey. Or states. Dakota, Oregon, Wyoming, Montana. Or characters from literature.

"Hey," said Cruz. "Earth to Thumps."

"Got something," said Archie.

Ulysses, Leda, Ishmael, Miss Marple.

"Last week, there was a fire at the plant in Sacramento." Archie pushed back so Cruz could see.

"And?"

Archie returned to the monitors. "And nothing. No follow-up story. No post-mortem."

Cruz stared at the monitor. "Which tells us what?"

"Secret government facility?" said Archie.

Cruz nodded. "A bit dramatic."

And there were always names from other parts of the animal kingdom. Otter, Bear, Badger, Tiger.

"Okay," said Archie, "how about a *secure* government facility?"

"Pancho," said Cruz, "you keeping up?"

"Secure government facility."

"Can we get everyone on the same page?" Cruz started slowly pacing the room. "We have a driver for Shield Industries."

"Frank Dodge," said Archie.

"Frank Dodge," said Cruz. "Steals a van from Sacramento and drives to the company's testing facility."

"A facility that's closed," said Thumps.

"Closed?"

"Woman named Bargain Hall," said Thumps. "Owns the paint store in Glory. When Duke and I drove out there, she told us the place has been closed for about eight months."

Archie held up a hand. "Why would you send a paint van to a closed facility?"

"When we got there, we found the van burned," said Thumps.

"And then three bigwigs from Shield show up," said Cruz.

"That's it," said Thumps.

"That's it?" said Archie. "Either of you have any idea what 'it' is?"

"All we're missing is the partridge in a pear tree." Cruz went back to his pacing. "First order of business is to find Raj."

"Except you don't know where Garza is," said Thumps.

"Anything else to add besides the obvious?" said Cruz.

"You *asked* for our help," said Archie. "So be nice."

"You're right. I shouldn't have involved you guys." Cruz walked the length of the room and out the door. "I'll take it from here."

Thumps and Archie waited for Cruz to reappear. Then they waited some more.

"That went well," said Archie.

"See what else you can find on Shield Industries." Thumps got to his feet. "Just in case."

"In case of what?" said Archie.

"Successful paint company gets sold and then suddenly goes belly up."

"No mystery," said Archie. "Companies buy up other

companies all the time and shut them down. Take out the competition. You ever play Monopoly?"

Thumps walked to the window and looked out. The seasons. Names for the kittens. Of course. Spring, Summer, Autumn, Winter. He'd check with Freeway when he got home, but he was sure she'd like the idea as much as he did.

22

ops was squatted down on the front porch, his ears up, his chest out, looking for all the world like a proud father. Freeway was curled up against the dog, while the kittens stumbled about on Pops's back, trying to find their way through his heavy coat.

A domestic montage. Slightly unsettling.

"I see you found each other."

Pops gave a low growl. Freeway didn't move.

"I'm going into my house." Thumps put a bit more emphasis on "my" in case the dog understood English and the concept of private property. "If you don't mind."

Pops seemed to mind. The dog was normally dozy and slow, but now he was bright and alert. His jaw set, his tongue tucked away and out of sight.

"Are you guarding Freeway and the babies?"

Thumps couldn't remember ever seeing the dog's teeth before.

Low growl.

"But you know that I'm a friend. Right?"

Louder growl.

Thumps was pretty sure that if he stepped over the dog, Pops wouldn't take his leg off. But he wasn't positive. In fact, trying to step over the dog would put more at risk than just his leg. He thought about going around the house to the back door, but that would just prolong the ongoing jurisdictional question.

"Pops!" Dixie was out his front door and headed across the lawn. "Are you being a bad dog?"

Pops kept his eyes on Thumps.

"He's just being protective," said Dixie. "First-time father and all."

One of the kittens started to wander off, and the dog reached out and nudged it back to Freeway with his nose.

"He's been like this all day," said Dixie. "It's kinda sweet."

"He's doing a good job."

"Pops won't bite, you know," said Dixie. "He's a big cream puff."

More growling.

"He just likes to hear himself talk."

One of the kittens popped out of the fur near Pops's head and began to whimper. Freeway slowly rolled over and opened her eyes. As soon as the kitten saw her mother, she tried to come down the side of the dog, lost her footing, and landed with a thud on the porch. Freeway licked her a couple of times and then curled back up against Pops.

"Pops and I were thinking that we might like one of the kittens," said Dixie. "If you're giving any of them away."

"Sure," said Thumps.

"Maybe the orange one," said Dixie. "I think Pops is partial to the orange one."

Pops let Thumps step over him and get through the door in one piece. Dixie was probably right. The dog *was* a big cream puff. And it was sweet seeing something that large take care of tiny kittens. His farting problems aside, Pops was a good sort.

Thumps stood in the kitchen and considered the same question he always considered at this time of the day.

What to eat?

He could scramble a couple of eggs, fry up some potatoes with onion. He could cook up a batch of quinoa and eat it with Parmesan and cottage cheese. Always a crowd pleaser. There were frozen chicken thighs and several cabbage rolls.

If he could find the energy to turn on a burner.

Thumps had given up on the concept of cooking anything and was contemplating a meal of crackers and cheese when the phone rang. Maybe call display wouldn't be a bad idea. He could vet calls before he answered the phone.

Claire, yes.

Hockney, maybe.

Archie Kousoulas, no.

Of course, it could be Archie inviting him to another meal. The food the other night had been lovely. But Archie's meals were never free. Being grilled by the little Greek about everything from his health to his love life would be the price of admission.

It wasn't Archie.

"Mr. DreadfulWater?"

Thumps waited.

"Look, sorry to call you like this, but I was hoping we could talk."

It took Thumps a moment to recognize the voice. Carl Mobley. One of the Shield Industries triumvirate.

"You should probably talk to the sheriff."

"Sure," said Mobley. "I get that, but I'd like to keep this unofficial for the time being."

Thumps wandered over to the cupboard to make sure he had crackers.

"If I talk to the sheriff," said Mobley, "then it gets official fast."

He had crackers. Whole grain and sesame seed. And a bag of potato chips. Thumps couldn't remember ever buying potato chips. Claire liked potato chips. Maybe she had brought them by.

"So I'm hoping we can have a conversation. Unofficial like."

Mobley paused for a moment, and Thumps thought he had lost the connection.

"Look, I'm out at a place called the Mustang. Going to have a burger and a beer. Why don't you join me?"

"At the Mustang."

"It's not the Tucker," said Mobley, "but have you seen the prices at that place?"

THE MUSTANG WAS QUIET. Lorraine Chubby was behind the bar. Little Hack was off somewhere, presumably with his father. Thumps wondered how a couple managed to juggle a child and get work done. Or two kids. Or three.

Freeway and the kittens were one thing. Four children would be quite another.

"You looking for Big Fish?"

"Nope."

Lorraine wiped the bar down. "He said you came by checking on strangers."

"That was the sheriff."

"Got one for you." Lorraine nodded in the direction of the jukebox. "Over there."

Carl Mobley was sitting by himself in the corner. He was bent over a beer and a burger. There was something stiff about the man. Nothing unfriendly, just a sense that he had spent time trying to find some sort of organization to the world and coming up empty.

"On his third beer," said Lorraine. "Keeps glancing at the door as though he's expecting someone."

"That would be me."

"You want a burger?"

"Who's cooking?"

Lorraine gave Thumps a sharp look. "Big Fish is at home with Hack. Yo-Yo is in the kitchen."

Yo-Yo was the best of the three cooks at the Mustang. He wasn't great, but he didn't burn the burgers the way Big Fish did, and he didn't leave them wounded and bleeding.

"You don't like my cooking?"

Thumps smiled.

"You overcook a burger, you ruin the meat," said Lorraine. "Any idiot knows that."

"Burger," said Thumps. "Hold the fries."

Lorraine grimaced. "You can't eat a burger without fries."

"I'm diabetic."

"When you tell Al to forget the hash browns," said Lorraine, her hands on her hips, "then you can talk to me about holding the fries."

MOBLEY HAD HIS head down over his beer, but Thumps knew the man had watched him from the time he came into the Mustang.

Mobley didn't stand. "Burgers are pretty good."

"Yo-Yo's cooking."

"Beer's cold." Mobley shifted in his chair. "That's about all you can ask for."

Mobley had a shoulder holster on under his jacket. Thumps could see the butt of a gun sticking out.

"Paint business dangerous?"

Mobley pulled his jacket shut. "Security's security. Don't matter if it's a paint factory or a bank."

"Lorraine know you're carrying?"

"She knows."

Lorraine didn't permit guns on the premises. Her fourth rule. Thumps wasn't sure why she had made an exception for Mobley.

"Retired Marine," said Mobley. "Evidently, the lady of the house has a brother who's serving."

Thumps didn't know that Lorraine had a brother.

"That's how I got the job at Main Street Paints back before it became Shield Industries." Mobley took a pull on his beer. "Twenty-one years and counting. You serve?"

Lorraine came out of the back.

"Burger." She set the plate in front of Thumps. "And fries."

"Real good food," said Mobley. "You can cook for me anytime."

"You want another beer?"

"No, me and Mr. DreadfulWater got business to talk."

"Thumps tends to be reluctant," said Lorraine. "Sometimes you got to put the spurs to him."

"That pretty much covers most people," said Mobley.

"But not Marines."

"Covers us too," said Mobley. "But we can fake it better than most."

Thumps knew that Lorraine had a soft spot in her heart for Big Fish Patek, and he was sure she was crazy about her baby. Finding out that retired Marines were even in the same neighbourhood as the first two was a surprise.

"Nice woman," said Mobley. "She married?"

"With a baby," said Thumps.

"We had enough small talk?" Mobley helped himself to one of Thumps's fries.

"We haven't gotten to the weather yet."

"Frank Dodge." Mobley's face hardened.

"The driver."

"I knew Frank. Maybe ten, twelve years. Man wasn't a brain trust, but he was hard-working, decent. Kept the peace, if you know what I mean."

Thumps nodded.

"You know much about Shield?"

Thumps tried the burger. Yo-Yo was good as gold.

"It used to be a family business. Nothing too large. Good place to work. Everyone knew everyone."

"Small shop."

"That's right," said Mobley. "Then the company got sold. After that, everything changed. Won't bore you with details."

"Okay."

"Here's the interesting part." Mobley pushed his beer off to one side. "Shield moves in and, suddenly, we're swimming in money. Government grants, private money, like we won the lottery."

Mobley paused and took a bite of his burger.

"First thing Shield does is build a new research wing. State of the art. High-end commercial and military. New personnel."

Mobley took another bite.

"Martha Burke and Graham Chandler. Burke is out of General Dynamics's executive pool. Chance for her to make her bones, as it were. Harvard Business School. Five years at Chase Manhattan. Runs a tight ship."

The fries were salty. Thumps squeezed some ketchup onto the side of the plate.

"Graham Chandler is an ex–alphabet agency spook. He's the liaison between General Dynamics and Shield. His sole responsibility is the Bubble. Manager and security rolled into one."

"The Bubble?"

"That's what we call the new complex," said Mobley. "The main plant belongs to me. But the Bubble belongs to Chandler."

"I thought you were head of security."

"Not in the Bubble." Mobley leaned forward. "You might wonder why we need two security guys. I mean, we make paint, for Christ's sake."

"And Rajan Garza?"

Mobley sat back. "You know about Dr. Garza?"

Thumps tried a fry with ketchup. The sweetness hid the salt nicely.

"Head of research in the Bubble," said Mobley. "Genius when it comes to paint and molecular compounds."

"I take it the Bubble is high security."

"Would you believe they have a walk-in vault?"

"For paint?"

Mobley looked around the Mustang, lowered his voice. "There's paint and there's paint."

Thumps tried to imagine a vault for paint.

"Know what I mean?"

Thumps had no idea what Mobley meant. He had just decided how to ask the question when Mobley's cellphone started vibrating.

"Shit." Mobley looked at the screen. "I got to go."

"Rajan Garza?"

"Right," said Mobley as he got to his feet. "That's the other part of our problem. When Dodge disappeared, so did Garza."

23

There was a football game on the big screen above the bar, and Thumps stayed at the table and nursed his burger and fries until the contest got into the fourth quarter and the outcome was pretty well assured.

Mobley had been surprisingly forthright with information. Thumps doubted that Burke or Chandler would have given him the time of day. Or Cruz for that matter. Thumps was sure his shadowy friend was only telling him part of the story.

"Hey, Thumps."

Big Fish Patek slid into the chair and helped himself to the fries.

"You find your friend?"

Thumps nodded.

"Great." Big Fish laid a couple of coupons on the table. "This entitles him to a free beer when he buys a medium pizza."

"Guy's dead," said Thumps.

"Damn." Big Fish pulled the coupons back. "Guess he's not going to be interested in the big line-dance contest at the end of the week."

"Does Hack bite?"

"What?"

"Nothing," said Thumps. "When I was out at Claire's place, Ivory bit me."

"Oh," said Big Fish. "And you're wondering if all babies do that."

"Just curious."

"Hack don't have any teeth yet," said Big Fish, "but Lorraine says he chomps the hell out of her nipples."

"Never mind."

"No," said Big Fish, "it's a good question. I'll keep an eye out and let you know."

Thumps's plate was empty. His glass was empty.

"That friend of yours," said Big Fish. "He the guy the sheriff dragged out of Deep House?"

"Yep."

"Hear he died of a heart attack." Big Fish cocked his head. "How the hell did he wind up in the canyon?"

"No idea."

Big Fish pointed to Thumps's plate. "You want more fries?"

***

THUMPS HALF EXPECTED to see Cruz's car parked in front of his house. Of course, the man could have parked it several blocks away, could be waiting for him in the living room, eating his food, playing with his cats, reading his novel.

The lights were on at Dixie's, the blinds drawn. As Thumps came up the walk, he saw Pops's shadow pass by the living-room window. There was some relief in the sighting. He worried that the dog might have found a way to break into his house in order to be with Freeway and the babies. The cat door had been an early attempt that failed. But how long would it be before the dog realized that the answer was to hit the door at speed? And once the dog got in, how would you get him out?

Of course, Pops could be the excuse he was looking for. Claire was known to have sympathetic moments. If he showed up on her doorstep, suitcase in hand, with a sad tale of being displaced by a vicious, farty hound, would she turn him away?

Probably.

The box on the porch was a surprise. There was a note taped to it.

For your kitty and the kittens, Dixie and Pops.

Inside the box was a bag of cat food for kittens, a bag for adult cats, two boxes of non-clumping kitty litter, a large cat basket, and an assortment of toys. The very things he had been meaning to buy but had forgotten.

Thumps brought the box into the kitchen, arranged the items on the table, and set about deciding where everything should go.

Freeway couldn't break into the cans, but in the past, she had ripped open bags. So the food would have to go into the closet. The kitty litter boxes could go in the laundry room, the cat basket in the living room as far away from his bedroom as the house allowed. There was the slim hope that Freeway and the kittens would find their own space preferable to a crowded bed.

Maybe it would help if he left the TV tuned to the nature channel.

One of the toys was a rubber mouse that squeaked when you stepped on it. Thumps squeezed it a couple of times to make sure that it worked.

"Freeway," he called out, "come see what I've got for you."

Nothing.

He went to the bedroom, rubber mouse in hand, and turned on the light. The bed was as he had left it, neatly made with the pillows in place.

And no cats.

The thought came out of nowhere. Was it possible that they had all trundled over to Dixie's house for a sleepover? Dixie wouldn't mind. Pops would be in heaven. And Freeway had already proven that her loyalties could be bought.

Probably too much to hope for.

More than likely, he'd find the cats in the living room, curled up under the sofa. As he came back through the kitchen, he picked up a stick with a feather at the end of a piece of thin wire.

"Hey, gang. Look what I have."

Thumps was reaching for the living-room light switch when a dark shape moved out of the shadows.

"Leave them off," said the figure, "and raise your hands. Please."

In the dim light, Thumps could just make out the dark shape pointed at his chest.

Thumps stood perfectly still. "Did you happen to see my cat?"

"Take your wallet out and throw it over here."

"Mother and four kittens?"

"Please do it now."

Thumps held his ground. "If I throw my wallet, everything will fall out."

"Don't make me shoot you."

"With my TV remote?" Thumps lowered his arms. "Worst you could do is change a channel."

"You must be DreadfulWater."

Thumps turned on the lights. "And you would be Dr. Rajan Garza."

24

Garza set the remote on the coffee table and sat down on the sofa. "You were expecting a man, weren't you?"

"Nope," said Thumps.

"Sure you were," said Garza. "Everyone does."

"You want coffee?"

"'Rajan' is one of those all-purpose names," said Garza. "My mother's idea of radical feminism."

"You mind if I sit?"

"Sit," said Garza. "It's your house."

Thumps took the easy chair. If Thumps was guessing, Garza was in her early forties. Dark hair. Not slender, not fat. Somewhere in between. High cheekbones, chin like a hammer. Handsome rather than pretty. Someone who was used to being in control.

"You're a scientist."

"Molecular physics," said Garza. "You know how to cook?"

"At Shield Industries."

"Because I don't."

Thumps flashed on Claire. She couldn't cook either, but at least she knew the difference between a remote control and a gun.

"I'm hungry," said Garza. "An omelette would be nice. If it's not too much trouble."

Maybe this was a new breed of women who had come into the world when he wasn't looking.

"With onion and cheese. Maybe some cottage fries."

Women who couldn't cook.

Garza put her feet up on the coffee table. "And please," she said, "try not to burn it."

A HALF-HOUR LATER, Garza was sitting at the kitchen table in front of a swiss, onion, and tomato omelette with home fries and honey-garlic sausage. Sourdough rye toast and rhubarb jam. Along with sliced bananas and grapes that had made the boat trip from Costa Rica or Peru more or less intact.

"This is lovely."

Thumps was of the opinion that if you were going to eat good food, you should take the time to taste it. Claire didn't ascribe to this particular belief. And neither, Thumps discovered, did Garza.

"Is there any dessert?"

"Dessert?"

"You know," said Garza. "Cake, cookies, pie, ice cream?"

"I have kitty num-nums."

Garza flattened her lips. "Cisco said you could be a bit of an asshole."

"No, I didn't."

Cisco Cruz stepped into the kitchen. Garza snatched up the knife and spun around.

"Careful," said Thumps. "She tried to shoot me with the remote."

"Damn it, Cisco, you know better than to sneak up on me."

"I said that he could be a bit of a boy scout."

Thumps didn't try to keep the annoyance out of his voice. "You broke in? Again."

"*Vato*, the back door was open," said Cruz.

"No, it wasn't."

"That looks good." Cruz pulled up a chair. "Am I too late?"

THUMPS WAS AT THE STOVE when Freeway appeared, the kittens tottering along behind her. The cat made a beeline to Garza and began rubbing herself against the woman's legs.

Garza moved her leg. "I'm not a pet person."

Freeway collapsed on the floor and rolled over on her back.

"She wants her tummy rubbed," said Thumps.

"Not happening," said Garza.

Thumps brought Cruz's meal to the table. "She has a gift for finding the person least likely to show her any affection."

"Hey, Raj," said Cruz, "that sounds a lot like you."

"Oh, shut up, *chango*."

Thumps put the plate down with a bang. "I'm glad to see you two are having a good time."

Cruz used his fork to pick up the piece of sausage that had bounced off the plate. "Easy, Pancho."

Thumps could feel the annoyance turn to anger.

"He's pissed off at you," said Garza.

"What did I do?"

Thumps held up a hand, the fingers spread. "One, you lied to me. Two, you lied to me. Three, you lied to me."

Cruz shook his head. "There's a difference between lying and not sharing."

Garza helped herself to a piece of Cruz's sausage. "Go ahead, cousin," she said. "I want to hear the difference."

"Cousin?"

"More or less," said Cruz.

"My father's brother," said Garza.

"So you're not . . . lovers."

Garza sat back in her chair. "Ewww."

"Four," said Thumps, "you told your cousin to meet you here, didn't you?"

"Sure," said Cruz.

"Without bothering to mention it to me?"

"An omission," said Cruz. "Not a lie."

"Not the point." Thumps sat down so he could glare at Cruz and Garza at the same time.

Cruz shrugged. "Would you have said yes?"

"Also not the point. I come home, find a stranger in my house who sticks a gun in my face."

"You said it was a remote."

"I was expecting Cisco," said Garza.

"Cisco Cruz doesn't live here," said Thumps. "I do."

"Okay," said Garza. "My apologies."

"Me too," said Cruz. "Okay, we good?"

"By the way," said Garza. "You make a hell of an omelette."

Thumps got out of his chair, went to the switch, and turned off the kitchen light. "Leave the dishes," he said. "I'm going to bed."

"Come on," said Cruz. "Don't be like that."

"And when I get up in the morning, I expect you two to be gone."

Garza looked at Cruz. "I thought you said I could stay here."

Cruz smiled at Thumps. "Yeah, I know," he said. "That's five."

Garza sat back in the chair and closed her eyes. "If you two are smart," she said, "you'll stay as far away from me as possible."

"Good news," said Cruz. "We're not that smart."

25

Thumps put Garza in the spare bedroom. Cruz got the living room. Thumps had never slept on the sofa, and he hoped that the man from Pie Town would find it lumpy and uncomfortable.

The next morning, Thumps was in the kitchen when Cruz appeared and helped himself to the coffee.

"Hockney still making that hot tar?"

"Maybe you should stay at his place." Thumps took a can out of the cupboard. "He has a nice cell that's vacant at the moment."

Cruz stretched one side and then the other. "Couldn't be less comfortable than your sofa."

"You going to tell me what's going on?"

Cruz sat down at the table. "Don't know myself. Have to wait for Raj to tell us."

"There is no us."

AN HOUR LATER, Garza padded into the kitchen, Freeway and the kittens trooping along behind her.

"Is that coffee?"

"You look like shit, cuz."

"You ever try to sleep with cats?"

Thumps didn't care for having two strangers sleeping in his house, but it had had its benefits. Freeway decided that variety was indeed the spice of life and had moved herself and the kittens into bed with Garza.

"Damn things purr." Garza got a cup from the cupboard and helped herself to the coffee pot. "And they have claws."

"Beans." Thumps held up the can. "And toast."

"No omelette? No potatoes?" Garza pushed her hair out of her face. "I have to have a good breakfast. Otherwise I'm useless."

"You can always go to Shadow Ranch," said Thumps with no hint of sympathy in his voice. "They have a breakfast buffet that would feed a village."

"Can't take the chance," said Garza. "I could have people looking for me."

"They're already here," said Cruz. "The dream team from Shield is in town."

"Here?"

"At the Tucker," said Cruz. "Burke, Chandler, and Mobley. Sounds like a law firm. Remember *Car Talk*? Dewey, Cheetham & Howe?"

"Chandler is here in town?"

Thumps dumped the beans into the pan and added some hot sauce.

"Supposedly, they're looking for one of their drivers who's gone missing," said Cruz.

Thumps watched Garza to see her reaction.

"One Frank Dodge," said Cruz. "You know him?"

Garza shook her head.

"Seems Mr. Dodge borrowed a van from the plant in Sacramento, drove it out to the test facility at Deep House."

Garza picked up Freeway and set the cat on her lap.

"You know anything about that?"

"They're not looking for a van driver," said Garza. "They're looking for me."

Thumps scooped the beans onto a plate and set it in the middle of the table. "Toast will be up in a minute."

GARZA DIDN'T WOLF the food down as she had the night before. She took her time with the toast and with the coffee, as though they would protect her from the questions that were waiting for her.

"Okay," said Cruz. "Time for some answers."

"I'm not done eating."

"You can talk while you eat," said Cruz. "Now, what the hell is going on?"

"I can't tell you."

Thumps buttered the toast and set the slices next to the beans. "More coffee?"

"Yes," said Garza.

"No," said Cruz.

Garza picked up each kitten in turn and set them on her lap next to their mother.

"Thought you weren't an animal person," said Cruz.

"I'm not," said Garza, "but they beat the hell out of most humans."

Thumps settled himself into his chair. "How about we guess, and you give us a sign to let us know if we're right or wrong?"

"This isn't a game, *vato*."

"But it could be." Thumps helped himself to a piece of toast. "Let's start with Frank Dodge for a hundred dollars."

Garza poked at her beans. "I told you I don't know Frank Dodge."

"Wrong answer," said Thumps. "Cisco Cruz, tell the audience what Dr. Garza gets."

"Well, Pancho," said Cruz, "if Dr. Garza was involved in our van driver's death, she could get forty years in prison."

"Death?"

"Let's see if she does better on the next question."

Garza put her fork down. "You two probably think you're funny."

"Hysterical," said Cruz.

Garza turned to Thumps. "Do you know what he used to do when we were kids?"

"Why are you here?" Thumps had another piece of toast. "Why Chinook?"

"Cisco told me to meet him here."

"No, I didn't. You said you were coming to Chinook, and would I meet you here. You said you needed my help."

Garza waved a hand. "Tomatoes, tomatoes."

"Another wrong answer," said Thumps. "Mr. Cruz, is there a prize for dishonesty?"

"There certainly is," said Cruz. "I walk, and Mr. DreadfulWater here goes back to taking pictures of mountains and rivers."

"We're family."

"That's the only reason I'm here," said Cruz. "So give me something to make me stay."

Garza pushed her plate away and began stroking Freeway. "Okay, what do you two geniuses know about solar power?"

FOR THE NEXT HOUR, Garza gave Thumps and Cruz a crash course on solar power, its applications, and the world of paint and ceramics.

Thumps made a second pot of coffee.

It didn't help.

He understood the individual words, but the combinations they created and the theories that they revealed left him longing for the simplicities of photography. Long exposure calculations, unsharp masks, and darkroom chemistry.

Garza was not a patient teacher, and she wasn't sympathetic. When she finished the lesson, she sat back, her arms crossed, enjoying the moment.

"So you two ready for the quiz?"

Cruz didn't blink. "You've developed a paint that collects solar energy."

"It's not a paint," said Garza. "It's a paint protocol that combines pigments and silicon crystals with ceramics."

"You apply it to a surface, and that surface becomes a solar panel."

"A highly efficient solar panel," said Garza. "Typical solar panels are able to convert fifteen to eighteen percent of sunlight to energy. Helios raises that percentage to almost forty percent."

"Helios?"

"The name of my protocol."

Cruz rubbed his forehead. "You named a paint?"

"Guys name their dicks."

"Not the same thing."

The coffee pot was empty. Normally, Thumps would make another one.

"Helios could change the face of energy production, especially for regions where people can't afford electricity produced by oil and gas."

"The poorer places of the world."

"Mr. Eshelman understood the value of my work. It wasn't about profit. It was about access to energy."

But fresh coffee would only encourage the Pie Town twins to stay.

"Is it cheap?"

"What?"

"Your protocol," said Thumps. "Is the paint thingy cheap to produce?"

Garza looked as though some of the wind had left her sails. "No. It isn't cheap. Not expensive, but not cheap. That was one of the things I was working on when the company was sold."

"To Shield Industries," said Cruz.

"Once Helios was perfected, the plan was to figure out a way to reduce the costs of manufacture and then give the process away."

Now Thumps was back up to speed. Molecular physics he did not understand. Greed he did.

"But corporate folks didn't want to give anything away."

Garza sagged in the chair. "It was worse than that. Shield decided that my protocol had other applications."

Cruz nodded. "As in military."

"Exactly," said Garza. "Shield began testing my solar protocol on drones."

"So they could stay airborne for longer periods of time."

"Almost indefinitely," said Garza. "Think about it. A fleet of perpetual drones patrolling a war zone."

Thumps brought the coffee pot to the table. "Or an urban protest."

"Goodbye, public domain," said Cruz. "Hello, profit."

Freeway was at her food bowl. The kittens were tumbling about on the floor in the middle of a no-holds-barred wrestling match, completely oblivious to the machinations of corporate America.

"About three weeks back, Martha Burke called me into her office. Graham Chandler and Carl Mobley were there." Garza's voice hardened. "They wanted all of my research and notes to be turned over to them, along with the test panels and any other test material."

"They fired you?"

"No," said Garza. "They said that they were worried about corporate espionage and wanted to make sure the process was secure."

"As in under their control," said Cruz.

"Exactly," said Garza. "They wanted to lock me out."

"And?"

"I agreed."

Thumps could see where this was going. "Sure, you did."

Garza allowed herself a small grin. "I said I'd get everything together, that it would take me a week or so, that all I wanted was to be part of the team."

Cruz chuckled. "And they believed you."

Garza picked up the coffee cup and pressed it against her face. "I thought so."

Cruz cocked his head. "But then . . . ?"

"But then," said Garza, "someone tried to kill me."

26

Garza had been walking home from a Zumba class when a car jumped the curb.

"Was just able to get out of the way in time," said Garza. "Don't know how he missed me."

"Could have been a drunk," said Cruz. "Or someone who lost control."

"The driver was wearing one of those black mask things."

"A balaclava?"

"I guess." Garza began picking at her finger. "Who wears that when they're driving?"

Cruz sat back. "Well, there's bad news, and there's good news."

"With you," said Garza, "there usually is."

"Maybe Thumps wants to take a run at it," said Cruz.

"Nope," said Thumps. "I just want to sit here and watch you two fight."

"He's shy," said Cruz. "What he was going to say is that if someone tried to kill you with a car, they're probably not professionals."

"And you know that, how?"

"Hit and run has too many variables," said Thumps. "Too many loose ends."

"And that's the good news?"

"It is," said Thumps.

"After the incident," said Cruz, "did you call the cops?"

"What for?" said Raj. "I couldn't prove anything. I didn't see the guy's face. The licence plate was covered with crap. It was a black SUV. How many of those are roaming around loose?"

"Okay," said Cruz. "What did you do?"

"What do you mean?"

"To precipitate the hit and run."

"Nothing."

"Wrong answer," said Cruz. "Mr. DreadfulWater, tell Dr. Garza what she wins for lying to officers of the law."

"You two are not officers of the law."

Thumps began putting the pieces in order. "After you were told to turn over all your research," he said, "how long was it before the car tried to hit you?"

"Three or four days," said Garza.

"And in that time," said Thumps, "what did you do?"

Garza went silent.

"I think you made copies of everything," said Thumps.

"What if I did? Helios was mine. My research. My discovery."

"Then why set the fire?"

"I didn't."

"Okay," said Cruz. "Bad news, worse news."

"They weren't trying to kill you," said Thumps.

"You weren't there," said Garza.

"He's right," said Cruz. "They're not stupid. They call you in for that chat, and within days there's a fire in the computer complex. Doesn't matter if you set it or not."

"They have their suspicions," said Thumps. "So they take a run at you. To see if you'll jump."

"Normal person," said Cruz, "someone with nothing to hide, would have gone to the police."

"But what did you do?" said Thumps.

"Nothing," said Garza. "I pretended everything was normal."

"Then shouldn't you be in Sacramento at the plant, doing the work you usually do?"

"I put in for vacation."

"When do you normally take vacation?"

"I've never taken a vacation," said Garza.

"You see the problem," said Cruz. "Meeting, replace files, fire, hit and run, vacation. A plus B plus C plus D equals E. As in *escape*."

"They can't prove anything."

Thumps was rethinking the coffee. The way things were going, his guests might never leave.

"They didn't have to prove anything," said Cruz. "You did that for them."

The edge of Garza's finger was picked raw. "Shit."

"Back to Frank Dodge," said Thumps. "How well did you know him?"

"Didn't know him at all."

"And why would he steal a van and drive it here?"

Garza shook her head. "No idea."

Cruz got up and walked to the kitchen window. "Going to be a beautiful day. Good day for a drive."

"Where we going?" said Garza.

"You're staying here," said Cruz. "Safe and out of sight. Uncle Thumps and I are going to do a little scouting."

"No, we're not," said Thumps. "And I'm not your uncle."

"Not mine, *vato*," said Cruz. "Hers."

"He's not my uncle," said Garza.

"Family," said Cruz. "Like it or not, cuz, he's family."

CRUZ INSISTED ON taking his car.

Thumps stopped at the curb. "You don't need me."

"Local knowledge," said Cruz. "You're my faithful Indian guide."

"You know, if I shoot you," said Thumps, "Duke won't arrest me."

"You don't have a gun," said Cruz.

"I could get one."

Thumps was not a car enthusiast. Cars got you from one place to another faster than riding a horse or walking. That was their sole purpose. The best of the bunch wasn't the fastest or the most expensive. The best cars, in Thumps's opinion, were the ones that didn't break down, the ones that started when you turned the key, the ones that ran until you stopped.

His second criterion was comfort. The Mustang, for example, was a good-looking car, but the seats were stiff and badly formed. And they were too close to the floor. Getting into the car was akin to falling into a well. Getting out was freestyling a rock face.

"You know, she's lying to us, Pancho."

Thumps watched the landscape rush by.

"We just don't know about what or why."

"There is no 'we,'" said Thumps.

"She was like that as a kid." Cruz downshifted to take a curve. "She'd make up stories all the time. Once, she told my mother that I had gotten into my auntie's makeup and used up most of her lipstick."

"Had you?"

"Kids are curious," said Cruz. "So not only is she a liar, but she's a rat as well."

"Then why are we helping her?"

"Family," said Cruz. "It's a reason not to get married."

The turnoff for Deep House was just up ahead. The test

facility after that. Maybe Thumps would take Cruz out to the rim of the canyon, show him the view, push him over.

"That's why you and me get along," said Cruz. "We're not married. No kids. Free as the wind."

"Lonely and unhappy."

"That comes later," said Cruz. "When we're old and realize what we've missed."

The Shield Industries paint-testing facility was exactly as it had been the last time Thumps was here. Chain-link fence, rolling gate, keypad, burned-out van, and trailer in the distance.

Crime-scene sticker.

The field of multicoloured panels was in full bloom, giving intensity and life to an otherwise drab landscape.

Cruz pulled the car up to the keypad.

"Code?"

"No idea."

Cruz reached into his jacket and pulled out a gun. It was a big gun. A .45 probably. Heckler & Koch or a Sig. Enough to blow a hole in almost any lock.

"Cover your ears."

"Four-two-nine," said Thumps.

Cruz slid the gun back into its holster. "And that's the other reason I brought you along."

"Plus you're okay company."

"Wonderful."

"You make me laugh."

Cruz parked the car next to the remains of the van. Thumps used the door frame to pull himself out. He'd stick with his Element, thank you very much. Getting in and out of that car wasn't an Olympic event.

"This used to be a Mercedes" said Cruz. "Who the hell does something like this to a Mercedes?"

"A Ford owner?"

"The single-wide's the facility office?"

"It is."

Cruz walked around the compound. Thumps stayed by the Mustang.

"How about we play show-and-tell?" said Cruz. "You tell me what you know, I'll tell you what I know, and we'll see how many of the pieces fit."

"Sheriff's not going to be happy, you snooping around his crime scene."

"Crime-scene stickers are just suggestions," said Cruz.

"I'll mention that to Duke."

"You go first," said Cruz. "The quicker we solve this, the faster you get back to your cat and her kittens."

Thumps looked out across the prairies toward Deep House. He couldn't see the rim of the canyon from here. It was flush with the land, invisible until you were on it. A geological surprise.

"Frank Dodge used to work as a driver for Shield Industries," Thumps began. "And then he's laid off, unemployed. Yet he's able to show up at the plant, check out a van, and drive it away without anyone noticing."

"Seems a little sloppy," said Cruz. "You'd think security would be better than that."

"He drives the van into the compound, dies of a heart attack, and winds up at the bottom of Deep House. Maybe he sets fire to the van before he has his heart attack, or maybe someone else sets the fire after Dodge is dead."

"Too many maybes."

"No way to know for sure," said Thumps. "But whatever the answer, Dodge wasn't the only person here at the facility."

"And with Dodge dead," said Cruz, "we need to find the other person."

"That's the sheriff's job."

"Ask the question, *vato*," said Cruz.

Thumps took a breath. "Why would an unemployed driver steal an empty van?"

"Oh yeah," said Cruz. "That is the big enchilada all right. You got an answer?"

"Something worth stealing."

"Shield's not going to show up in force to run down a driver or a van," said Cruz. "They have to be after Garza or what was in the van."

"Or both."

"You believe her about that solar paint thingy?"

"Helios?" Thumps paused. "Maybe."

"Okay," said Cruz. "So let's go look at this famous Deep House."

"Not worried I might push you in?"

"Won't be the first time someone has tried," said Cruz.

27

Deep House was not so much a canyon as it was a wound. As though someone had stretched the earth until it split open. A jagged gash that ran out for about two miles, never more than a hundred yards wide.

Something that looked as though it could be fixed with a Band-Aid.

Or a zipper.

"What do you mean there's no road?"

"There's no road," said Thumps. "If you want to drive to the rim, you're going to have to drive overland."

"Through that shit?"

"Scrub," said Thumps. "We call it 'scrub.'"

"This is a high-performance car," said Cruz. "With a custom paint job."

***

THE WALK FROM THE TEST facility to the canyon rim took just under half an hour. Cruz was no happier on foot than he had been in the car.

"If I had known we were going to go native, I would have rented a horse."

"Gives us a chance to commune with nature."

"If I want to commune with nature," said Cruz, "I'll go to a park."

"This is more authentic."

"With food vendors," said Cruz, "a place to sit in the shade, and ducks."

"Watch your step," said Thumps. "You don't want to stumble into a hole or kick a prickly pear."

"A what?"

"It's like a cactus," said Thumps. "Boy from New Mexico should know all about cacti."

"Any rattlesnakes?"

"Sagewort, rabbitbrush, needle and thread, bluebunch, blue grama." Thumps rattled off the names as he and Cruz shuffled through the prairie grass.

"I'm getting crap on my boots."

"Mountain tarweed," said Thumps. "Hard to get that off leather."

"You're enjoying this, aren't you?"

* * *

THUMPS STARTED AT the south end of the canyon rim and made his way north. Cruz stayed on his heels.

"How big was Dodge?"

Thumps had to think about that. Dead bodies always looked smaller, the way a ball looked when you let the air out.

"Two hundred, 210. Why?"

"So we can rule out someone carrying Mr. Dodge from the test facility in order to dump him in the canyon."

"Think that's a safe bet."

"And if they drove, we should be able to find tracks."

Thumps stopped in his tracks. "Why?"

"Why what?"

"Why dump Dodge in the canyon?"

"Okay," said Cruz, "run with it."

"If someone murdered Dodge, getting rid of the body and burning the van would make sense."

"Destroy the evidence."

"But Dodge died of a heart attack." Thumps looked out at the clouds on the horizon. "So why go to all this trouble? Why make it look like foul play when it wasn't?"

Cruz moved on ahead. Thumps stayed where he was and took in the view. Yellow-brown prairie, white clouds, blue sky. And no wind. A gentle reminder that he should never go anywhere without his cameras.

"Over here," Cruz shouted.

***

THERE WAS NO mistaking the sign. Here, the grass had been crushed flat, the tracks running across the prairie back toward the test facility.

"Okay," said Cruz, "one mystery solved."

"We know how," said Thumps. "We just don't know why."

"We can't ask Dodge." Cruz stopped as though he had been hit in the head with a brick. "Did you rat me out?"

"What?"

Thumps didn't see it at first. And then he did. A low cloud of dust bubbling up out of the landscape and heading for them.

"Damn it, DreadfulWater."

Even before he could see the vehicle, Thumps knew who it was.

"I didn't say a word."

The dust cloud and Sheriff Duke Hockney's cruiser arrived at the same time. The car stopped. The cloud kept coming and buried the world in a tidal wave of dust and dirt.

Thumps and Cruz turned away. Not that it did any good.

"Well, well, well." Hockney stepped out of his cruiser, bright and spotless, his hat set at a jaunty angle on his head. "What do we have here?"

"Morning, Duke," said Thumps.

"Don't 'morning' me, DreadfulWater," said the sheriff. "And Mr. Cisco Cruz. Delighted to see you again."

"Morning, sheriff."

"Don't suppose there are any outstanding warrants for your arrest?"

"Not this week."

"And I suppose you two are out here looking at the wild-flowers and the birds."

"Thumps wanted to show me the canyon," said Cruz. "Supposed to be the number one sight in the area to see."

Hockney smiled and nodded his head. "And I suppose Shield Industries's test facility is number two on Expedia?"

Cruz put his hands in his pockets and waited.

"Here's what I find peculiar." Duke started chuckling. "I'm sitting in my office, enjoying my first cup of coffee, looking forward to a day when I've got nothing to do, when I get a call from that nice lady who owns the paint store in Glory."

"Bargain Hall?" offered Thumps.

"The very same," said Duke. "And guess what she tells me?"

"She got a notification on her cell."

"She got a notification on her cell," said the sheriff. "Seems that someone accessed the test facility."

Thumps figured he was safe for the moment. Cruz would try to strangle him later, when the sheriff wasn't looking.

"Someone accessed the facility," repeated Duke, "in spite of the very large and very prominent crime-scene sticker on the gate."

"Probably a false alarm," said Thumps.

"That was a possibility. But I drive out anyway, and what do I find?" Duke paused for effect. "My sticker has been removed, there's a nifty Ford Mustang parked in the facility, and I find you two wandering about out here amongst the flora and fauna."

"You know much about tarweed?" said Cruz. "You do not want to get it on your clothes."

"You want to tell me what you're doing?"

"Flora and fauna," said Cruz. "Wildflowers and birds."

Duke looked at the tire tracks that stopped at the rim of the canyon.

"Appears someone else had the self-same idea."

"Happens from time to time," said Cruz.

"Since I don't expect a straight answer," said Duke, "how about I do some guessing?"

"Free country," said Cruz.

Thumps stood to one side, feeling like a spectator at a tennis match of long and boring rallies. There were days when he might have enjoyed watching Duke and Cruz exchange lobs from the baseline. Today was not one of those days. Today, he simply wanted to get back in the car and go home.

"Cruz has a cousin," said Thumps in a bold move to speed up the match. "She works at Shield."

Duke and Cruz stopped their lobbing.

"Dr. Rajan Garza." Thumps ignored Cruz's death stare. "She's head of research and development."

"Ninja assassins have cousins?" said the sheriff.

"Evidently," said Thumps.

"You know," said Duke, "I feel like a cup of coffee. You boys feel like a cup of coffee?"

Cruz turned to Thumps. "Is threatening someone with his coffee a misdemeanour or a felony?"

"My office. In an hour." Hockney climbed into his cruiser. "The ride back into town should give you two chuckleheads enough time to get your stories straight."

Thumps watched the black-and-white bounce across uneven ground on its way to the paved road. Cruz reached down and pulled a prickly pear spine out of his boot.

"Shit," he said. "Least old John Wayne could have done is give us a ride back to my car."

28

The sheriff's office was warm. The percolator was bubbling away, the room filled with the alarming smell of blistered coffee beans. The sheriff was sitting behind his desk, his fingers tented under his nose. Thumps took the chair on the right, Cruz the chair on the left.

"Ground rules are simple," said Duke. "You lie to me, I throw you in jail."

Claire and the new man. Now that Thumps thought about it, Roxanne Heavy Runner would probably know the guy who had taken his place. Not that Claire was a *place*. She wasn't a piece of real estate that had been foreclosed. Or a territory that had been invaded. That, Thumps realized immediately, was very old-fashioned thinking.

Still.

"You leave something out, I throw you in jail."

Thumps knew better than to ask Roxanne outright. But he could ask Cooley. Roxanne was his auntie, and Cooley would probably escape with only minor bruising.

"You annoy me or criticize my coffee, I throw you in jail."

Thumps wasn't sure knowing was going to do much good, but it seemed to him to be the natural place to start.

"You two are joined at the hip," said the sheriff. "What happens to one, happens to the other. We clear?"

And where had Claire found this new man? She wasn't the social type, and now that she had Ivory, her ability to roam about the countryside auditioning potential partners was severely limited.

"We do something you don't like," said Cruz, "and you throw us in jail."

"Now, you see," said Duke, "you're already pushing my annoyance button."

THUMPS LET DUKE and Cruz carry on without him. They'd sort things out or Duke would throw the man from Pie Town into a cell simply because he could and because it would please him no end.

Great Falls.

That had to be the answer. Claire was seeing someone in Great Falls. Friends in that city had introduced her to someone, and what had been a spark was now a flame.

What had been a spark was now a flame. Thumps remembered the phrase from an old black and white movie he had watched one late night when he couldn't sleep. He and Claire had never been sparks or flames, and maybe that was the problem. Maybe a warm, gentle smoulder wasn't enough. Maybe a conflagration was needed. A passion so hot that it burned away good sense and turned caution to ash.

What was odd was that, in terms of personal relationships, Claire was more sloth than greyhound, slow-moving and exact. A new man seemed all too quick and frivolous, an impulse buy at the checkout counter.

"DreadfulWater. You paying attention?"

"We piss you off, you throw us in jail."

"We're way beyond that now," said Duke. "You guys are regular shit magnets."

"Prosaically put," said Cruz.

"Let me make sure I've got this right." Hockney took a deep breath and sucked in his stomach. "Mr. Frank Dodge, formerly of Shield Industries, steals a van, which he drives to the test facility, whereupon he drops dead of a heart attack, burns the van, and then jumps into Deep House."

"Astounding recall," said Cruz.

"That cell with your name on it?" said Duke. "It's still available."

"Good reminder," said Cruz.

"In the meantime, your cousin Dr. Rajan Garza gets involved in a pissing contest with her employer, whereupon she steals corporate secrets, is almost killed in a hit-and-run, takes a vacation, and winds up here in our fair city."

"She didn't steal anything," said Cruz. "The documents she took belonged to her. Her research."

"And if that wasn't enough of a cluster, I get Shield's holy trinity of Burke, Chandler, and Mobley camped out at the Tucker in expensive suites, eating expensive food."

"They're not looking for Dodge," said Cruz.

"Seeing as Dodge is dead."

"Seeing as Dodge is dead," said Cruz. "Which means they're looking for Raj."

"What about it, DreadfulWater," said Duke. "Am I missing any pieces?"

Now that Thumps thought about it, there weren't all that many pieces to begin with and most of them didn't fit with each other.

"What I'd like to know," said Duke, "is what this research was about."

"You'll have to ask Raj about that," said Cruz.

"And you know where I might find Dr. Garza?"

"No idea," said Cruz.

The sheriff sauntered over to the percolator and poured himself a cup of coffee.

"I got a meeting with the three musketeers from Shield tonight," he said. "They're going to buy me dinner. How about that?"

"Order the most expensive thing on the menu," said Cruz.

"Maybe I'll mention your name. See if that flaps the curtains." Duke held the cup up, as though he were going to make a toast. "Now get the hell out of my office."

THE MUSTANG WAS parked at the curb. Cruz worked his cell with one hand and opened the door with the other. Thumps didn't stop or break stride. He walked past the car and on down the street.

"Hey, Pancho, where you going?"

Thumps kept walking. "I have things to do."

"You're not going to help me?"

"Nope."

"What about *mi prima*?"

Thumps stopped and turned back. "She's lying to us."

Cruz caught up with Thumps. "Of course she's lying to us. But she's still my cousin. You know what her mother will do to me if something bad happens?"

"If Duke finds out that she's staying at my place . . ."

Cruz held up the phone. "Good news," he said. "She's not there."

"Maybe she's not answering her phone."

"Naw. Raj has always thought she was smarter than anyone else. Woman is a meticulous planner. When we were kids, she was always the mastermind. She'd put together these elaborate schemes for doing stuff like . . . robbing banks."

"Robbing banks?"

"You know, where all the money disappears and no one knows how it was done."

"Whole family like that?"

"Point is, she's not going to sit around and wait. By the time we got to Deep House this morning," said Cruz, "she was long gone."

"Where is she going to go?"

"She'll find somewhere to hole up," said Cruz. "She knows how to find me."

"So she's safe for the time being."

Cruz's face darkened as though he had seen something farther down the street that he didn't like. "No," he said. "Soon as she gets settled, she's going to be making up some elaborate plan to slay the dragon and save the damsel."

"You said she was smart."

"Remember those plans of hers I told you about, robbing banks?"

"They wouldn't have worked?"

"Worse," said Cruz. "Would have gotten everyone killed."

"Okay."

"And all of this?" Cruz waved a hand around in a lazy arc. "All of this feels like one of her plans."

***

THUMPS WAITED UNTIL Cruz got back in the Mustang and drove off down the street before he headed for the pharmacy.

Chintak Rawat had bought Chinook Pharmacy from Harry Lomax when Harry retired and moved to the coast of Oregon to live with his daughter. Rawat arrived from Toronto and landed with a thud, kicking up all the available bigotries.

After all, Lomax had been a local boy. Born and raised in Chinook.

White.

Rawat was an invading brown army from Mars.

Folks in Chinook had been cool to Chintak, and rather than continue to support a local business, they drove to the big-box stores in Great Falls and Helena to get their drugs and dental floss. Thumps had worried that the man from Toronto and the business he had purchased with his life savings would fail.

But then the price of gas had gone up, and economics proved to be more powerful than prejudice.

THE INSIDE OF the pharmacy was bright and spotless. Thumps strolled to the back, checking the displays in case Rawat had branched out into cat toys. Chintak was standing behind the counter, immaculate in his starched white pharmacy jacket.

"Ah, Mr. Thumps," said Rawat. "Your advice was most propitious."

Thumps took a step back from the counter. Not offering

advice was one of his cardinal rules. No matter how tempting it was to provide counsel, he knew the chances were excellent that any suggestions would result in misfortune and unintended consequences.

"I have spoken to Mr. Stas and Mr. Cooley, and they are delighted with your idea."

"My idea?"

"Of course, the formulation was mine," said Rawat. "But it was inspired by your patience and understanding."

"Do you have any cat toys?"

"Ah," said Rawat, "sadly not. Nor is this the first such inquiry. I had not thought a pharmacy a proper place for animal toys, but I may have been hasty in that conclusion."

Thumps wondered if the kittens would like to play with a box of Q-tips. Or bat a bottle of vitamin C around the house.

"A celebratory dinner," said Rawat. "At the Golden Harvest. Chinese buffet and beer. At which time, Mr. Cooley and Mr. Stas can regale us with tales of the hunt."

Or chase a toothbrush on a string.

"This will, I hope, allow me to participate in the ritual of male bonding without the expectation that I shoot something."

"Nothing like buffet and beer for male bonding."

"It's what friends do," said Rawat. "Is it not?"

"Absolutely," said Thumps.

"Then," said Rawat, "I will say no more about it."

29

The walk home gave Thumps time to think about Claire, about what had become of their relationship and what, if anything, he wanted to do about it. He had seen enough nature shows to know that many animals fought for mates, that battles to procreate could be savage and deadly.

One of the episodes had lingered on two sets of elk horns locked together, bleached and ghostly, the aftermath of a fight for a female that had left both combatants dead.

Thumps DreadfulWater. Bull elk.

No, that wouldn't do. Thumps couldn't think of anything sillier than two men fighting over a woman. He wasn't stupid. He knew that no matter how impressive the posturing, women made their own decisions.

Of course, a nice car or a good job didn't hurt.

And if he did want to fight for Claire, how would he go about doing that? Archie would be more than willing to help him. The little Greek would probably have a book on the subject.

Or a do-it-yourself video.

If he were an elk, he would just beat the shit out of Claire's new man. Thumps smiled at the thought. It was nothing more than a juvenile, testosterone-driven fantasy, something that maturity and good sense would ignore.

Still.

THUMPS HAD NO IDEA what he was going to find when he got back to the house. Cruz and Garza playing gin rummy at the kitchen table? Pops with Freeway and the kittens snuggled up on his bed? Archie, Ora Mae, and Roxanne in the living room dispensing advice on how he should live his life?

Claire and her new boyfriend parked in front of his house?

So he was relieved to find no car at the curb and no one in his house. No Cruz. No Garza. No Greek chorus. No Claire and her boyfriend.

No cats.

At first, he thought Freeway had just taken the kittens into hiding, but after looking for them in every conceivable nook and cranny, he guessed that they had gone to Dixie's house for a visit.

Cruz was in the wind. Garza was in the wind. All of it good news. Best of all, he had the house to himself. He padded to the bedroom and crawled onto the bed without taking off his shoes. He wasn't going to go to sleep. He was simply going to rest his eyes and think about his life and how he would like to live it.

WHEN THUMPS WOKE, it was dark. How had that happened? It was the diabetes, of course. That was the obvious answer. The exhaustion, the general aches and pains, the periodic dizziness, the need for naps.

Not that he was against naps. But lately, these sudden collapses felt less like luxurious breaks from a busy schedule and more like dying.

Seven o'clock. The clock on the nightstand said seven o'clock. And he was hungry. He lay on the bed and tried to remember what he had in the refrigerator that could be thrown into the microwave or dumped into a pot.

Okay, plan B.

First, a shower. When was the last time he had taken one? A quick shave. Deodorant. A spritz from a bottle of something he bought in the last century but still smelled fine.

The shirt he had worn to Pappous's was hanging on a hook. Thumps sniffed the underarms. There was something there, but it wasn't obvious. Dark slacks. Sportcoat. And suddenly, what had been a haggard and fatigued photographer was now a bon vivant about town. A *flâneur*, if Thumps remembered his high-school French correctly.

* * *

THE LOBBY OF the Tucker had been redecorated since the last time Thumps had been in the hotel. The dark wood had been replaced with copper panelling and heavy-cream walls. He wasn't sure he liked it, but then he was never comfortable with change.

The old Tucker had been snooty and aloof. Why change it? The new Tucker didn't look any less exclusive or less expensive.

There were two restaurants in the Tucker. The Quick Claim and the Mother Lode. The Quick Claim was the breakfast and lunch spot, while the Mother Lode looked after the evening trade.

But the pandemic had changed that. The Quick Claim had closed, and if hotel guests wanted to eat before six, they now had to venture out into the wilds of Chinook and forage for themselves.

Thumps didn't make it past the front desk before he was stopped.

"Good evening, sir," said a young man who was easily twice Thumps's size. "Are we a guest at the hotel?"

Thumps wondered if Cooley had a larger, older brother whom he didn't know about. There was a gold plate on the man's jacket that said "Joshua."

"We are not."

"While the pandemic has abated," said Joshua, "we are still restricting access to the hotel to our clients and to our dinner guests."

"I'm here for dinner."

Joshua took out a small tablet and tapped the screen. "Name?"

"Thumps DreadfulWater."

Joshua smiled. "Didn't you used to be sheriff?"

"Temporary."

"Your name is not on my reservation list."

"I'm meeting friends."

"And these friends are?"

"Martha Burke?"

"No," said Joshua.

"Graham Chandler?"

"Again, no."

"Carl Mobley?"

Joshua checked the tablet and sighed. "You know, we do offer takeout."

"Shield Industries," said Thumps. "The reservation might be under Shield Industries."

"Ah," said Joshua. "Here it is. For four."

"That's the one," said Thumps.

"And the four have already been seated."

"When I made the reservation," said Thumps, his face flat and calm, "I didn't know that the sheriff would be dining with us."

Duke had actually put on a sports jacket and a tie. Thumps was sorry he hadn't brought a camera to capture the moment for posterity.

"Special Deputy DreadfulWater."

Duke held out a hand and waved him over. If Thumps didn't know better, he could have thought that the sheriff was happy to see him.

The same couldn't be said for the folks from Shield.

"Mr. DreadfulWater," said Martha Burke. "What a surprise."

Burke was dressed in a dark grey business suit that was a complement to Chandler's navy pinstripe. Thumps wondered if the two of them had consulted on attire ahead of time.

"The sheriff invited me."

Mobley was the odd man out. Windbreaker, slacks, plaid shirt, a working man's version of business casual.

"My right-hand man," said Duke, not missing a beat. "Big case like this, I need all the help I can get."

Chandler tried to manage a little warmth. "Good thing we were given a large table."

"Sit down, Mr. DreadfulWater," said Burke. "We were just about to order."

Thumps had always thought you could tell a great deal about people by the food they ate. Duke had the prime rib. Burke went for a crab salad and the fish special. Chandler had the strip loin. Mobley, the burger and fries.

"Carl always orders the burger," said Chandler.

"I like burgers," said Mobley.

Thumps debated between the Vienna schnitzel and the risotto with chicken and caramelized onions.

"You can imagine our surprise," said Burke, "when the sheriff here told us about Frank Dodge and our van."

"Man dumped in a canyon," said Chandler. "Van burned. All in all, quite disturbing."

"Folks were kind enough to fill me in on Dr. Rajan Garza," said Duke.

"Don't think I know the name," said Thumps.

"No reason you should," said Duke, the edge of his voice sharp enough to cut steel. "Dr. Garza is one of Shield Industries's top research scientists."

Thumps played it out. "Is this Dr. Garza connected to Frank Dodge?"

"Good question," said Duke.

"Naturally, we want to talk to Dr. Garza," said Chandler, ignoring the question.

"But she seems to have gone missing," said Burke.

"Was supposed to be on vacation in Puerto Vallarta," said Mobley. "But she never made her plane."

"We now know that she flew here," said Chandler.

Duke turned to Thumps. "Ain't this something. Dead driver, burned-out van, missing scientist. All right here in Chinook. Next thing you know, we'll be knee-deep in ninja assassins and top-secret projects."

"How's the prime rib?" asked Mobley.

"Perfect," said the sheriff. "Just perfect."

"We're concerned that Dr. Garza may have had an episode," said Burke. "She's quite brilliant, but unfortunately, she has a history of erratic behaviour."

"Geniuses," said Chandler. "They're not necessarily stable."

Duke ladled the butter onto his baked potato. "So I take it Dr. Garza took something that she shouldn't have taken."

Burke shook her head. "Nothing like that. But she does have knowledge of our formulae and protocols that we would prefer to remain within the company."

Duke turned the potato black with pepper. "Anything in particular?"

The risotto with the chicken and caramelized onions was excellent. But the only way it was worth the price on the menu was if it came with a complimentary weekend in Venice.

"Our first order of business is to find her," said Burke.

"Well," said the sheriff, "now that I know she's missing and could be in some difficulty, you may rest assured that Special Deputy DreadfulWater and I will do everything in our power to find her."

For dessert, Thumps was going to try the chocolate mousse with whipped cream.

"We've already checked the accommodations in the area," said Chandler.

"Could be staying with friends," said the sheriff. "Or she might be doing that Airbnb thingy."

"That's what we figure," said Mobley.

"The problem I have," said Duke, "is trying to figure out where Frank Dodge fits into all this."

"It does look suspicious," said Chandler. "But I think we have to assume that Dr. Garza's disappearance and Mr. Dodge are two separate events."

"Both Garza and Dodge taking off at the same time?" said the sheriff. "Both of them coming here with the three of you hard on their heels?"

"We were hoping for a little co-operation," said Burke.

"You can ask my special deputy," said Duke as he mopped up the *au jus* with a wedge of bread. "I'm nothing but co-operation."

THE CHOCOLATE MOUSSE was delicious, worth every penny, provided it came with two tickets for a Mediterranean cruise.

Duke tried to chip away at the front that Burke, Chandler, and Mobley had thrown up, but to little effect. In the end, he consoled himself with the apple strudel and ice cream.

The conversation wandered away from Dodge and Garza to travel and where everyone wanted to go now that they could.

"Valencia," said Burke. "I've been to Madrid and Barcelona. The virus hit it hard, but it's a beautiful country."

Chandler was going to spend two weeks in Singapore and Hong Kong. "Always wanted to see that part of the world."

"Fishing," said Mobley. "Friend of mine has a lodge on the Rogue in Oregon."

"What about you, sheriff?" said Burke. "You got a special place?"

"Backyard," said Duke. "Hammock and a bottle of beer."

No one asked Thumps about his plans, and he didn't volunteer.

"It's been a lovely evening," said Burke. "We'll have to do this again."

"After we find Dr. Garza," said Chandler.

"Count on me," said the sheriff. "Not going to sleep until that happens."

THUMPS WAS ALREADY out the door and halfway down the steps when Duke caught up to him.

"You enjoy that expensive free meal?"

"I did," said Thumps. "What about you?"

"Worth every penny," said Duke, "provided you tossed in tickets to the Super Bowl."

Thumps was stuffed. He should have skipped dessert, but he was glad that he didn't. The chocolate mousse had been thick and rich, the whipped cream real.

"You want a ride home?"

"Better walk."

"Could have passed on the mousse," said Duke.

"I have a fast metabolism."

"Yeah," said Duke, "I can see that."

The sheriff's cruiser was parked down the street. Thumps walked with him until they got to the car.

"How come you didn't tell them about Cruz?"

"Nothing to tell." Duke opened the door. "As I recall, he's here for the flora and the fauna."

30

The house was just as empty as when he had left it. No Cruz, no Garza.

No cats.

He had his bed all to himself, didn't have to worry about rolling over and crushing the kittens. Didn't have to put up with wiggly furballs tucked in against his neck. Didn't have to listen to decibel-busting purring into the early hours. Nothing but a dark room filled with blissful silence.

All things considered, Thumps expected to get a full night's rest. Maybe even sleep in. So why was he up at two and at three and at five. Finally, at six thirty, when the light outside was more than a rumour, he found himself wide awake with nothing to do and no place to go.

Well, that wasn't exactly true. If he was going to be up at this ungodly hour, he was going to need a full breakfast to help him get through the day.

THERE WERE STOOLS available at Al's. Wutty Youngbeaver was in his usual seat, flanked by Russell Plunkett and Jimmy Monroe. The three of them were looking at a series of snapshots of a yellow school bus.

Thumps slid past the men, with no thought of asking them about the photographs.

"Look who's up early." Al brought the coffee pot with her. "Hear you had a good time at the Mother Lode last night."

"Expensive place."

"Do tell," said Al. "Also hear that someone else paid the freight."

"Breakfast, please," said Thumps. "The usual."

"When you talk to your little buddy," said Al, "I'd probably make the complimentary nature of the meal the main bullet point."

"Archie?"

"Don't know he's going to be all that happy, you sleeping with the enemy."

"I'm not sleeping with the enemy," said Thumps.

"I don't have to worry," said Al, "'cause Pappous's doesn't serve breakfast."

"I didn't go there because I wanted to go there."

"Last person to use that excuse didn't get out of Nuremberg alive."

"It was business," said Thumps. "I was helping the sheriff."

Al started chuckling. She chuckled all the way back to the grill. Out of the corner of his eye, Thumps saw Wutty leave his seat and come sliding along the stools. There was the chance he was heading for the pay phone on the wall at the end of the café.

"Thumps, my man."

And there was the chance that he wasn't.

"Take a look at these."

Wutty laid out six snapshots of himself standing in front of a yellow bus.

"Be honest. I want your unbiased, professional opinion."

Three were slightly out of focus. Wutty had his eyes closed in another. The last two had the top part of his head cut off.

"Pretty terrible, right? Bet you could do better." Wutty was smiling and bobbing his head. "How about tomorrow?"

"What?"

Wutty turned and held up a thumb, and Russell and Jimmy gave him a thumbs-up back.

"Eleven o'clock," said Wutty as he retreated to the front of the café. "At Stas's garage."

Al arrived with breakfast. "You actually said yes to doing his publicity photography for free?"

"I did not."

"So why does he think you did?"

"Did you cut back on my potatoes?"

"You know what carbohydrates are?"

"Delicious," said Thumps. "Especially when fried."

"Sugar in disguise," said Al. "They're just sugar in disguise."

"She's right, you know."

Thumps hadn't seen the sheriff come in, didn't even know that the man was within striking distance. And then there he was, sitting on the stool next to him.

"Macy can tell you all about carbohydrates." Hockney helped himself to Thumps's home fries. "What you need in your diet is more kale."

"Those are my potatoes."

"You had a big meal last night."

"You want breakfast, sheriff," said Al, "or are you just taking up valuable space?"

"Coffee, please," said Duke. "To go."

"Stop eating my potatoes."

"Don't you want to know where we're going this bright and lovely morning?"

Thumps watched Al pour coffee into a takeout cup and snap the lid on.

"I don't know where you're going," said Thumps, "but wherever it is, I won't be going with you."

"Make that two coffees to go," Duke called out to Al. "Special Deputy DreadfulWater and I are bound for Glory."

Glory was an old gold-mining town that had been on the verge of oblivion when it was discovered by a Hollywood location scout. Thumps couldn't remember the name of the movie, but it was a period piece with a big battle scene that pretty much destroyed the turn-of-the-century storefronts along Main Street.

By the time the movie wrapped, the leading lady had taken a liking to the town and the surrounding mountains. She rounded up a flock of her friends from Los Angeles, who descended on Glory and bought up much of the land.

Thumps couldn't recall if the movie had been a success, but Glory rose from its own ashes on the wings of vacation homes and condominiums that sprang up around town and in the surrounding foothills. The remains of the wonderful old buildings along Main Street were bulldozed and replaced with wonderful new buildings that were exact replicas of the originals.

Thumps leaned up against the window and watched as they climbed into the mountains.

"We really going to Glory?"

"That's what I said."

"There's nothing in Glory but expensive real estate and expensive people."

"Most of the big players have gotten out," said Duke. "Word is the place has been taken over by accountants and dentists."

And then Thumps remembered. "Bargain Hall."

"And people say you're slow."

***

GLORY PAINT AND MILLWORK was just off Main Street in a building that had once been a church. The place still had a steeple, though the cross had been removed.

"Whenever Macy tries to paint a room in the house, she generally goes through six or seven cans trying to find the right colour."

"Maybe," said Thumps, "buying paint from a church would increase your chances of success."

"Pray for the right colour?" said Duke.

"Probably same odds as using paint chips."

BARGAIN HALL WAS behind the counter, sorting through a stack of invoices. "Well, well," she said. "If it isn't the Lone Ranger and Tonto."

Duke turned to Thumps. "I'm guessing I'm the Ranger."

"Don't suppose you boys came all this way for paint."

"In a manner of speaking," said the sheriff, "we did."

Thumps wondered if Duke was going to circle around the problem, riding the thermals, keeping the warm air beneath his wings.

"Special Deputy DreadfulWater here was wondering why there are paint panels in Deep House."

Or whether he would just swoop in for the kill.

"Paint panels?"

"Paint panels," repeated Duke. "From the test facility."

Thumps could see that Hall was getting ready to lie.

"And my special deputy was wondering exactly how they got there."

Bargain leaned on the counter. "I suppose someone put them there."

Duke looked around the store. "Got a nice store here. Don't imagine the pandemic helped any."

"Get to the point, sheriff."

"As I recall," said Duke, "you told me that the company would send paint panels out for testing, and that you would send paint panels back so that the folks in Sacramento could check the colours and the formulas against the weather."

"That's the theory all right," said Bargain.

"So what am I missing?"

"You guys want tea?" Bargain went to the front door and locked it, turned the sign around. "I feel like a cup of tea."

The back of the store was set up as an apartment. Living room, small kitchen, bathroom, one bedroom.

Duke helped himself to the larger of the chairs. "You live here?"

"It's what I got." Bargain set a plate of cookies on the table. "When Jerome was alive, we had a small house just outside of town."

"Jerome your husband?"

"Died. One year, three months."

"Sorry," said Thumps, knowing how difficult it was to make such expressions of sympathy sound sincere.

"When Jerome was alive, he ran the store. I kept the books."

"World's a tough place for small businesses," said Duke.

"I tried to sell," said Bargain. "But no one wants a paint business. I had to sell the house to stay afloat."

"And now you're running the business."

"No choice," said Bargain. "It's what I got."

Both Thumps and the sheriff lingered over their tea in silence, waiting for a way to ask the question.

"It was Jerome's idea," Bargain said at last. "Before, when it was Main Street Paints, everything was great."

"And then Shield came along."

"Then Shield came along," said Bargain, "and the business went to shit. First, they cut the discounts they had been giving us on paint."

"But they still wanted you to look after the test facility."

"Too right, they did," said Bargain. "They still sent out samples and expected us to keep all the records, didn't they? Expected that we'd help them load the return panels as well."

"Just like before," said Duke.

"Same work," said Bargain, "half the pay. Then last year, they stopped sending panels. Just before Jerome passed, they sent us a memo saying we should dispose of the remaining panels."

"The panels that were already here."

"Four hundred and twenty-four," said Bargain. "Each one is half a sheet of three-quarter plywood. You know how much that weighs?"

Thumps tried to remember the last time he had picked up a sheet of three-quarter plywood.

"Thirty-one pounds," said Bargain. "We were supposed to take the panels to the landfill."

"Landfill free?" asked Duke.

"Hell, no," said Bargain. "Oh, Shield sent us out a lump sum to take care of the disposal costs."

"But they weren't paying you for your time or effort."

"Not even close," said Bargain. "I was against it, but Jerome thought that dumping some of the panels into the canyon would make up for the way they were treating us. Besides, the canyon was part of the facility lease."

"You remember the colours?"

"Colours?"

"Of the panels that were dumped into Deep House."

"You kidding?"

The sheriff rubbed the side of his nose. "For instance, were there any silver panels in the lot."

"Silver?" Bargain looked at Duke and then at Thumps. "We never had any silver panels."

Thumps finished the last of his tea. "What are you going to do now?"

"About the test facility?" Bargain smiled. "Not a damn thing.

Only reason I went out when my cell went off was to give who-ever was there a piece of my mind."

"That's when you found the driver dead."

"What?"

"You drove his body to the canyon and dumped it in, drove back to the facility, and set fire to the van." Duke paused to take a breath. "To let the folks at home office know how you felt about the way they had treated you."

Bargain looked at Thumps. "Is he really the sheriff?"

"He is," said Thumps.

"Jerome used to come up with some stupid ideas," said Bargain, "but you take first prize. Why the hell would I do any of that?"

"You were angry with Shield," said Duke. "Natural reaction."

"What planet do you live on?"

"Other people have asked that very same question," said Thumps.

"Do I strike you as a person who would waste her time cook-ing up some cockamamie scheme like that because some cor-poration treated her badly?"

"People get angry," said Duke. "They do stupid things."

"Can't argue with that." Bargain held her arms out. "Guess you better slap the cuffs on me."

Duke smiled. "Right now, I'll settle for another cookie, maybe some more tea."

<h1 style="text-align:center">31</h1>

Thumps and the sheriff were halfway back to Chinook before either of them spoke, and then it was Duke who broke the silence.

"Thoughts?"

"She didn't do it."

"I know she didn't do it," said Duke. "I still had to ask."

"The cookies were good," said Thumps. "Homemade."

"Some people," said Duke, "when they make chocolate chip cookies, use milk-chocolate chips."

"She used bittersweet chips."

"Hence the good cookies," said the sheriff. "Tea was good as well."

"So you're back to where you started."

"Not completely," said Duke. "I now know how those paint panels got to the bottom of the canyon."

"That's true."

"Not knowing could have kept me up at night."

Thumps was working on something clever to say about counting paint panels instead of sheep when the sheriff's cell began buzzing.

"Speak . . . Okay . . . No, it's not a problem . . . In the car . . . Yeah, okay, be there in twenty."

Thumps closed his eyes. "Wife?"

"Beth," said the sheriff.

Thumps opened his eyes. "Beth?"

"Wants us to stop in."

"Drop me off at my house," said Thumps.

"No can do," said Duke. "She specifically said she wanted to see the both of us."

"No way, I'm not going into that basement," said Thumps.

"Some days," said Duke, "I just love this job."

BETH WAS WAITING for them on the first floor of the old Land Titles building. Thumps couldn't remember the last time he had been in Beth's medical office.

"Gentlemen."

"I think she's talking about us," said Duke.

"Sit."

Beth was dressed in a white lab coat. Her hair was pulled

back and tight to her head. A look that was both severe and professional, frightening and reassuring.

"Have you boys been having fun?"

"Thumps is a bit grumpy," said Duke.

"He took me to Glory."

"I assume," said Beth, "that you're talking about the place and not the metaphor."

"Paint store," said Duke. "Maybe you know it."

"Because I paint my apartment so often?"

Both Duke and Thumps knew this was not a question to be answered.

"You wanted to see us?"

Beth opened a drawer, took out a pill bottle, and set it on the desk.

"Either one of you know what this is?"

"Pill bottle?" said Duke.

"And do you know who they belong to?"

Duke turned to Thumps. "Your turn," he said.

"Frank Dodge?"

"Amazing," said Beth. "And here I thought you two were just pretty faces."

"We are pretty faces," said Duke.

"Do you know how I know that this belongs to Frank Dodge?"

Thumps held up his hand. "You found it in a pocket?"

"And?"

"And it has Dodge's name on it?"

Beth picked up the bottle and turned it around in her hand. "Better yet, it has the name and address of the pharmacy that filled the prescription."

"And you called the pharmacy," said the sheriff.

"I did," said Beth. "As I had surmised, Mr. Dodge had contracted the COVID virus. Had a pretty rough time of it. He recovered but came away with atrial fibrillation."

"Friend of mine had that," said Duke. "Had to take blood thinners."

"And that's what these are," said Beth.

"This is all very interesting," said Duke, "but we already know that he died of a heart attack."

Beth ignored the sheriff. "So I called the pharmacy, and Sarah and I got to chatting."

"Sarah?"

"The pharmacist in Sacramento."

"One professional to another."

"Exactly," said Beth. "And Sarah told me a couple of interesting things."

"Which you're going to tell us," said Duke.

"Which I'm going to tell you," said Beth, "if you stop interrupting me."

Thumps sat back in his chair, content to be a spectator.

"Dodge was unemployed and broke," said Beth. "Sarah said he was always complaining about the cost of his medications.

Said that a country as rich as the U.S. should damn well have a decent health-care system."

Thumps thought of the costs of his diabetes medication. Dodge had every right to complain.

"We talking socialized medicine?" said Duke.

"You know that if you two lived in Canada, the cost of your operation and your buddy's diabetes medication would be covered."

"Sure," said Duke, "but you'd have to live in Canada."

"So Sarah and I got to talking about Mr. Dodge, and it seems that he suddenly came into some money. He got this prescription filled a couple of weeks before he wound up in my morgue, and he paid for the medication with cash."

"This is going somewhere, right?"

"Keep your badge on," said Beth. "Anyway, the day he picked up the prescription, he also asked for a copy of his pharmacy records, said he was going to be moving. Sarah told him that if he told her where he was going, she could have the records emailed to a pharmacy near his new address."

The sheriff shifted position in the chair.

"Guess where Dodge was going."

"I'd have to guess he wasn't going back to Sacramento," said Duke.

"Mexico," said Beth. "Sarah said he was headed to Mexico."

"Destination of choice for the middle class," said Thumps. "Cheap living and the beach."

"Before the pandemic hit," said Beth, "Gabby and I were thinking of going to Cancun."

The sheriff got to his feet. "That's all very interesting, but it doesn't tell us why he wound up here or what he was being paid to do."

"I don't do why or what," said Beth. "And sit down. I'm not done."

Flights to Mexico might be cheap. Maybe Claire would like to go to someplace with sun and sand. Puerto Vallarta, the Mayan Riviera, Cabo San Lucas. They could take Ivory with them. She'd love the ocean. And if he remembered correctly, children under a certain age could fly free.

"Take a look at this." Beth took an X-ray out of a large envelope and clipped it to a light screen. "What do you see?"

The image was of a large bone.

"This our Mr. Dodge?" said the sheriff.

"No," said Beth. "This is Harold Shipman."

Thumps felt the air go out of the room.

"Shipman?"

"His left tibia to be exact," said Beth.

"Looks broken," said Duke.

"That's because it is," said Beth.

"We knew this already," said Thumps. "He tried to cross the Slump, fell, and broke his leg. Died of exposure."

"Nothing too good for a serial killer," said Duke.

"Yes, we did," said Beth. "But take a close look. You see that faint white smear right at the break?"

Duke got right up to the light screen and squinted at the image. "You saying what I think you're saying?"

"I'm not saying anything," said Beth. "State medical examiner caught it. Kicked it back to me for my opinion."

"And you think the smear is lead," said Duke.

"That's certainly one answer," said Beth.

Thumps stared at the image. "Is there another option?"

Beth pulled the X-ray off the screen and slipped it back into the envelope. "I just thought you should know."

"You think Shipman was shot?"

"I don't think anything," said Beth. "I just thought **you** should know."

"What are we supposed to do about this?" said Duke.

"Again," said Beth, "I don't do the what."

"So if Shipman's broken leg was the result of a gunshot, then it wasn't death through misadventure. It was murder."

"If the mark on the X-ray was from a bullet," said Beth. "In my opinion, it's inconclusive."

"And what's the state examiner going to say?"

"My call," said Beth. "Last thing the state lab wants is to reopen a closed case."

"So that's that," said Duke.

"That's that," said Beth. "I just thought you should know."

32

The wind was up when Thumps and the sheriff stepped out of the old Land Titles building. Duke had to hold on to his hat.

"Well," said the sheriff, "that was interesting."

"Dodge or Shipman?"

"Both," said Duke. "Though I'm going to file Shipman under 'intriguing, but requiring no further action.'"

"And Dodge?"

"We need to talk to Cruz and his cousin."

"Dr. Rajan Garza."

"Why does everyone think that lying to an officer of the law is a good idea?"

"It's appalling."

"Present company included," said the sheriff. "You could have told me that Cruz was in town."

"Didn't have the chance."

"Or that his cousin was on the run from the Shield folks."

"That was an omission."

"You got any more omissions I should know about?"

"Not a one."

"And you wouldn't happen to know where Cruz and Garza are hiding?"

"Cruz doesn't hide. He just moves around."

Duke turned his face away from the wind. "We need to find them. Got a feeling this thing is about to blow up."

THE HOUSE WAS still empty. Thumps was tempted to go next door to make sure that Freeway and the kittens were there and in good health, but instead he shaved quickly and ran a comb through his hair.

Clean shirt, clean jeans, clean socks.

He wasn't sure that Claire was going to be home. In fact, there was every chance that she would be off somewhere. Visiting friends. Shopping. Out with the new man.

Still, the drive would be nice and he might see something along the river to photograph. He hadn't really done much fieldwork in the last few months, and it wouldn't hurt to stand in the middle of a landscape and listen to the sound of a shutter.

Claire's pickup was parked by the barn. Thumps pulled up next to the Russian olive that Claire had planted to brighten the surroundings. It hadn't worked. It was the nature of Russian olives, with their thin, grey leaves and spindly branches, to look as though they were perpetually dying, and the one in Claire's yard was more gifted than most.

Claire came out the door before Thumps reached the house. Ivory was in her arms.

"Dog," said Ivory.

"Didn't expect you."

It wasn't the warm welcome Thumps had hoped for, but it was a start.

"Just learned something," said Thumps. "Maybe it's important. Maybe it's not."

It wasn't a smile, but it was a start.

"Then I guess you better come in."

"Dog," said Ivory.

Claire's kitchen was not going to win a good-housekeeping award. The table was awash in crayons and art paper. The sink was stacked with dirty dishes, cups, and glasses. There was a fry pan on the stove that had been recently used but not cleaned. There was a faint fragrance in the air. Something floral with a citrus undertone.

Claire bounced Ivory on her hip. "You want coffee?"

"Sure."

Ivory gave a big yawn, and her eyes drooped.

"She was almost asleep when you arrived."

"Sorry."

"How about I try to put her down, and you make yourself useful."

"As in clean the kitchen?"

"That would be useful."

Truth be told, Thumps didn't mind doing housework. He filled the sink with soapy water and began working his way through the plates and the bowls, the glasses and the utensils. There were lipstick marks on one cup that required an extra soak and scrub. The patina on the fry pan turned out to be a layer of burnt fat on top of another layer of burnt fat.

Thumps was just contemplating taking the burners off the stove and scrubbing them as well when Claire came out of the bedroom.

"She doesn't mind a nap," said Claire. "Just have to remind her."

"She's getting big."

"I like her just the way she is."

"I made a fresh pot of coffee."

Claire glanced at the fry pan. "What did you do to it?"

"Cleaned it."

"What happened to the patina?"

"That was burnt fat."

Claire helped herself to the coffee. "Am I going to get a lecture?"

"Nope."

"About cleaning my house?"

"I like doing dishes."

Claire sat in the chair and let her shoulders slump. "So why are you here?"

"Beth Mooney," said Thumps.

"Beth okay?"

Thumps realized he had started this wrong. "No, there's nothing wrong with Beth. It's the state medical-examiner's office. They sent her a report."

"This about the autopsy on Harold Shipman?"

Thumps tried not to look surprised.

"Beth called me," said Claire. "Wanted to give me a heads-up. Wanted me to pass the information on to Moses and Cooley."

"Okay."

"You think Shipman was shot? You think that's how his leg got broken?"

"Beth says the X-ray is inconclusive."

"Shipman was a serial killer."

"He was."

"That night," said Claire, "he was going to kill me and Ivory."

"He was going to kill us all."

Claire wrapped her arms around herself. "And then you let him go."

There it was. The piece that Thumps had been missing.

"You had him," said Claire, "and you let him go."

"I didn't let him go."

"You could have shot him." Claire began rocking back and forth. "You should have shot him."

"He's dead."

"He could have escaped."

"There was no chance of that," said Thumps.

Claire stopped rocking. There were tears in her eyes. "You went back, didn't you? You went back and found him."

Thumps shook his head. "It doesn't matter."

"It matters to me. I need to know I can count on you."

Thumps tried to think of something to say. "I should probably go."

Claire got up and walked to the window. "Cruz and his cousin were here."

"Yeah," said Thumps, "I know."

"No, you didn't."

"Too many dirty dishes. Lipstick on a coffee cup. You can still smell perfume in the air. You don't use lipstick or perfume."

"I have friends, you know."

Thumps waited.

"Cruz saved my life. That time at Buffalo Mountain."

"Mine too."

"They needed a place to stay for a night," said Claire. "Couldn't say no."

"You know where they went?"

"No idea."

"He knows I'll find him."

Claire nodded. "He said you'd say that."

Claire left the front door open, so she could hear Ivory, and walked Thumps to his car.

"If you wanted to come out this weekend," said Claire, "I wouldn't say no."

"Overnight?"

"We could give it a try. I know Ivory would like having you around."

"She run out of things to bite?"

Claire laughed. "Give it a few years, and biting will seem like a walk in the park."

The sun was hot. The sky was high and bright. The Russian olive in the yard was doing its best impression of a corpse.

"What about the new man?"

"Roxanne is right." Claire touched Thumps's face with her hand. "You guys really are dense."

33

Thumps drove back along the river, and when he got to the scenic turnout, he stopped.

So Claire thought he had killed Shipman, thought he had shot the man in the leg, ensuring that the serial killer would never leave the reservation alive.

Now that he thought about it, Beth had floated the same question.

Thumps stood by his car and took in the panorama. In the afternoon light, the river bottom wasn't all that picturesque. The view was much better at night when the Ironstone would turn silver and glowing under a full moon.

Cruz and Garza had spent the night at Claire's place. Thumps hadn't anticipated this, but it made sense. No one would connect Rajan Garza with Claire Merchant. They might connect Claire with Cruz, but the only two people who knew that Cruz was even in town or that Cruz and Garza were family were Thumps and the sheriff.

Why hadn't they stayed on the reservation? And where would they go? Some place unexpected. Some place where Garza wouldn't be exposed until Cruz could figure things out.

Thumps got back in the car. Sometimes driving helped him to think. Sometimes it didn't. Most of the time, it just wasted gas and wore out the tires.

BY THE TIME Thumps pulled into Chinook, he had a plan. Of sorts. What less enlightened folk might call a "tree shaker," and the tree he figured he'd shake was Shield Industries.

Thumps hoped that the gatekeeper who had stopped him when he had come to the Tucker for dinner would be on break or in the bathroom or somewhere other than where he was.

Joshua. Standing in the middle of the lobby looking right at him.

"Good afternoon, Mr. DreadfulWater."

Thumps found the man's memory somewhat unnerving.

"Afternoon."

"Are we here for a late lunch?"

"We're here to speak with one of your guests."

"Name of the guest?" said Joshua.

Thumps had hoped to surprise the tree. Having his presence announced wasn't part of the plan.

"Martha Burke."

Joshua took out an electronic device that could have been a small tablet or a large cellphone.

"Ms. Burke is in our spa and currently unavailable."

"How about Graham Chandler?"

"I believe that Mr. Chandler is at the bar. Do you know where that is?"

"I do."

"Enjoy the rest of the day."

CHANDLER WAS BY himself at a round table in a semicircular booth. "Mr. DreadfulWater." He raised a hand and gave a delicate wave. "Please. Join me."

Thumps pulled a chair up to the outside edge of the table. In case he had to beat a quick retreat.

"To what do I owe the honour?"

"Dr. Rajan Garza," said Thumps, giving the tree a vigorous shake.

"May I offer you a drink? Scotch? Wine? Antifreeze?"

Thumps was pretty sure he didn't like Chandler, but the man did have a sense of humour.

"Have I been annoying?"

"Not yet," said Chandler, "but I have the distinct feeling that you could become an irritant."

"That's the sheriff's job."

Chandler glanced around the bar. "And just where is the good sheriff?"

"Probably out sheriffing," said Thumps. "He does that from time to time."

Chandler sat back. "You mentioned Dr. Garza's name. Have you located her?"

"I'm not looking for her."

Chandler waited.

"That appears to be your job," said Thumps. "I'm just curious."

"You know what they say about curiosity and cats."

"If that were true," said Thumps, "there would be no cats in the world."

"I believe it was intended as a metaphor," said Chandler. "A caution to mind your own business."

"You came to us," said Thumps. "You asked for our help."

"You have the local knowledge that we do not," said Chandler. "We hoped that you could be of assistance."

Across the room, Thumps saw Martha Burke come into the bar. She paused for a moment and then came straight to the table.

"Mr. Thumps and I were just discussing cats," said Chandler.

Burke stayed standing. "Cats?"

"Metaphorically speaking," said Chandler. "In actual fact, he wants to ask us about Dr. Garza."

Burke looked as though she hadn't been getting enough sleep. "Does he?"

"In particular," said Chandler, "he wants to know why we're looking for a scientist who is on vacation."

"Quite the curious fellow," said Burke.

"And I suspect that neither he nor the sheriff are going to stop asking questions until they have the answers."

Burke rubbed the back of her neck with one hand. "I'm going to lie down for a bit," she said. "I'll leave you to deal with Mr. DreadfulWater."

Chandler waited for Burke to disappear into the lobby. "Do you know what she did before she came to Shield?"

"Warden at a women's prison?"

"That's not nice," said Chandler.

"Head of the Girl Scouts."

"Somewhere in between," said Chandler. "Think Fortune 500, but with guns."

"Military."

"Military," said Chandler. "So let's begin."

"Garza."

"Rajan Garza." Chandler turned his glass around. "Dr. Rajan Garza was already at Main Street when General Dynamics bought the company and created Shield Industries. Do you know much about holding companies and corporations?"

"Nope."

"Okay," said Chandler, "let's try this. Why do you suppose a multinational corporation such as General Dynamics would buy a company such as Main Street Paints?"

"Because that's what corporations do?"

Chandler smiled. "There's that."

"Rajan Garza."

Chandler nodded. "Woman is a genius. Do you know any-thing about solar energy?"

"As much as the next guy."

"Garza has developed a paint and ceramic protocol we call Helios that can turn almost any surface into a solar panel."

"Cool."

"Very cool," said Chandler. "A solar panel with a much higher efficiency than standard solar panels. I'm sure you can imagine some of the applications."

"Energy source for very poor countries?"

"Of course not." Chandler signalled the bar for another drink. "Shield is hardly a non-profit."

"But Garza wants to give the protocol away?"

"It would appear," said Chandler. "Garza was supposed to hand in all her research. Notes, test results. We anticipated that she would keep copies of everything."

"Makes sense," said Thumps.

"And then shortly before Garza disappeared, we had a fire in our server room, and the Helios files were lost."

"You must have a backup," said Thumps. "Isn't there always a backup?"

"Quite right," said Chandler. "It will take time, but I'm told that we can retrieve the lost files. At the same time, we discov-ered a problem with the test panels."

Chandler's drink arrived, and the empty glass disappeared.

"We had eight test panels. Locked in a vault."

"And now they're gone."

"Was that a guess?"

"More or less," said Thumps.

"And now they're gone." Chandler tested the drink, made a face, and set it to one side.

"Frank Dodge?"

"Too much of a coincidence," said Chandler. "In order to get the panels out of the plant, you would need a vehicle."

"So you think that Garza set the fire, and Dodge took the panels, and they agreed to meet up here in Chinook."

"Cuffs and collars," said Chandler. "Cuffs and collars."

"Did they know each other? A driver and a research scientist? Were they friends?"

"Had to be," said Chandler.

"If you still had the panels and the expertise, could you recreate the process?"

"Sure." Chandler took another sip of his drink. "I guess. It would take us some time."

"So if Garza has the research and the panels, she controls Helios."

Thumps yawned. He was tired, and he was hungry. Chandler had been remarkably open. But as Thumps went over the information that the man had been willing to share, he realized that Chandler hadn't told him much that he didn't already know.

"If I were a suspicious man," said Chandler, "I might think that you know where Garza is hiding."

Thumps got out of the chair. "I don't have a dog in this fight."

"Could be a finder's fee." Chandler help up his glass in a salute. "Just in case you needed some encouragement."

The full-length windows at the far end of the room were ablaze with late-afternoon light.

"Keep that in mind," said Thumps. "I'll surely keep that in mind."

34

Thumps got to Al's early the next morning.

"Where is everybody?"

"Church," said Al. "Unless of course you mean Mr. Wutty Youngbeaver, CEO of Screaming Eagle Tours?"

Thumps could hear the threat of story in Al's voice.

"Don't you want to know what happened?"

"Nope," said Thumps, "just breakfast."

"You ever have one of those ideas that you know can't miss, a plan that can't fail?" Al tossed a dishtowel over her shoulder. "And then it does. It shouldn't, but somehow it flat out falls apart?"

"Scrambled eggs and whole-wheat toast."

"Something too good to be true."

"Sausage. Extra crispy."

"So yesterday, Wutty takes a busload of erstwhile adventurers from California out to Deep House, where he regales them with apocryphal stories about the canyon that he probably makes up on the spot."

"Lots of hash browns, salsa."

"And then they all get back on the bus and head out to the lake for lunch."

"Maybe the sourdough toast instead of the whole wheat."

"So they're sitting around Red Tail Lodge, trying to decide what they're going to order, and guess what?"

"And coffee. Please."

"Wutty counts bodies," said Al, "and discovers that he's missing one."

Thumps sat up straight. "He lost a customer? In Deep House?"

"Just wanted to give a heads-up," said Al. "Seeing as how you and the sheriff are such experts at hauling bodies out of the canyon."

"Wutty go back?"

"He did."

"He find the missing tourist?"

"There you are." Archie Kousoulas burst through the door like a bull out of a chute.

"Best part will have to wait." Al headed back to the grill. "You might want to use the back door."

"You don't have a back door."

"There's that."

Thumps sagged on the stool. There were times when he wished the café *had* a back door. Not that a back door would have done any good. The rear of Al's was hard up against the rear of the civic centre, and a back door, if there had been one, would have opened onto a brick wall.

Archie sat down on the stool with a thud.

"You had dinner at the Mother Lode?"

"I did."

"When you could have eaten at Pappous's?"

"You're not open," said Thumps. "I was a guest. Didn't get to pick the venue."

"What did you have?"

Al was standing at the grill. But she didn't look to be in any great hurry to bring him his breakfast.

"Can't remember."

"Risotto with chicken and caramelized onions," said Archie. "Who makes something like that?"

"It was good."

"The French. That's who."

"Archie . . ."

"They throw a bunch of leftovers into a pot with a bucket of brown sauce and give it a fancy name that ends in *eaux*."

"Risotto is Italian."

"Did you even mention my restaurant?"

Thumps considered lying.

"And don't even think of lying."

"One breakfast special." Al slid the plate between the two men. "You want coffee?"

"Sure," said Archie. "And some toast while Benedict Arnold here tells me about the chocolate mousse."

Thumps took a paper napkin from the dispenser, set it beside his plate, and picked up his fork. "I don't talk while I'm eating."

"Fine," said Archie. "You eat. I'll talk."

Even if he ate slowly, there was little chance that Archie would get bored and go away.

Al was back with coffee, an extra plate, and a fork. "You might want to help your buddy with the potatoes."

Thumps moved his plate out of harm's way. "I don't need any help."

"So I did some more research after you and the hitman left." Archie leaned in and lowered his voice. "Seems as soon as Shield took over Main Street Paints, a bunch of money begins to flow into the company. Over the last two years, we're talking a little north of half a billion."

"Half a billion?"

"The government money is public record. That's just what came in the front door."

"Any idea what the total might be?"

"No way to know," said Archie. "But I can tell you one thing. More to this than just paint."

Al was back with the pot. "You boys kiss and make up?"

Archie pushed his cup forward. "Hear Wutty's got a new business."

"Screaming Eagle Tours." Al tried to keep a straight face. "I was just telling Thumps the sad tale when you came in."

Thumps mixed the salsa into the potatoes. "Wutty lost a tourist."

"You're kidding."

"Nope," said Al. "Took sixteen of California's finest out to Deep House for a look-see. But when he got to Red Tail Lodge, he only had fifteen."

Archie reached across Thumps's arm and helped himself to a forkful of potatoes. "Who'd he lose?"

"Turns out, he didn't lose anyone," said Al. "When Wutty counted heads at the beginning, he counted himself, and when he got to the lodge, he didn't."

Thumps smiled. "He counted wrong?"

"He did."

"When did he figure it out?"

"He didn't. Russell and Jimmy tumbled to the mistake," said Al. "I expect they'll tell him once he gets out of the hospital."

"Hospital?"

"Went into the canyon to find his lost lamb, didn't he?"

"He get hurt?"

"Fell off a boulder," said Al. "Messed up his leg. Had to be rescued."

"That's embarrassing," said Archie.

"Any chance the boys will spare his feelings?" Thumps knew the answer even before he asked the question.

"Not a chance," said Al. "Expect we'll be hearing about this for the next couple of months."

"If it weren't for bad luck . . ."

"Hee-haw." Al pointed the coffee pot at Archie. "Going to come to the grand opening. Bringing my niece and her husband."

Archie turned to Thumps. "See. This is what friends do."

"But I don't want to be finding any of that octopus in my food."

"Grilled calamari," said Archie. "It's delicious."

"I don't care if you dip it in dark chocolate," said Al. "Minute Jenny and Felix and I walk into your restaurant, you make sure all your soft-bodied molluscs are locked up."

Thumps picked up the napkin and tossed it into the air, as though he were calling a penalty at a football game.

"Lucrecia."

Al and Archie froze.

"Name of that kitten you wanted," said Thumps.

"Lucrecia." Al worked the word around in her mouth. "Mean little shit, is she?"

"Takes no prisoners."

* * *

"You're giving your kittens away?" Archie made a face. "And you didn't ask me if I wanted one?"

"Freeway has four," said Thumps. "There's enough to go around."

"Don't know that I want a kitten," said Archie, "but you should have asked."

"What's she look like? You got a photo?"

"Mostly black. One white stocking."

Al nodded. "Mice won't even see her coming."

"Maybe having one around the bookstore would be a good idea," said Archie. "Lots of bookstores have cats."

"I might call her Lucy for short," said Al. "What would you call yours?"

"Leonidas," said Archie, "the hero of Thermopylae."

"Lucy and Leo," said Al. "That's nice. You want more coffee?"

Al filled Archie's cup, and the two of them began planning the lives of their kittens in earnest.

"We couldn't breed them," said Archie, "'cause they're brother and sister."

"But they could be friends," said Al. "Nothing to say they couldn't be friends."

Thumps eased himself off the stool as the kitty discussion picked up pace and enthusiasm.

"Lucy could visit Leo at the bookstore," said Archie, "and I could bring Leo by the café."

Thumps made it to the door before the two of them got around to sleepovers and picnics.

He was on the street, safe and sound, when the phone began to ring.

35

Thumps didn't have a phone, and so when the phone he didn't have began to ring, it was a surprise.

And then he remembered.

Cisco Cruz.

Cruz had given him the phone.

Thumps pulled it out of his pocket, turned it away from the bright sunlight so he could see the screen. He half expected the message to be an offer to reduce the monthly payments on the credit card he didn't have or to warn him of a virus that had affected the computer he didn't own.

When he had been acting sheriff and had been required to carry a cell, he had gotten more than his fair share of such messages on a daily basis.

But the message on the phone was none of these.

* * *

Cisco Cruz was waiting for him. "What took you so long?"

Thumps held up the phone. "*Tuck gar now*? What kind of a message is that?"

"You're here."

"You think I spend my day waiting for you to summon me?"

"You're here."

The Tucker garage was an underground affair. Grey concrete, stale, damp air, dim light. With cars lined up along the walls like horses at a feed trough. Cruz was leaning against a late-model pickup.

"Raj has disappeared. Again."

"You mean you knew where she was?"

"Sort of."

Thumps waited.

"I might have stashed her in the hotel."

"The Tucker?"

"Figured it was the last place Shield would look."

The sound of a car door came from somewhere in the garage. Cruz stepped back into the shadows at the rear of the pickup. Thumps followed him.

"Got her a room," said Cruz.

"Under your name?"

"Of course not," said Cruz. "Leo Carrillo."

"Do all your aliases come from that TV program?"

"Easy to keep track of them."

Thumps tried to remember the other characters from the

show. Loco and Diablo. But those were the horses.

"And it gave us a safe house," said Cruz. "Somewhere we could talk."

"You know, she's not sharing with the rest of the children."

Cruz leaned against the pickup. "I mentioned that."

"And?"

"She claims she didn't know Dodge. Says she never went out to the test facility."

"You believe her?"

"I do," said Cruz. "Which leaves us with three problems."

Thumps arranged the pieces in his head. "If Garza didn't hire Dodge to steal the test panels, someone else did."

"That's one."

"Let's call him Mr. X," said Thumps. "The guy who hired Dodge."

"Or Ms. X," said Cruz.

"Martha Burke?"

"Maybe."

"Okay, just plain X."

"Gender-neutral, *cabrón*," said Cruz. "Wow. The modern man."

Thumps had read that chess savants could close their eyes and see the board, imagine all the moves.

"X hires Dodge to drive the test panels from Sacramento and bring them here. I'm guessing Dodge was supposed to call X when Dodge got to the test facility."

"But X doesn't hear from Dodge," said Thumps, "because Dodge is dead."

"So X has to break cover and come to the facility to see what's happened." Cruz paused. "The goose, the fox, and the sack of grain."

The riddle was a classic of logistical thinking. A farmer has a goose, a fox, and a sack of grain that he has to get across a river. But he can take only one of the three with him in the boat at a time. If he leaves the goose with the fox, the fox will eat the goose, and if he leaves the goose with the grain, the goose will eat the grain.

"Paint panels," said Cruz. "A dead body and one too many vehicles."

The farmer takes the goose over first and leaves the fox with the grain. Then he goes back and picks up the grain, takes the grain across, and picks up the goose. Back he goes with the goose, picks up the fox, leaving the goose behind, and takes the fox to the side of the river with the grain. Finally, he goes back one last time and picks up the goose.

"X comes to the facility, finds Dodge."

"What to do?" said Cruz. "What to do?"

Thumps closed his eyes. "He drives Dodge and the panels to Deep House and dumps everyone and everything into the canyon."

"Panels and Dodge out of sight, out of mind."

"Then X drives the van back to the facility, sets it on fire, and drives off into the sunset. In, out, in, out. Which would account for the four gate notifications on the Sunday."

"You know," said Cruz, "this plot is complicated enough and crazy enough to be one of hers."

"But it's not."

"No."

"Just as well," said Thumps. "You said her schemes never worked."

"And then there's the second problem." Cruz stretched his arms over his head. "How did they know she was at the Tucker?"

"Who says they knew?"

"Raj isn't in the room," said Cruz.

"Just because she's not in the room doesn't mean she's been blown."

"She took my car. She knows better than to screw with my car. Only reason she would do something like that is if she was scared."

"Her phone?"

"Got rid of it that night at your house," said Cruz. "No way they could have traced her that way."

"Your phone."

"*Ese*, those *pendejos* don't even know I exist."

Thumps let Cruz find it on his own.

"*Mierda*. She called me."

"Before the hit and run. Before Dodge and the panels went

missing." Thumps checked the logic in his head. "They were watching her. She was already under surveillance. Computer. Phone."

"They knew about me before I got to town."

"Only explanation that makes sense."

Cruz pushed off the side of the pickup. "Which brings us to the third problem."

"Which is?"

"How you're going to explain all this to the sheriff."

"Me?"

"*Vato*," said Cruz, "he's your friend."

36

The sheriff was not particularly pleased to see Thumps and Cruz when they arrived at his office. And he was well on his way to apoplectic when Cruz finished filling in most of the blanks.

"You recall that little chat we had couple of days back?" said the sheriff. "The one about you two chuckleheads causing me undue discomfort?"

"Something about a sleepover in a cell," said Cruz. "As I recall."

"And if I had something to charge you with, that's where you'd be."

"At least now we can see the outline."

"Of what?" Duke sucked on his lips. "We got a missing scientist. A body in the county morgue. And three executives living the high life in a fancy hotel. Those all the dots you got?"

Thumps and Cruz waited patiently for Duke to run out of steam.

"You connect them, and what do you have? Simple theft. Dr. Garza steals corporate documents and prototypes. Shield wants them back. End of story."

Thumps could feel his eyes begin to droop. Any minute, he was going to start yawning.

"And you don't even know where Garza is."

"Nope," said Cruz.

"And you wouldn't lie about something like that."

Cruz shrugged. "I might."

"Okay," said Duke. "How about this. I'll ride herd on the musketeers from Shield, and you two find Garza."

"And then?"

"We put them all in a locked room with hammers for a couple of days and then beat the truth out of the survivors."

Cruz got to his feet. "So you're not going to arrest us?"

"Tight budget," said the sheriff. "I arrest you, I have to feed you."

THE AFTERNOON WAS still warm, but the air was moving toward evening. Thumps zipped his jacket as he and Cruz headed down the street. Cruz stopped at the corner.

"We need a car."

Thumps put his hands in his pockets. "Because Garza stole yours."

"Borrowed."

Thumps could feel the annoyance creep into his voice. "You might have mentioned this to the sheriff."

"What was he going to do?"

"Car like that," said Thumps, "I have to guess it's got a tracking system."

"What are you, some kind of electronic genius?"

"So it has a tracking device, and you know where it is."

"Yeah." Cruz held up his cellphone. It showed a miniature map with a blinking red dot in the middle of nowhere. "That's why we need a car."

THERE WERE FOUR pickups parked to the side of the Mustang, and a handful of bikes lined up at the railing. Cruz's car was around the back, next to the fighting ring.

Thumps got out of his car. "This was easy."

Cruz snorted. "You think we're going to pop in and find Raj having a burger and a beer, humming along with Dolly Parton?"

"Dolly Parton?"

"If you figured out that my car has tracking," said Cruz, "so did Raj."

* * *

Lorraine was behind the bar. Big Fish and Hack were nowhere to be seen. Thumps wasn't sure that parents working shifts at a bar was a particularly good idea, but he couldn't come up with a better solution.

"You looking for Big Fish?"

"Nope."

"Good," said Lorraine, "'cause he's playing daddy-mommy at the moment."

"How's he doing?"

"Better than expected," said Lorraine. "The two of them got a lot in common. Main difference is that Big Fish don't shit his pants."

"Good to know."

"And if he did, he'd be the one to clean it up." Lorraine gave Cruz a long look. "You military?"

"Another life, another time."

"Then the first beer is on me."

Thumps looked around the bar just in case Raj was buried in the shadows.

"I expect that you would be Cisco Cruz." Lorraine held up a set of keys. "Woman said you'd be stopping by."

"Yes, ma'am."

"She said you might be a bit pissed, but not to indulge you."

"My cousin," said Cruz.

"Figured it might be a family matter." Lorraine set a beer down on the bar. "I took my father's motorcycle once. Never did hear the end of that."

Cruz nodded. "Get far?"

Lorraine smiled. "All the way to the Oregon coast. Hell of a ride. Might have gotten away with it, 'cept I had to lay the bike down on 242 outside of Sisters."

"You get hurt?"

"Wrecked my knee. Dented my pride. Messed up a custom paint job."

"Dad wasn't too pleased?"

Lorraine tapped the bar for luck. "Let's just say it's a good thing I was an only child and he didn't have a spare."

Thumps could see he was going to have to step in before the two of them began to take off their clothes and compare scars.

"The woman who left the keys," said Thumps, "she didn't happen to say where she was going?"

"Nope," said Lorraine. "Didn't say much at all. And then she disappeared."

"Disappeared?"

"She was sitting right over there," said Lorraine. "I went back to the kitchen to get an order, and when I came out, she was gone."

"How long was she here?"

"Twenty minutes, half an hour," said Lorraine.

"She make a phone call?"

"Might have," said Lorraine. "Can't say I was watching her."

Cruz finished his beer. "She say anything else?"

"Nope," said Lorraine. "She comes in, gives me the keys, and she's gone. Didn't even finish her wine."

Cruz pushed off the stool. "Probably should get going. Not going to find my cousin sitting here."

"Ask me," said Lorraine, "don't think she wants to be found."

CRUZ'S CAR WAS LOCKED. There was a note on the driver's seat.

Everything is under control.

Cruz handed the note to Thumps.

"Remember those elaborate schemes I told you about?"

"You think this is one of them?"

"Ta-dah," said Cruz. "Ta-dah."

Cruz wandered over to the ring, leaned on the ropes. "What's this for?"

"Lorraine set it up. Boys want to fight, they have to bring it out here."

"A fist fight in a sandpit?" said Cruz.

"Slows everything down," said Thumps. "Trying to move in the sand wears you out. Most fights don't last more than a minute or so."

"My fights don't last that long," said Cruz. "So what's our next move?"

"Find Raj, I guess."

"Not going to be easy," said Cruz. "She's got someone help-ing her."

"That she does."

"Any ideas?"

"Maybe," said Thumps. "What are you going to do?"

"Go back to the hotel." Cruz slid in behind the wheel. "Wait for Humpty Dumpty to fall off the wall. Rush in with all the king's men and pick up the pieces. You?"

Thumps stretched to one side and then to the other. "Go home, feed my cats, sit on the porch, and watch the sun go down."

Cruz started the car. "You know, I'm tempted to cut her loose and just head back to New Mexico."

Thumps nodded. "Only she's family."

"Yeah." Cruz tapped the accelerator. "But all things considered, we're not that close."

Thumps was just pulling the seat belt into position when his pocket began to buzz.

"You going to answer it?"

Thumps made a mental note to give the phone back to Cruz at the first opportunity.

"You have to press the green button."

"Only if I want to answer the phone."

"Could be opportunity," said Cruz.

Thumps didn't think anyone would mistake the sheriff's voice for opportunity.

"Where the hell are you?"

"Out of state."

"Very funny." Duke huffed a couple of times. "Is the ninja assassin with you?"

Thumps wanted to ask Duke how he had gotten this number, but he was sure he wasn't going to like the answer.

"The Tucker," said the sheriff. "Now."

37

Cruz dropped him off in front of the Tucker.

"You're not coming in?"

"My invitation was lost in the mail."

"Having to chase you down," said Thumps, "probably won't put Duke in a good mood."

"I suppose I'll have to get him something nice."

DEPUTY DEANNA HEAVY RUNNER was waiting for him.

"I thought I was pretty good at pissing off the Dukester," said Deanna, "but you do tend to raise the bar."

"Where is he?"

"Fourth floor," said Deanna. "The Remington suite."

"They've named the suites?"

"Last year," said Deanna. "Hotel thought a suite name would be more exciting than a number."

"Want to give me a hint?"

"Where's the fun in that?"

"You know you don't have to channel your auntie."

"Auntie Roxanne?" said Deanna. "You know, you're one of her favourite people."

Thumps looked, but he couldn't find a trace of sarcasm on Deanna's face. Maybe the gene skipped a generation.

"Auntie Roxanne is always saying how much she appreciates your advice."

And then again, maybe it didn't.

Duke Hockney, Beth Mooney, Martha Burke, and Carl Mobley were standing in the newly minted Remington suite. Graham Chandler was on the sofa.

And he wasn't going to get up.

"About time." Hockney waved him over. "Follow my lead. Pretend you know what you're doing."

Beth squatted down next to the body. "Shot once in the chest, once in the head."

"I told him he was playing with fire," said Burke, "but Graham wouldn't listen."

"I just don't believe it," said Mobley.

"What don't you believe?" said Duke.

"That Garza would kill anyone."

"So maybe it wasn't Garza," said Burke. "It was probably her cousin. This Cisco Cruz."

There it was. The only way that Shield could know about Cruz was if they had Garza under surveillance. They had caught the calls she made. Had been waiting for the pair to show up.

"The sheriff didn't tell us," said Burke. "Graham knew about Cisco Cruz before we arrived."

"We've been monitoring Dr. Garza for the last while," said Mobley. "Computer. Phone. Chandler was going to let Cruz lead us to her. That was the plan."

"What happened?" asked Duke.

"It's not like on TV," said Mobley. "We could track their cellphones, but we could only narrow the signals to a general area. I'm guessing they figured out that we were tracking them."

Burke's sorrow suddenly turned to anger. "Graham was arrogant. He fancied himself a Sherlock Holmes, a Hercule Poirot."

Mobley turned to the sheriff. "We need to find Garza and Cruz before anyone else gets hurt."

"You might have let me in on the plan," said Duke. "Might have been able to prevent this from happening."

"You saying this is our fault?"

Thumps left Duke to deal with the corporate brain trust and drifted over to Beth and the body.

"Looks like stippling around the head wound."

"Does it?"

"Which would mean the second shot was from close range."

"If it is stippling," said Beth in the voice she reserved for small children and bureaucrats, "that would be a reasonable assumption."

Chandler was dressed in dark slacks and a white shirt. The gun at his waistband was a compact automatic, a Sig Sauer or a Glock. It had never left the holster.

"Position of the body is interesting."

"Is it?" said Beth.

"All comfy on the sofa. Not a care in the world. What do you suppose that tells us?"

"Tells me I'm not a crime-scene analyst," said Beth. "And neither are you."

Thumps stood up. It was a slow process. He could feel his knees crack, hear the joints groan. When had that started?

"Who found the body?"

"Ms. Burke," said the sheriff. "And Mr. Mobley."

"This is Chandler's suite?"

"It is," said Burke. "Graham didn't come down for dinner, and he didn't answer his phone."

"So Martha came up," said Mobley. "Knocked on the door, didn't get an answer."

"We got security to let us in," said Burke.

"And no one heard the shots?"

"There are six suites on the floor," said Duke. "Three are empty."

"Graham, Martha, and I have the others," said Mobley.

"Rajan Garza," said Burke. "Cisco Cruz. One of them murdered Graham, and you just stand here?"

Thumps let Duke ask the question.

"Why?" said the sheriff.

"What?"

"What reason did Garza or Cruz have to kill Chandler?"

Burke looked at Mobley. "Garza stole sensitive corporate property. She and Cruz were afraid that Graham would catch them."

"Sure," said Duke, "but he hadn't caught them, had he? So far as I can tell, he wasn't even close to finding them. For all he knew, they might have already left town."

Mobley held up a hand. "What's your point?"

"My point," said Duke, "is why kill a man who couldn't find you? More to the point, why would Chandler let either Garza or Cruz into his room?"

"What are you getting at?" said Burke.

Duke shrugged. "No sign of forced entry. Could be Chandler knew his killer, didn't see the danger, and got shot for his trouble."

"You think that Carl or I killed Graham?"

"Special Deputy DreadfulWater," said Duke, "you have anything to add?"

"Chandler's gun," said Thumps. "It's still in the holster."

"So it is," said the sheriff. "So it is."

* * *

DUKE LEFT IT TO DEANNA and Lance to take statements from Burke and Mobley and to help Beth with the body.

The sheriff didn't say a word until they got to the elevators.

"We could take the stairs," said Duke.

"We could."

"Macy is on this exercise kick. Wants to lose twenty pounds."

"Nothing wrong with a little exercise."

"When I had that operation," said Duke, "I lost ten pounds."

"You're looking good," said Thumps.

"And then I gained it back."

There was a ding, and the elevator doors opened.

"You ever go on a diet?"

"Thought about it," said Thumps.

"Moderation." Duke stepped into the elevator. "Macy says the key is moderation."

THUMPS FOLLOWED DUKE out of the Tucker and up the street to the sheriff's office. The place was dark. Hockney unlocked the door and turned on the lights.

"Hello."

Someone had left a large box of doughnuts on Duke's desk.

"Dumbo's," said Duke.

Morris Dumbo was a mean-spirited bigot, a skinny scrub brush of a man who made the best doughnuts in the state. There were tables at Dumbo's, but most people opted for takeout. So far as Thumps was concerned, sitting in the toxic gloom of the café was akin to sharing pizza with Donald Trump in an adult video store.

"Don't forget moderation," said Thumps.

"Two instead of three," said Duke. "That sound about right?"

There was an envelope next to the box. Duke opened it and took out the card.

"Well, shit." Hockney handed Thumps the note. It was short and succinct.

Didn't do it.

Duke raised the lid on the box of doughnuts. "I'm supposing that this is courtesy of your friend, the felon."

"Killing Chandler isn't Cruz's style."

Duke helped himself to a chocolate-coated cake. "And you know this how?"

"Whoever shot Chandler shot him in the chest first," said Thumps. "Then they walked in close and shot him in the head."

"Charming."

"Cruz would have shot him in the head and saved the second bullet."

"And Garza?"

"She's not lethal." Thumps helped himself to a glazed old-fashioned. "Woman can't even load a remote."

"Burke?" said Duke. "Mobley?"

The old-fashioned was delicious. Thumps hoped he could stop at one.

"They've been lying to us. Garza, Burke, Mobley, Chandler. They've been lying to us the whole time."

"You know why?"

"Maybe."

Duke licked his fingers. "You ever hear that doughnuts make you smarter?"

"Can't say I have."

The sheriff put his hand in the box and came up with a glazed. "Still, there's no point in being dismissive without doing our due diligence."

"But in moderation." Thumps selected a maple bar. "Everything in moderation."

38

The next morning, Thumps got to the café as Al was turning on the grill.

"What happened? You forget to sleep in?"

"Places to go," said Thumps, "things to do."

He had left the sheriff's office the night before in good order, but when he got home, everything went sideways.

The kittens were back, waiting for him in a yowling huddle on the bed, stinking of farty dog. Freeway was desperately trying to lick her babies clean with little effect.

Thumps got a plastic bin from the laundry room and filled it with warm, soapy water. One by one, he washed Freeway and each of the kittens, drying them in a large bath towel. But there was little help for it, and Thumps spent the night with his face buried in the pillow, breathing through his mouth.

"HEAR THERE WAS trouble at the Tucker." Al poured a cup of coffee. "Someone mentioned your name."

"You might want to put a bunch of sausages on the grill," said Thumps. "Make up an extra batch of pancake batter."

"Rumour is the sheriff is looking for that hunky buddy of yours."

"Cooley and Stas are meeting me here."

"Rumour is there's a woman involved," said Al.

"This rumour got a name?"

"You know I don't abide rumours," said Al. "Though Archie *is* right more times than not."

"Did Mr. Kousoulas happen to say who did it?"

"The dead guy at the Tucker?" Al took a cellphone out of her apron. "Why don't you call him and ask him yourself."

"Breakfast," said Thumps. "The usual. Please."

COOLEY AND STAS arrived together.

"Hello, hello," said Stas. "This is where the free breakfast is going, yes?"

"Yes," said Thumps. "Breakfast is on me."

"I'm pretty hungry," said Cooley. "I didn't eat much this morning."

"And then we are to be the posse," said Stas. "Yes?"

"Tow truck's ready to go," said Cooley.

"And I have rifles," said Stas. "For the shoot 'em up."

"Won't be any shoot 'em up," said Thumps.

"If you boys are going off to a shoot 'em up," said Al, "you're going to need coffee."

Jimmy Monroe and Russell Plunkett arrived just before eight. Wutty Youngbeaver brought up the rear, hobbling into the café on a pair of crutches.

"What's two plus two," said Jimmy.

"Three," said Russell, "if you don't count yourself."

Wutty tried sitting on his regular stool, but the cast got in the way.

"Going to have to sit in a booth," said Russell. "The embarrassments just keep on coming."

"Fractured his fibula," said Jimmy.

"That's the small bone in his leg," said Russell.

"What do you get when you put sixteen people on a bus?" said Jimmy.

"That's one dumb joke," said Wutty. "You see anyone laughing?"

"Counting wrong," said Cooley, "is better than actually losing one of your paying customers."

"See," said Wutty. "Cooley understands the intricacies of big business."

Russell leaned out of the booth. "Wutty thinks he should get a free breakfast, seeing as how he got hurt on the job."

"Maybe three free breakfasts," said Jimmy, "seeing as how Russell and me have to look after him."

"Sort of like Make-A-Wish," said Wutty.

"Now that," said Al, "*is* funny."

THE THREE OF THEM were still going at it when Cooley and Stas finally stopped eating and got off their stools.

"You guys should sign up for the tour," Wutty called out as Thumps got to the door. "It comes with lunch at Red Tail Lodge."

"If Wutty doesn't lose you in Deep House first," said Jimmy.

"You hear anyone laughing?" said Wutty. "You hear anyone laughing?"

IT WAS A SHORT WALK to Stas's garage. Thumps had seen any number of standard wreckers, pickup trucks with a boom mounted on the bed, the kind that went out on calls for flat tires and dead batteries.

The tow truck parked in front of the garage was not one of those.

"1957 Mack," said Cooley. "B series. Not many of them still on the road."

"Old truck," said Stas. "But good. Like me."

"Gas mileage is shitty," said Cooley, "and the cab is tight."

The problem was the massive steering wheel and the two gearshifts on the floor that took up much of the legroom. You could squeeze three people in the cab, but only if the third person was a gerbil.

"I figure I'll follow you," said Cooley. "That way, we'll have two vehicles, and Thumps won't have to sit on my lap."

Stas opened the door and swung himself up into the cab. "Saddle up, partner," the big Russian shouted. "We'll head 'em off at the pass."

THUMPS HAD ALWAYS admired the styling of cars from the 1950s, and the Mack wrecker was no exception. While it was a bit on the bulbous side, the rounded lines and curves softened the metal body and made Thumps think of a giant pillow on wheels.

Unfortunately, this impression was destroyed by the ride.

"Cummins diesel," Stas shouted over the engine noise. "Leaf springs. Very strong."

By the time they hit the city limits, Thumps was convinced

that the truck didn't have any springs at all. If it did, then they weren't working. He braced himself on the dash, wedged his shoulder against the door to keep from being thrown about like a frog in a flood.

"You must use two hands to shift." Stas shoved his left arm through the wheel and worked the second shift with his right. "So exciting to drive."

By the time they got to the north edge of the canyon rim, Thumps had decided that if he couldn't drive back with Cooley, he was going to walk back to town.

Cooley was first to the edge of Deep House.

"This the place?"

The tracks were fainter now, but Thumps could still see where the van had cut through the prairie grass.

"They came from the test facility to this spot," said Thumps. "I think this is where Frank Dodge was thrown into the canyon."

"In Russia," said Stas, "this is done all the time."

"Dodge was dead before he was dumped."

"In Russia," said Stas, "dead is not necessary."

Cooley went to the edge and looked down. "So how we going to do this?"

Stas backed the wrecker as close to the edge as he could go.

"Here we extend the boom arm," he said. "There are loops in the line. It is best you put one foot in a loop and hold on to each other."

Thumps wasn't all that keen on being lowered into the canyon on a wire.

"Very close," said Stas. "Like dance with lovely lady."

Then again, he wasn't about to hike into Deep House on foot a second time.

"Come on," said Cooley. "It'll be fun. Like bungee jumping, only in slow motion."

Stas played the line out. Cooley stepped into the loop first, steadied the swing.

"Okay," said Stas. "Step on and grab Cooley."

As soon as Thumps put his foot in the loop and grabbed on to Cooley, he knew this was a bad idea. The line began to swing back and forth.

"You know, if we throw our weight around," said Cooley, "we could really get this going."

All the way to the bottom, Thumps kept a death grip on the wire with one hand and on Cooley's belt with the other.

And his eyes closed.

"Next time Moses needs tea," said Cooley. "I'm going to use the wrecker."

"Please don't move."

"Can't wait to be pulled up," said Cooley. "I'll bet if we yell, we'll get an echo."

In addition to walking back to town, Thumps was prepared to walk out of Deep House.

"Where did you guys find the body?"

"Right over there," said Cooley. "Sheriff figures Dodge hit

some rocks on the way down and wound up near the panels."

Thumps stepped off the loop, thankful to be on solid ground.

"You got a particular colour we're looking for?"

"Maybe," said Thumps.

Cooley began walking the shelter. "We got red panels and yellow panels. There are a couple of blue panels over there and some dark green ones over behind those boulders."

Cooley looked up at the rim of the canyon.

"I'm guessing that they took off like Frisbees when they were tossed over the edge. No telling where they all went."

There were a good many panels, scattered on the ground like jackstraws.

"And we got silver." Cooley set one of the panels up against a rock. "Not sure I'd want to paint a room silver."

"Can we get one of these back to the top?"

"Sure," said Cooley. "The silver panels are smaller than the others, so no problem."

"Great."

"You can go up first, and then I'll come up with the panel."

"How about you go up with the panel," said Thumps, "and I'll walk out."

Cooley helped Thumps position his foot in the loop. "That's the best way to handle fear," he said. "Humour."

Being lowered into the canyon by cable had been terrifying, but at least Thumps had had company. Being able to hold on to Cooley had been reassuring, and the big man's weight had kept the line from swinging.

Going up and out was a different story. As Stas took up the slack on the winch, Thumps found himself dangling like a fish on a line, swaying from side to side, in danger of slipping or being slammed into the canyon wall.

Clearing the rim was one of the happy moments in his life, and as the big Russian worked the boom and swung Thumps back to firm ground and safety, he couldn't recall another.

"Just like elevator."

Stas sent the cable down a second time, and Thumps watched as Cooley and the panel were pulled out of Deep House.

"You have to try it." Cooley tossed the panel on the ground and stepped out of the loop. "I'll work the winch."

Thumps picked the panel up and set it against the side of the wrecker. The surface was thick and hard like volcanic glass. But the silver colour wasn't steady. It was mottled, as though someone had not taken the time to mix all the pigments together.

"Первый блин—комом!" Stas stepped into the loop and gave the cable a hard jerk. "The first pancake is a lump."

"If you swing from side to side," said Cooley, holding his arms out and flapping his fingers, "it'll feel like you're flying."

39

For the next hour, Stas and Cooley took turns on the cable, dropping into the canyon, popping out, swinging back and forth, pushing off the canyon wall, twirling in mid-air. It was like watching two ten-year-olds on a scary ride at Disneyland.

"You are wishing a turn?" said Stas.

"I'm fine."

"The spinning is an excitement."

"I'm fine."

Stas finally called a halt to the merriment when the winch motor began to overheat.

"This has to be today's best idea." Cooley slipped his foot out of the cable loop. The big man picked up the panel, brushed it off. "So is this what you wanted?"

"I think so."

"You know what?" Cooley ran his hand along the rear fender of the wrecker. "We could come out here of a weekend and use the winch to haul some of the trash out of Deep House."

"This is idea," said Stas. "There are many good things in canyon."

"Scrap metal."

"Car parts."

"I could use a sofa," said Cooley.

"Yes, yes," said Stas. "But now, I must return to garage. Cars are desiring my attention."

"You go ahead," said Cooley. "I'll take Thumps home."

Stas climbed into the wrecker. "So much fun," he shouted. "We must do this again."

Cooley loaded the plywood sheet into his pickup. The sun caught the face of the panel, the glare intense and painful, and Cooley had to turn it face down in the bed.

"Wouldn't want to paint a house this colour," he said. "Could blind the neighbours."

"I think it's a new kind of solar paint."

"Like for solar energy?"

"Could be a good source of energy, especially in the poorer places in the world."

"Like reservations."

"Sure."

"Or a weapon," said Cooley. "A solar laser. Get the right angle, and you could disintegrate invading space aliens."

Thumps looked out across the prairies. In the distance, he could just make out the shape of the trailer at the test facility.

"It's kinda cool," said Cooley, "but what are you going to do with it?"

Thumps tipped the panel up. "This look right to you?"

Cooley shrugged. "When you open a can of paint, you're supposed to stir it real good, so the colour comes out even."

Thumps set the panel back down. "You mind if we make a stop before we go home?"

"Maybe we can get something to eat," said Cooley. "Swinging around on a cable can work up an appetite."

Glory Paint and Millwork had a Closed sign in the window.

"Says their hours are 9:00 to 6:00," said Cooley. "Monday to Saturday."

Thumps knocked on the door.

"Maybe they went for lunch."

Thumps cupped his hands and peered in the window. The store was empty and dark.

"Maybe we should get lunch," said Cooley.

"There's an apartment around back," said Thumps. "Let's check that first."

Bargain Hall was in the backyard, breaking down cardboard boxes.

"Well, well," she said. "If it isn't Tonto and Tonto."

"Afternoon, Ms. Hall."

"It's Mrs.," said Bargain. "Jerome and me wasn't much for societal innovation."

"Yes, ma'am."

Bargain shielded her eyes. "Who's your sidekick?"

"Cooley Small Elk," said Cooley. "How come the store is closed?"

"'Cause it's closed," said Bargain. "Closed. Done. Finished."

Thumps frowned. "You're closing the business?"

"No business left," said Bargain. "Bank's foreclosing next week. I got less than a month."

"I'm sorry."

"I'm not," said Bargain. "Paint was Jerome's thing. I'm going to head out to Northern California. Got a sister in Crescent City. Figure I'll start there."

"I was hoping to pick your brain," said Thumps. "Got a puzzle you might be able to solve."

"Cost you lunch," said Bargain. "Busting boxes is hard work, and my brain don't function on an empty stomach."

"And that," said Cooley, "is today's second-best idea."

***

THE HAPPY DAYS Coffee Shop was new construction done up to look like a soda shop from the 1950s. A long line of stools at the counter, Formica and chrome tables, tuck and roll Naugahyde booths, and an ornate Wurlitzer jukebox that was roped off with a sign that said "Please Don't Touch."

Bargain led them to a booth.

"I'll warn you now," she said, "it ain't cheap."

"Thumps doesn't mind," said Cooley.

"Course, nothing in this town is cheap anymore."

"Have whatever you want," said Thumps.

And then he looked at the menu. Hot dogs were $12.50. Burgers were $18.00. There was a steak sandwich special for $26.00.

"Looks like you got to order fries separately," said Cooley.

Bargain ordered the chicken-fried steak and mashed potatoes. A salad with a cherry milkshake and a piece of berry pie. Cooley had two cheeseburgers and a side of fries.

"Might as well get a root beer float while I'm at it," said Cooley. "Haven't had one of those in quite a while."

Thumps did a rough estimate in his head.

"Most of the folks who used to live in Glory have left," said Bargain. "I'm one of the last of the old-timers."

Then he ordered the soup and salad.

"All you got left are expensive people and dentists," said Bargain. "They don't live here, of course. They just own the land."

Cooley nodded. "Place looks like the restaurant in that old TV show."

"Entertainment lawyer built this place," said Bargain. "Called it an 'homage to nostalgia,' whatever that means. He'd come up a couple of weekends during the summer. Then he stopped. That was it. Haven't seen him since."

The soup was thin and salty.

"Towns like Glory ain't toys," said Bargain. "You can't just pick them up and put them down when something new and more exciting comes along. Town's a living thing."

The salad was all lettuce, with one thin slice of tomato.

"But that's the way it is. Disposable world. Towns, people. You know the good news about going to Crescent City?" Bargain paused and used the long-handled spoon on the milkshake. "Once you get there, ain't nowhere else to go."

"All in all," said Cooley, "these burgers are disappointing."

Cooley lifted the panel out of the truck, so Bargain could get a good look at it.

"Where'd you find this?"

"Bottom of Deep House," said Thumps. "Someone threw it in off the rim."

"Don't look at me," said Bargain. "This ain't one of ours."

"You sure?"

"Sure, I'm sure," said Bargain. "The test panels we got were all four by fours. This is a two by four."

"So it's the wrong size."

"Wrong colour too," said Bargain. "Feels more like glass or ceramic. This some kind of special paint?"

"It is."

"What's it for?"

"Solar energy."

"Don't go buying stock," said Bargain. "Less you feel like losing your money."

"They didn't stir the pot well enough," said Cooley.

"More than that," said Bargain. "You see the discolouration here and here?"

"Is that a problem?"

"Bring that panel around back," said Bargain, "and I'll show you."

There was a small workshop behind the paint store. Bargain unlocked the door and turned on the lights.

"Put it on the bench." Bargain picked up a jigsaw.

"You're going to cut it?"

"You want to know or not?"

Cooley held the plywood down while Bargain cut a small square off the edge.

"Whatever it is," said Bargain, "it's pretty hard. That blade is toast."

Cooley put the panel to one side.

"See that?" Bargain held the piece up to the light. "It's layered. Five, maybe six separate coatings. Some sort of ceramic or glass. All laminated together."

"Sounds complicated."

"Wouldn't call it paint." Bargain picked at the edge with her fingernail. "Problem is, the laminations aren't holding. You can see where they're beginning to separate."

"So it's coming apart."

"That's why you're getting the blotchy variations in tone."

"Any idea how that could happen?"

"The separating?" Bargain picked at the edge some more. "Moisture. Heat. Exposure to the sun. Could be anything."

Cooley cleaned the top of the table saw. "When do you plan to head out to California?"

"Not right away," said Bargain. "Got some stuff out at the trailer. Binoculars, a camera, some of my bird books. If they haven't locked the place down or moved it, I may spend a week out there."

"Sort of a vacation."

"That's right," said Bargain. "Walk the rim of the canyon, watch for birds, take some photographs. It's quiet out there. A couple of days under that sky all alone, and the rest of the world disappears."

Thumps slipped the piece of plywood into his pocket.

"What are you going to do when you get to the coast?"

"You mean a job?" Bargain sighed. "I'll find something."

"One of my aunties is a greeter at a Walmart," said Cooley. "Another one works at McDonald's."

"Maybe I'll do nothing," said Bargain. "Maybe I'll walk into the ocean, float all the way to Hawaii."

Cooley took the panel back to the truck. Thumps and Bargain walked along behind.

"You get any more notifications?" asked Thumps. "For the test facility?"

"The other morning," said Bargain. "Went out 'cause I was curious. What with all that's been happening."

"And?"

"Couple of big shots from Shield in Sacramento. They wanted to look at what was left of the van, check out the trailer."

"You talk to them?"

"The one guy, kind of arrogant, wanted to know why the test panels were still there."

"The other big shot a woman?"

"Another guy," said Bargain. "Older. Nice enough. But he didn't seem to give a shit." Bargain stopped at the corner. "Should get back. Got a lot of packing. Amazing how much crap you accumulate in a lifetime."

"You want any help?"

Bargain's face softened. "That's sweet. But no, I got to figure out what part of my life I keep and what part I throw away."

*　*　*

THUMPS CAUGHT UP with Cooley as the big man was loading the panel into his pickup.

"Nice lady," he said. "Sad to see someone lose everything."

"She'll be okay."

"Hope she gets to Hawaii." Cooley slammed the tailgate shut. "Always wanted to see that part of the world. But if I go, I think I'd probably fly."

<h1 style="text-align:center">40</h1>

When Thumps and Cooley arrived at Blackfoot Autohaus, Stas Black Weasel was in the first bay at his workbench.

"Catalytic converter." The big Russian cut a piece of metal tube in half. "Piece of shit."

"We had lunch in Glory," said Cooley. "Thumps treated."

"Lunch?" Stas tossed the shorter piece into the trash. "Happy Days place?"

"That's the one," said Cooley. "The food wasn't all that good."

"But expensive," said Stas. "Everything in Glory is expensive."

With tax and tip, the bill had come to almost $150.00. Thumps had checked the total twice before conceding defeat.

"Kids wish for us to go to Orlando," said Stas. "I tell family, we go to Glory. Same prices, but don't drive so far."

"But there aren't any theme parks in Glory," said Cooley. "No Splash Mountain. No Expedition Everest. No Incredible Hulk Coaster."

"Rocking A Ranch," said Stas. "Horse rides, paintball buffalo hunting, swimming pool and waterslide, whitewater rafting."

"Didn't think it was open," said Cooley.

"Now it is." Stas handed Thumps a brochure. "Pretty good early-bird family special. One price fits all."

The brochure was a handsome thing. The horseback riding was of little interest. If Thumps was ever overcome by the urge to sit on a horse, he could always go out to the reservation and whistle. And driving around in a golf cart with a paintball gun, shooting at bales of hay dressed up to look like buffalo was just plain silly.

But then, he was no longer ten.

Thumps was trying to imagine plunging through whitewater in a rubber boat when the cellphone in his pocket began to vibrate. The damn thing was really starting to get annoying.

"You have a cellphone?" Cooley looked as though he had just watched a spaceship land.

"It's not mine," said Thumps.

"I have cellphone," said Stas.

"But you don't answer it," said Cooley.

Evidently, no one with a cell bothered with complete sentences.

S Office. Now.

Thumps stared at the screen for a moment. He supposed that there was a way to respond to messages. If he had any inclination to do so.

"I have to go."

"Why don't you give me your number," said Cooley. "That way, we can text each other."

"My kids have cellphones," said Stas. "This is all they do. Text, text, text."

"I'm giving it back today."

"And when they are not texting," said Stas, "they are taking pictures."

Thumps slipped the phone back into his pocket.

"Pictures of what they eat," said Stas. "Pictures of what they're doing. Some are funny. Many disgusting."

"You don't know the half. There's this one guy on the internet, takes photos of the inside of fast-food dumpsters." Cooley shook his head. "Never knew maggots could get that big."

COOLEY DROPPED THUMPS off in front of the sheriff's office.

"What did you think about that idea?"

"Taking photos of maggots in dumpsters?"

"Pulling trash out of Deep House," said Cooley. "It's our land. Least we can do is keep it clean."

As Thumps crossed the street, he could feel his hip begin to stiffen. A by-product, he told himself, of swinging from a cable.

By the time he reached the sheriff's office, he was limping.

Duke Hockney was behind his desk. Martha Burke and Carl Mobley were sitting on the hard-backed chairs that the sheriff kept for visitors, chairs so uncomfortable that no one stayed long.

Which was, after all, the point.

"And there he is," said Duke.

Thumps was tempted to ask how the sheriff had gotten the phone number for the cell Cruz had given him. There was only one answer.

"Why does he need to be here?" said Burke.

"Mr. DreadfulWater's been trying to help," said Mobley.

"At least," said Burke, "he didn't get anyone killed."

"Chandler's not my fault," said Mobley. "Don't you try to lay Chandler on me."

"Special Deputy DreadfulWater is here," said Duke, "because I want him to be here."

"You have your murderer," said Burke. "What more do you need?"

Thumps felt as though he had arrived in the middle of a movie and had missed a large part of the plot.

"Murderer?"

"The sheriff has arrested Cisco Cruz," said Mobley.

"Garza and this Cruz character were in it together," said Burke. "As soon as we find Rajan, we'll be able to put an end to this sorry mess."

"You arrested Cruz?"

"I did," said the sheriff. "In a manner of speaking."

Thumps waited.

"He walked in, gave himself up."

Thumps tried to imagine such a scenario. "He gave himself up?"

"In a manner of speaking."

"He's here? In a cell?"

Duke leaned a little farther back in his chair.

"Which is how you got the cellphone number."

"He asked that I text you," said Duke.

"Can I talk to him?"

"No, you cannot," said Burke.

Thumps took the piece of the paint panel out of his pocket and held it out for Burke and Mobley to see.

"You got something to share with the rest of the children?" said the sheriff.

"You recognize this?"

Burke stiffened.

"That what I think it is?" said Mobley.

Thumps set the piece of panel on Duke's desk. "How about we bring Mr. Cruz out here, so we can have a proper conversation."

The sheriff held up a set of keys. "He's in the Jesse James suite."

"Sheriff," said Burke, "I strongly object."

"Noted," said Duke. "Anyone want coffee?"

* * *

CRUZ WAS IN the first cell. He was stretched out on the bench with his arms crossed on his chest. Thumps stood at the bars and waited.

"Pancho."

"Thought you were going to stay out of trouble."

Cruz sat up. "I said I'd try."

"You gave yourself up?"

"Nope," said Cruz. "I came to find you."

"And Duke threw you in here."

"Can you believe it?"

"Where's Garza?"

Cruz came to the bars. "No idea. But when I find her, we're going to have a long talk."

"I think I know what happened."

"You here to let me out?"

Thumps held up the keys. "Only if you promise to behave."

DUKE AND MARTHA BURKE were still arguing. Mobley was trying to play referee. He had just called unnecessary roughness on both teams when Thumps and Cruz came into the room.

"You are going to handcuff him?" said Burke. "Aren't you?"

The sheriff took his gun from his holster and laid it on the desk. "I have your word you won't try to escape?"

Cruz held up three fingers. "Scout's honour."

"Good enough for me," said Duke. "All right, Special Deputy

DreadfulWater, the floor is yours. And this better be good."

Burke shifted in her seat. "Is this really necessary?"

"That," said the sheriff, "is what we're about to find out."

Thumps tried to imagine how Moses would tell the story. That would take days. Best to stick with the short version.

"Frank Dodge, an employee who was laid off, shows up at Shield Industries, commandeers a transport van, and drives it to the company's test facility just north of town. I believe that Dr. Rajan Garza arranged for this to happen. Dr. Garza was convinced that Shield Industries was going to take her solar-energy protocol and weaponize it rather than use it to help meet the energy needs of Third World countries. I believe that when the van left the plant, it was carrying the Helios test panels that were kept in a paint vault. I believe that Dr. Garza then copied all of her research and set fire to the computer complex at the plant."

"Busy lady," said Duke.

"The idea was for Dodge to meet Dr. Garza at the test facility and hand over the panels. But something went wrong. Frank Dodge died of a heart attack shortly after getting to the test facility, and when Dr. Garza arrived to make the exchange, she found Dodge's body along with the van and the panels. A dilemma. She now had two vehicles, the panels, and a dead body. She knew that Shield probably had already discovered what had happened and would be trying to find her, so she did what she thought would keep the plan intact. She drove the van to the edge of Deep House and pushed Dodge's body into the canyon. Then she removed the panels from the van and threw them in as well. It wasn't the best of plans, but it was the only one that had a chance of working. Then she drove the van back to the test facility and set it on fire."

Burke made a tsking sound. "And just how did she hope she was going to make this convoluted scheme work?"

"Time," said Thumps, "and misdirection."

"Burning the van was supposed to distract us," said Mobley.

"If she was trying to make off with the research and the panels," said Burke, "why throw them into the canyon?"

"Because she had nowhere else to put them," said Thumps. "She figured she could go back later and retrieve them."

"Dicey plan," said the sheriff.

"But somehow Chandler found out," Thumps continued. "There was a confrontation in Chandler's room, and Garza killed him."

"So now," said Burke, "how about we find Dr. Garza before she kills someone else?"

"Don't you want to know why Garza killed Chandler?"

"She was angry," said Mobley. "Sometimes that's enough."

"No argument there," said the sheriff. "Pissed off people do stupid things."

Moses had a way of waiting until the moment felt right before he moved on with a story. Thumps didn't have the old man's skill, but he could feel the tide in the room shift.

"That's not why she killed him."

"You just said—"

"Garza didn't kill Chandler because he was trying to steal her protocol. She killed him because he had falsified the test results."

Thumps looked to see if the colour drained from Burke's face. It didn't. So much for that particular cliché.

"The problem with Helios was that it didn't work."

Burke held herself in check. "What are you talking about?"

"Shield Industries has gotten a great deal of money from the federal government for Garza's solar-energy protocol. I'm guessing millions of dollars."

"That's classified," said Mobley.

"Here's what I think." Thumps picked up the piece of panel. "I think that Garza had difficulties with the protocol. I think it worked well enough, but she couldn't keep the layers of paint and ceramic from separating."

Thumps tossed the piece of the panel to Burke.

"Isn't that right?"

Burke handed the piece to Mobley. "I have no idea what this is."

"Sure, you do," said Thumps. "You and Chandler were worried that Garza might not be able to solve the problem of delamination, but you weren't willing to shut off the flow of government dollars. So the two of you began to falsify the test results."

Mobley turned on Burke. "What the hell!"

"Shut up, Carl."

"You're saying that Helios is worthless?"

"As if you didn't guess."

"No," said Thumps, "I don't think that Carl knew. And neither did Garza. At least not at first."

"But she figured it out," said Cruz.

"Yes," said Thumps, "she figured it out."

"She would have been really pissed."

"Furious, I would imagine," said Thumps. "It was bad enough that her protocol didn't work, but she stood to have her reputation ruined as well. All over greed."

"You have no idea what you're talking about." Burke was on her feet. "And if you pursue this publicly, I'll bury you in lawsuits."

Mobley handed the panel piece to Thumps. "So it really doesn't work?"

"It works," said Thumps, "but then it doesn't."

"One man dead," said Mobley, "a good scientist's reputation ruined, just so you could get rich."

"You're fired, Carl."

"Fuck you, Martha."

"Children, children," said Duke. "Now that we've all had our storytime, why don't you take your differences somewhere else."

Cruz cocked his head. "You're not going to arrest her?"

Duke shrugged. "For what? Being greedy? Being stupid? I'm

sure the feds will want to look into Ms. Burke's part in all this."

"And they won't find a thing," said Burke. "In the meantime, I suggest that we find Dr. Garza. She's a thief and a murderer. In case you've forgotten."

"Not forgetting anything," said the sheriff. "Might even think of arresting you."

"For what?"

"Well, you did lie to an officer of the law."

"Omissions," said Burke. "Not illegal."

"True enough," said Hockney. "But I wonder how General Dynamics is going to feel about your omissions."

"I bring in money. That's all the hell they care about." Burke strode across the office. "How about we concentrate on Garza, so I can blow this one-horse town and get back to civilization."

Burke slammed the door behind her with a bang that sounded for all the world like a gun going off in a closet.

Mobley got out of his chair, went to the coffee pot. "She's right, you know. All corporate cares about is the profit."

"Out of coffee," said Duke. "Going to make some new tomorrow. Sorry."

"Just as well." Mobley put his jacket on. "Maybe I'll get a good night's sleep."

"What are you going to do?"

Mobley stopped at the door. "My job is to find Garza. After that, no idea. Go back to Sacramento. Face the music."

"You were just doing your job," said Duke.

"Doesn't matter," said Mobley. "Security was breached. That's on me."

THE SHERIFF WAITED until he was sure that Burke and Mobley were gone. Then he leaned back, put his feet on the desk, and did a drum roll on his thighs.

"That was some performance."

"Yeah, Pancho," said Cruz. "You outdid yourself this time."

"Felt like I was in one of those shows where the detective gathers all the suspects in one room and solves the crime."

"*Death in Paradise*," said Cruz. "*Murder on the Orient Express*."

"I used to think that summation gatherings were a bit on the cheesy side," said the sheriff, "but now I see the appeal."

"We still have to find Raj," said Cruz.

"I'm going to leave that little job to you two," said Duke. "You created this mess. You can clean it up."

"So I'm not under arrest."

"In a manner of speaking," said Duke.

"You going to give the powers that be a call?" said Cruz. "Fill them in on Ms. Burke's extracurricular activities?"

"Could," said the sheriff.

Thumps slowly got to his feet. "You think she's right? That she'll walk clean?"

"Maybe," said Duke. "But she's dead wrong about the town. We have always had more than one horse."

41

Thumps stood on the sidewalk and watched the light fade. There was a coral glow to the edge of the horizon with a darkening dome of sky floating above it. He had read somewhere that the red and orange colours were caused by pollution in the atmosphere, which was somewhat disheartening.

"You know what makes those great colours?"

"I do," said Thumps. "So don't tell me."

"A romantic," said Cruz. "Who knew."

"I like sunsets. I don't need to know how they're made."

Cruz smiled. "Sort of like hot dogs."

Cruz bringing up the topic of hot dogs reminded Thumps that he was hungry. Evidently, it had the same effect on Cruz.

"I'm starving."

"Duke didn't feed you?"

"Mentioned something about his budget," said Cruz.

"I know just the place."

"*Mira*. Last time you took me out, we wound up at the racist doughnut joint."

PAPPOUS'S WAS EMPTY. Archie was sitting at a table by himself, surrounded by plates of food.

"Slow night?"

"We're closed." Archie made a note on a pad of paper. "Grand opening is Saturday."

Cruz cast his eyes over the dishes. "These samples?"

"I'm testing the menu."

"We can help," said Cruz.

Thumps recognized several of the items. "Dolmades, right?"

"Try that," said Archie, "and tell me what you think."

Cruz pulled up a chair. "Octopus?"

"Just eat it."

"I don't do octopus."

Thumps could see tiny suckers on tiny arms. "Octopus are highly intelligent creatures."

"They're also delicious," said Archie.

"Are these babies?"

Archie pushed his glasses up his nose. "Try this."

"What is it?"

Archie put the pencil down and stared at the two men. "Food

is an adventure. If you know everything that you eat, where's the adventure?"

"I don't want an adventure," said Cruz.

"Your friend is a Philistine," said Archie. "You know that?"

"Thumps doesn't like adventures, either," said Cruz.

"It's salted cod," said Archie. "With skordalia."

"It sort of looks like hummus."

"Why are you two here?"

"No reason."

"Did you come to apologize?"

Thumps was trying to think of the right answer when the phone in his pocket began to vibrate. Thumps looked at the screen.

The sheriff.

Where Are U?

"Here." Thumps set the phone on the table. "I'm returning the damn thing."

"You got a text message, Pancho."

"I don't get text messages anymore," said Thumps, "because I no longer have a phone."

Cruz held the phone out. "What should I tell him?"

"Lie."

Cruz put the phone near his face. "We're at Pappous's."

"You can talk to a phone?"

"Of course you can talk to a phone." Archie headed back to the kitchen. "Try the rest of the dishes. I'll bring out some more."

* * *

THE SHERIFF DIDN'T waste any time getting to the restaurant.

"Should have known you two would be eating."

"You didn't feed me," said Cruz.

Duke helped himself to the calamari. "Remember that little theatre production you put on for Burke and Mobley?"

Cruz cut a dolmade in half. "You mean the one where Rajan Garza plays a homicidal maniac and the evil mastermind behind a major breach of corporate security?"

Duke reached over and took the other half. "Does any of that bullshit survive the first act?"

"Raj is up to her armpits in this mess," said Cruz. "But she didn't kill Chandler."

"Maybe she thought it was Chandler who was trying to kill her," said Duke.

"Then why would she go to his room?" said Cruz. "To give him another chance?"

"Maybe she wanted to take him off the board."

"She's a scientist," said Cruz, "not a ninja assassin."

"Do we know if she has a gun?"

"She doesn't," said Cruz.

"She pointed a remote at me," said Thumps.

"We need to find her," said Duke.

"Easier said than done," said Cruz.

Archie came out of the kitchen with plates of food on a trolley. "The big plate is roast spring lamb with lemon and oregano. The potatoes are cooked in lamb fat and the zucchini is fried in butter."

Cruz poked at hard lumps in a brown sauce. "These what I think they are?"

"Why all the questions?" said Archie. "You're food tasters. So taste."

"I got no problem with that." Duke helped himself to some of the salted cod and skordalia. "Nothing I like better than garlic."

"The lamb's delicious," said Thumps.

Archie handed him a menu. Thumps looked down the prices. "You're kidding."

"What did the risotto at the Tucker cost you?"

Cruz held up a plate. "This looks good."

"It's all good," said Archie. "That's *ravani*. It's a syrup-soaked cake."

"And this?" asked the sheriff. "Has a nice lemon taste."

"*Kourabiedes,*" said Archie. "Very tasty with an espresso."

"It's like shortbread," said Duke.

"In Greece, it's normally made during Christmas."

"It's not Christmas."

"And we aren't in Greece." Archie pulled up a chair and sat. "Have you three found that scientist yet?"

"Well, now that you mention it." Duke put his cellphone on the table. "Guess what I just received?"

Thumps didn't have to guess. "A notification from the test facility."

"Seems that someone has opened the gate."

"When?"

"About twenty minutes ago," said Duke.

"And you're going to go out there to check on it."

"I am," said Duke, "and you're coming with me."

"Take Cruz," said Thumps. "I want dessert."

"*Ravani* is too sweet for a diabetic," said Archie.

"Can't take the man from Pie Town," said the sheriff. "He might shoot someone."

"I'm not going to shoot my cousin," said Cruz. "My aunt would skin me alive."

"I trust Thumps," said Duke. "I don't trust you."

"Fair enough." Cruz shrugged. "Okay, I'll stay here and have dessert."

"You stay," said Archie, "and you have to try the octopus."

"All right." Duke helped himself to several keftedes. "Saddle up."

"You guys need extra firepower?" said Cruz. "I got a Remington M24 with a scope, a Mossberg tactical, and a couple of Glocks in my trunk."

"Jesus, DreadfulWater," said the sheriff, "you got any other friends like him?"

"Might even have a couple of vests that'll fit."

"Not going to be any shooting," said Thumps.

"Anything you break," said Cruz, "you buy."

"Don't forget," said Archie. "Grand opening on Saturday. I'll be taking names."

As soon as they got into the cruiser, Duke went to lights and siren. By the time they hit the long stretch of open road north of town, the sheriff had the car up to warp speed.

"Good to burn the carbon off the cylinders," said Duke.

"That still a thing?"

"Who knows."

Thumps assumed that the sheriff was going to go to silent running as they got close to Deep House. But he didn't.

"No sense trying to sneak up on the complex," said Duke. "Can see us coming a mile away."

"And we have to open the gate."

"Exactly," said the sheriff. "So if someone *is* in the trailer, best to let them know who it is has come to call."

The sheriff cut the siren before they got to the fence. But he left the flashing lights on.

"Let's wait here to see if anyone comes out."

The trailer was dark. If there was anyone there, they were doing a good job of not being seen.

"You see a car?"

"Could be parked around back."

Duke turned the car off and got out. "Spotlight's in the trunk. Let's do this slow and easy."

For the next while, the sheriff and Thumps walked the fenceline, playing the spotlight on the trailer and around the panel field.

"In the dark," said Duke, "all those colours are kinda creepy."

"Cruz's Mustang," said Thumps. "Behind the trailer."

"Guess that answers the question about someone being home."

"What do you want to do?"

Duke put the spotlight back in the trunk and took out the bullhorn.

"Cover your ears. Thing tends to squeal when I turn it on."

"Someone at the window," said Thumps. "Right side."

Duke brought the bullhorn to his mouth. "Knock knock."

"Knock knock?"

"Shows we're friendly." Duke pressed the button. "This is Sheriff Benjamin Hockney and Special Deputy Thumps DreadfulWater. We're going to open the gate and come in."

Hockney punched in the code, and the gate slid away.

"Leave the car here," said Duke. "Shut the gate behind us."

"Do I get a gun?"

"Promise not to shoot me?"

"In that case," said Thumps, "never mind."

Duke stopped just short of the trailer and worked the megaphone. "I want whoever is inside to open the door and come out with their hands up. No need for this to end badly."

One of the windows in the trailer slid open.

"How do I know you are who you say you are?"

"It's me, Raj. Thumps."

"Who's my cousin?"

"Cisco Cruz."

"What does Cisco call you?"

Thumps hated questions for which there were more than one answer.

"*Cabrón?*"

"The other one."

"Pancho."

"Send Pancho in," shouted Raj. "I won't shoot him."

Duke let the megaphone hang from the wrist strap. "*Cabrón?* Doesn't that mean 'asshole'?"

"You're thinking of *pendejo*," said Thumps. "It's an easy mistake to make."

"You going to go in?"

"Can't stand out here all night."

Duke handed Thumps his service revolver. "Here, take this," he said. "Just in case. I got another one in the car."

Thumps shook his head. "You're right. I might shoot you."

42

Dr. Rajan Garza was wearing the same clothes that she had been wearing when she showed up at Thumps's house and threatened him with the remote.

This time, she had a gun.

"How did you find me?"

"Gate has an alarm."

"Why'd you bring the sheriff?"

"You're a fugitive."

"Where's Cisco?"

"Having dessert at Pappous's."

"Figures." Raj waved the gun at the sofa. "People are trying to kill me, and he's feeding his face."

Duke touched the brim of his hat. "Appreciate it if you pointed that somewhere else."

Raj started pacing. "I'm hungry. I haven't had a bath in days. My clothes stink. And now you show up."

Thumps smiled. "See. Your luck is changing."

"I'm not going to turn my research over to Shield." Raj brought the gun back up. "Chandler can spit in one hand and wish in the other, and see which gets filled first."

"Chandler's dead." Thumps watched Raj's face.

"What?"

"Shot in his hotel room."

Raj looked at the gun in her hand. "And the sheriff thinks . . ."

"That you're a suspect?" Thumps tried to look sympathetic. "Yes."

"I didn't kill Chandler," said Raj. "I haven't seen that *pendejo* since I left Shield."

"I'm guessing 'asshole' in this case isn't the affectionate version." Sheriff Duke Hockney filled the doorway, his gun pointed at Raj. "Please put your gun on the table."

"You can't arrest me."

"Actually," said Thumps, "he can."

"This is crazy," said Raj. "I'm the victim."

"Please don't make me shoot you," said Duke. "You have no idea how much paperwork that entails."

Raj set the gun on the coffee table. "How much is Burke paying you?"

"Don't I wish." Duke took out his handcuffs. "I haven't had a decent bribe in years."

"You won't think you're so funny when I sue you for false arrest."

Thumps picked up the gun, held it to his nose. "Where did you get this?"

"None of your business."

"It's been fired."

"Not by me," said Garza.

Duke cuffed Garza's hands behind her back, turned to Thumps. "Maybe you want to bring the car around, save us a walk."

Thumps got as far as the door. It was black out. He could see the front gate and the outline of the sheriff's car. But there was something else. Something moving in the darkness.

He quickly stepped back inside, turned off the lights.

"We got company."

"Cisco!" Raj shouted.

Duke pushed Raj to the floor. "Stay there."

"Cisco!"

"And shut up."

Thumps could see two figures coming up from the gate.

"Dr. Garza, is that you?"

"It's Mobley," said Thumps. "I think Burke is with him."

"Rajan," Burke called out. "Are you in there? Are you okay?"

Duke motioned Thumps away from the door.

"Sheriff," Mobley shouted. "It's me and Martha. We're coming in."

Duke moved to the door. "Stop where you are, Mr. Mobley. You too, Ms. Burke."

"We just want to make sure that Dr. Garza is okay."

"She's under arrest." Duke raised his voice. "Turn around and go back to your car."

"What about our property?" said Burke.

"Everything's under control," said the sheriff. "We'll all meet up at my office in an hour."

Thumps watched as Mobley and Burke turned and went back through the front gate.

"They're going."

"Okay," said the sheriff. "Now maybe we can get some answers."

"I'm not helping you," said Garza. "How do I know you're not working for Shield?"

Thumps stood next to the window. "How about this. The sheriff and I are going to have a little conversation, and all you have to do is listen."

"But jump in at any time if you feel the urge," said Duke.

Thumps watched in the distance for a door light to go on, listened for an engine to start. Nothing.

"You developed a paint protocol," Duke began. "Something called Helios. Was going to change the face of solar energy."

"Burke and Chandler were going to sell it to the military."

"No, they weren't," said Thumps. "Because the protocol didn't work."

"It worked."

"Maybe for the first little while," said Thumps. "But then the layers began to separate."

"I could have fixed the problem," said Raj. "I told Burke and Chandler that I just needed more time."

"But they couldn't take that chance," said Thumps. "As a project in development, Helios was a gold mine."

"They falsified the test results," said Raj. "They didn't want the research money to stop."

"And they signed your name to those reports."

"What was I supposed to do? If I said anything, they'd bury me and the project."

"I don't get it," said the sheriff. "Why did you steal your own research and the test panels? What was that going to accomplish?"

It would have been nice if the test facility had security lights around the perimeter, so Thumps could see what was going on just beyond the fence.

"Wasn't her idea," said Thumps.

"Frank Dodge?" Duke thought about it for a moment. "Frank Dodge was her partner in this?"

Out in the darkness, Thumps heard a trunk shut.

"Dodge?" Raj frowned. "Didn't even know the man."

"Not Dodge," said Thumps. "He wouldn't have known about the falsified reports, couldn't have told you what Shield planned to do with your protocol. He couldn't have disabled security or changed the transport logs. Dodge couldn't have opened the vault. He was just a driver, just in it for the payday."

The shot ripped through the roof of the trailer before Thumps heard the crack.

"Get down!"

Duke pushed Garza behind the refrigerator. "Rifle rounds."

"That was high," Mobley shouted. "The next one won't be."

Thumps picked his face up off the floor. "You might want to call for backup."

Duke shook his head. "They couldn't get here inside twenty minutes, and my cell is in the cruiser."

Thumps checked the clip in Raj's gun.

"What about that cell of yours?"

"Gave it back to Cruz. Remember?"

Garza tried to sit up. "Why is Carl shooting at us?"

"I think he wants to kill you," said the sheriff.

"It was Carl," said Thumps, "wasn't it?"

"Raj," Mobley shouted, "come on out. We can still make this work."

Garza started to move. Duke pushed her back to the floor.

"You take one step out that door and he'll kill you."

The second shot came through the window, tore a hole in the back wall.

Duke rolled onto his side. "This trailer isn't going to stop shit."

"Pistols are no good," said Thumps. "He's too far away."

The cupboard next to the sink blew up.

"I can do this all night," Mobley shouted. "Send Garza out."

Another shot. This one went through the refrigerator just above Duke's head.

"This guy is beginning to piss me off."

"Let me go," said Garza. "I can get Carl to stop."

"Ask him about Burke."

"We want to talk to Burke," Duke shouted.

"We had a disagreement. She's currently indisposed."

"Should have taken your buddy up on his arsenal," said Duke. "Would really love to have that Remington right about now."

"Time's up!"

The report was loud, a snapping two-part crack. And then silence.

"He missed?"

"Wasn't Mobley," said Duke. "We got a second shooter. Anyone we might know?"

The sound of the shot and a car window exploding arrived at the same time.

Another long silence.

"Okay," Mobley shouted. "Stop shooting!"

Duke got to his knees. "Can you see anything?"

"You want me to look?"

"Just a quick peek."

"Why don't you take a quick peek?"

"You're closer to the door," said Duke.

Garza rolled up into a sitting position. "Could you take these damn handcuffs off me?"

There was a bullet tear in the wall near the door. Thumps put his eye to the hole. The light from the trailer didn't reach the fence, but it didn't matter. It was enough to see Carl Mobley on his knees, his hands locked behind his head.

"You're not going to believe it," said Thumps.

"Try me," said Duke.

"Remember that friend of ours, was eating with us at Pappous's?"

"The *pendejo* from Pie Town?"

Garza struggled to her feet. "You two talking about my cousin?"

Thumps nodded. "I think he finished his dessert."

43

It took most of the night to sort things out, but by four in the morning, Martha Burke was on her way to the hospital with a concussion, Carl Mobley was in the back of Deanna Heavy Runner's cruiser, Rajan Garza was in Duke's, Mobley's Buick rental was missing a rear window, and the trailer had holes in it that hadn't been there the day before.

Duke and Thumps were no worse for wear.

Cisco Cruz was nowhere to be found.

"Your pal always disappears like that after a gunfight?"

"He's shy," said Thumps. "Wants other people to get the credit."

"While avoiding being charged with discharging a firearm in a dangerous manner and vandalizing a vehicle."

"There's that," said Thumps.

***

WHEN THUMPS AND Duke got back to the office with Rajan Garza in tow, Cisco Cruz was sitting in the sheriff's chair behind the sheriff's desk.

"Move it or get shot."

"Just keeping it warm for you."

"How'd you get in?" said the sheriff. "Door was locked."

"Your deputy let me in," said Cruz. "I helped her tuck Mr. Mobley in for the night."

"And just where were you this evening," said Duke, "when the shit hit the fan?"

"Dessert," said Cruz. "*Galaktoboureko*. Sort of a custard pie."

"Fine help you were." Garza squirmed in the chair. "Wait till I tell Mom."

Cruz was unfazed. "Would that be before or after you're indicted for corporate espionage and murder?"

Garza stopped moving. "Murder?"

Thumps held up an evidence bag. Inside was a gun.

"This is the weapon you had out at the trailer," said Thumps.

"It's not mine."

"And yet," said Duke, "it was in your possession."

"We don't have ballistics yet," said Thumps, "but I'm betting it's the gun that killed Chandler."

"Carl gave it to me," said Garza. "For protection."

"I'm betting he'll say he's never seen it."

"I've got nothing to say," said Garza. "And you have no reason to hold me."

Thumps went to the percolator and shook it. Empty.

"Make a new batch in the morning," said Duke. "Drinking coffee this time of night will just keep you awake."

"It's almost morning." Thumps came back to the chair and sat with a thud. "Wasn't your idea, was it?"

"Whatever," said Garza.

"Jesus, Raj," said Cruz, "they're trying to help you."

"It was Mobley." Thumps tried to get comfortable.

"You don't know what you're talking about."

"It was Mobley who tried to run you down in Sacramento."

"Carl wouldn't do that."

"Wanted to make you paranoid," said Thumps. "Get you to run. He just didn't count on your calling Cruz."

"Lot of good that did me."

"Saved your life, actually." Thumps turned to face Garza. "Mobley was the one who told you Shield was going to sell Helios to the military. He was the one who came up with the plan and arranged for Dodge to get into the plant and take the panels from the vault. He was the one who got you to download the files. Who set the fire at the computer complex? You? Him?"

Garza looked straight ahead.

"You thought he was a friend, helping you out."

"He was."

"Jesus," said Cruz, "you're no better at this than when we were kids."

"Mobley wanted the protocol for himself," said Thumps.

"What he didn't know was that Helios didn't work. He didn't know that Burke and Chandler had rigged the test results."

"And once he had the research and the test panels," said Cruz, "the plan was to sell Helios and quietly slip away. Leaving you to take the fall."

"But things went sideways." Thumps put the evidence bag back on the desk. "Dodge died, and he had to improvise."

"What's going to happen to Shield?" Garza still had an edge of annoyance to her voice. "They're going to walk, aren't they?"

"Chandler's dead," said the sheriff. "Burke is in the hospital with a severe concussion. Mobley's in a cell. Nobody's doing much walking from what I can see."

"You still don't get it, do you?" Cruz took a deep breath and let it out slowly. "Mobley didn't come to the test facility tonight to rescue you. He came to kill you. He was going to kill everyone."

"You have no idea what you're talking about." Raj was still defiant, but the facade was beginning to crack.

"Look at it from Mobley's point of view," said Thumps. "Suddenly, his plan has gone to hell. Helios doesn't work. The big payday he had been dreaming about is up in smoke. The only play left is to trim the loose ends."

"Dodge was dead." Cruz used his fingers to cut the air. "Snip. One loose end. Chandler must have found out about the security breach and called Mobley on it. Snip, snip. Two loose ends. Almost home free."

"You were supposed to meet him at the test facility tonight," said Thumps. "What did he tell you? That he had found a place for you to go where you could take Helios, where you would have the time and research facilities to work out the flaws? Europe? South America?"

"He promised me." Garza put her head in her hands. "He promised me."

"You were the last loose end," said Cruz, his voice low and calm. "After he killed you, he would have thrown your body in the canyon and left the gun in the trailer to find. Your fingerprints would be on the gun, so we would assume you killed Chandler and ran."

"But we got in the way," said Duke. "He didn't expect to find us at the trailer when he arrived."

"So now he had to kill everyone," said Thumps. "And he would have if your cousin hadn't intervened."

"Not me." Cruz held up his hands. "I was having dessert."

Duke rubbed at his eyes. "Then you wouldn't mind giving us a look at that Remington."

"I think it was stolen."

"And you reported the theft?"

"Deputy Heavy Runner," said Cruz. "She took all the particulars."

Garza was rocking back and forth in the chair, her arms held in place by the cuffs.

"What's going to happen to my cousin?"

Duke used his key to take the cuffs off Garza.

"You letting her go?"

"Got nothing to hold her on," said Duke. "Being stupid's not a crime. Look at our last president."

"Shield will fire her," said Thumps, "but I don't think they'll prosecute."

Garza rubbed her wrists. "I suppose you think I should thank you."

"You do what you want, Dr. Garza," said Duke. "Just get the hell out of my town."

Cruz stretched his legs. "Am I free to go as well?"

"Sure," said Duke. "I'm pretty much out of cells."

"You still have one free," said Cruz.

"I'm thinking of putting Special Deputy DreadfulWater in that one."

"What'd I do?"

"Do you know how long it's going to take me to write up a coherent report on tonight's little shootout?"

"Not my circus," said Thumps. "Not my monkeys."

"By the way," said the sheriff, "how was that dessert?"

Cruz helped his cousin to her feet. "It was okay," he said. "A little too sweet for my tastes."

"You tell Archie that?"

"I did."

"And?"

"He was a good sport about it."

"No, he wasn't," said Thumps.

"You're right," said Cruz. "He wasn't."

Duke went to the door and held it open. "I got coffee to make, criminals to catch. Get out of here before I shoot the lot of you."

44

It was almost six in the morning by the time Thumps got home. Freeway and the kittens were curled up in the middle of the bed. There was no point in trying to sleep, so he got into the shower instead and stood under the hot water until it ran cold.

All that planning and scheming. And for nothing. Graham Chandler was dead. Martha Burke was in a coma. Carl Mobley would most likely go to prison for the rest of his life. Rajan Garza would never find another research position.

And for what? Helios. A golden goose that, in the end, couldn't fly.

THE KITTENS WERE waiting for him. When he pulled the shower curtain open, there they were, all four of them, lined up in front of the tub, their eyes wide with surprise, as though they had come upon an alien creature, all naked and wrinkly.

Which they had.

He dried himself off and padded back to the bedroom, the kittens bouncing along behind him on parade. Freeway hadn't moved. She had seen him naked any number of times and was not impressed.

The kittens, on the other hand, were keen to make the most of the situation. They tumbled around his feet, clawed at his socks as he tried to put them on, pounced on the cuffs of his pants, pulled at the laces of his shoes.

Thumps wondered if kittens were just a smaller version of children. Maybe he'd name one of the kittens Ivory. And then again, maybe he wouldn't.

IN ADDITION TO STOOLS, Al's had plywood booths. That no one used. Except the occasional tourist who got lost and wandered in off the street. Jimmy Monroe, Russell Plunkett, and Wutty Youngbeaver normally sat on the three stools directly across from the grill, but when Thumps got to the café, the three men were in the first booth, looking uncomfortable and out of place.

"It's embarrassing," said Jimmy, "but Wutty's got to keep his leg elevated."

"It's just for a week," said Russell.

"What's sixteen minus one?" said Jimmy.

"It wasn't funny then," said Wutty. "It's not funny now."

Al arrived with the coffee pot. "Hear you had some fun last night."

"Breakfast," said Thumps. "The usual."

"Hear shots were fired," said Al. "Hear you and the sheriff had to be rescued."

"Breakfast," said Thumps. "The usual."

"Wutty wants me to ask you about the trailer. Wants to know how badly it was shot up, and if you can see the bullet holes from the fence."

"The trailer?"

"Figures to work it into the next tour." Al put a growl in her voice. "The Canyon of Death and the Trailer at the O.K. Corral one-day tour."

"Wutty's still running tours?"

"He is."

"What about his leg?"

"Russell's doing the driving," said Al. "Jimmy's doing the counting."

Thumps turned to the booth. On one side, Wutty was sitting by himself with his leg propped up on his jacket. On the other, Russell and Jimmy were banging shoulders and laughing.

"What's the difference between fifteen and sixteen?"

"Depends who's counting."

"It's still not funny," said Wutty. "Still not funny."

***

THUMPS WAS HALFWAY through his breakfast when Cruz came into the café and slid onto the stool next to him.

"Figured I'd find you here."

"Here I am," said Thumps.

"Wanted to say goodbye before I left."

"How's Garza doing?"

Cruz shrugged. "Just dropped her off at the airport. She still doesn't get it. Still thinks she's the victim."

"She going back to Sacramento, face the music?"

"Albuquerque," said Cruz. "Face her mother."

Thumps couldn't help it.

Cruz tried to look stern. "It's not funny."

"Her mother going to kill her?"

Now Cruz was smiling. "Personally, I'd rather go to jail."

Al brought two breakfasts. "This is for saving his ass."

Cruz shook his head. "I wasn't there. I was having dessert at Pappous's."

"Shut up and eat."

THUMPS AND CRUZ ate in silence. Jimmy and Russell continued to give Wutty a hard time, coming up with variations on math, each one worse than the last.

"Those three always like that?"

"They are," said Thumps.

"Must be nice to have friends."

"It is."

"I wouldn't know," said Cruz. "You're about the only friend I have."

"Appreciate that."

"And you're not all that good."

Al came back with the coffee. "Nice to see you boys getting along."

"Yes, ma'am."

"And when do I get my cat?"

"They're still babies."

"Damn, DreadfulWater," said Al. "Hope you're not getting all attached."

"I hear the longer kittens stay with their mother," said Cruz, "the better behaved cat you get."

"Don't want a cat with manners. I want an apex killer." Al headed back to the grill. "And don't take too long. Cat's an impulse buy, and I might lose my impulse."

Thumps leaned on the counter, settled into his coffee. "Where you going to go now?"

"Not sure," said Cruz. "Guess I'll figure that out once I get there."

"You could stay around here while you're figuring."

"What am I supposed to do in this one-horse town?"

"Got more horses than that."

Jimmy and Russell were starting on Wutty again.

"What happens when you take one from sixteen?"

"You wind up with a broken leg," said Jimmy.

Cruz got off the stool, patted Thumps on the shoulder. "Pancho," he said, "just because you got horses' asses don't mean you got horses."

45

Ameet Zalera had come back through Chinook, had dropped off a Fuji body and two lenses for Thumps to try. So for the rest of the week, Thumps got up each day before dawn and drove out to Deep House. The area wasn't as dramatic as the river valley to the south or the mountains farther east, but as he worked the rim of the canyon with his field camera and the Fuji, he discovered a world he had never imagined. Under the early-morning sky, the long, deep cut in the flat land created momentary images of light and shadow that left him calm and at peace.

On Sunday, he drove out to Claire's house with flowers and chocolate, a cardboard box filled with sandwiches, fruit, cheese, and a bottle of wine. Several blankets and pillows, a pair of canvas chairs, and a folding table.

Roxanne had suggested a picnic.

"Good for the baby to get out of the house," Roxanne told him. "Little girl like that can use all the sunshine she can find."

Thumps wasn't sure that Claire would be keen on a picnic.

"Already talked to her," said Roxanne, "so we got that question settled."

Roxanne had even picked out the site.

"High ground, so you can see the river and the mountains at the same time. So you know you're home."

Claire was sitting on the porch, reading a book. Ivory was practising climbing the stairs.

"She can go up just fine, but she still likes to slide down on her bottom."

"Look at you," said Thumps. "Climbing stairs all by yourself."

"Dog," said Ivory.

"Speaking of which," said Claire, "how are Freeway and the kittens?"

"Great."

"You just leave them at home?"

"When I'm not there," said Thumps, "they go to my neighbour's house. He's the one with the big dog."

"Freeway's okay with that?"

"Pops is a cream puff."

"That's the dog who farts?"

"He's got a good heart."

Ivory made it to the top of the stairs, scrambled to her mother's side, and buried her head in Claire's lap.

"She's tired," said Claire. "She was up last night."

"You want to stay home?"

"No," said Claire, "but maybe we could take a few extra things with us."

"Sure."

It took Thumps several tries to pack all the "extra things" into his car. He squeezed the toys and the diaper bag and the portable toilet into the back with the food and strapped the collapsible playpen and the sleeping tent to the roof rack.

The car seat accounted for most of the delay. Getting it out of Claire's truck took a certain amount of contortion and strength, while putting it in the Element was an exercise in logic and frustration.

Ivory cried through much of the packing, and she cried as Claire strapped her into her seat, and she cried all the way out to the buttes overlooking the river.

And then she fell asleep.

Thumps and Claire sat in the car and watched the clouds build up on the horizon.

"We could just stay here."

"I'd love to leave her in the seat and let her sleep."

"But we should get out and enjoy the day?"

"Yes," said Claire, "we should."

Thumps expected that Ivory would stay asleep, but the moment he opened the door to get her out, she woke up.

"Dog."

"You play with her," said Claire. "I'll unpack."

Playing with a two-year-old, Thumps discovered, consisted of chasing her through the prairie grass while she worried the whole of creation with her shrieks.

"Growl at her," Claire called out. "She likes that."

Thumps was stunned by the number of moving parts there were to one small child. Feeding, changing diapers, singing songs, in the playpen, out of the playpen. In the end, Claire had to crawl into the tent and cuddle with Ivory before she would fall asleep.

"And that is what my day is like."

"Exhausting," said Thumps.

"It'll get better," said Claire, "and it will get worse."

"And yet people have children."

"Most don't know any better," said Claire. "Until it's too late. And then you either step up, or you don't."

"Archie's having his grand opening this weekend."

"This about a date?"

"Sure."

"How do you feel about children in restaurants?"

"Archie will want to spoil her."

"You're just hoping that she'll bite him."

THUMPS MADE A NEST of the blankets and the pillows, and the two of them stretched out under the sky.

Claire snuggled up against him. "You've certainly had an exciting time."

"Not what I'd call excitement."

"Rescue the damsel, solve the mystery, catch the bad guy."

"Wouldn't call Rajan Garza a damsel," said Thumps. "And we got shot at."

"Sure," said Claire, "but he missed."

Thumps rolled up on his side. "Land return still on track?"

"More or less," said Claire, "but the state is now insisting on another environmental study before they sign off. They want to explore a joint management proposal for Deep House."

"As in landfill?"

"Maybe," said Claire. "Guess who wants the contract?"

"Shield Industries?"

"So you're not just a pretty face." Claire smiled. "We go to court next month to stop it."

Thumps lay back on the blanket. "And in the meantime?"

"Land is ours," said Claire.

"I heard Cooley and Stas are working on a way to haul the garbage out of the canyon."

"I heard that too," said Claire.

"What's going to happen to the test facility?"

"Wutty came to council with a plan to make it part of his Canyon of Death tour." Claire turned onto her side. "Wants to keep the fence and the paint panels and the trailer with the bullet holes intact."

"What'd council do?"

"What they always do," said Claire. "They formed a committee."

Every so often, Claire stuck her head into the tent to make sure Ivory was still breathing.

"Sometimes she's so quiet, I think she's died."

"But she's okay."

Claire walked out to the edge of the butte. Thumps followed along.

"You know why I picked this spot?"

"I thought Roxanne picked the spot."

"She did," said Claire, "after I told her where the right spot was."

"It's a good spot."

Claire shielded her eyes. "This is as close as you can get to the Slump."

"Looks like more of it has collapsed."

"What do you think," said Claire, "seventy-five, hundred yards?"

"About that."

"Not a long shot for someone who knew what they were doing."

The wind came up, not strong but building. Thumps could see an arch forming on the western horizon. By tonight, it would be a full-blown chinook.

Claire put her arm around Thumps and pulled herself in close.

"I need to know," she whispered.

THEY MADE LOVE that night for the first time in months. Thumps lay in bed and listened to Claire breathe. Later, when Ivory cried out, he got up quickly and changed her. He warmed the bottle and fed her, rocked her back to sleep, held her in his arms until the morning light nudged the house awake.

Then he went into the kitchen and started the coffee.